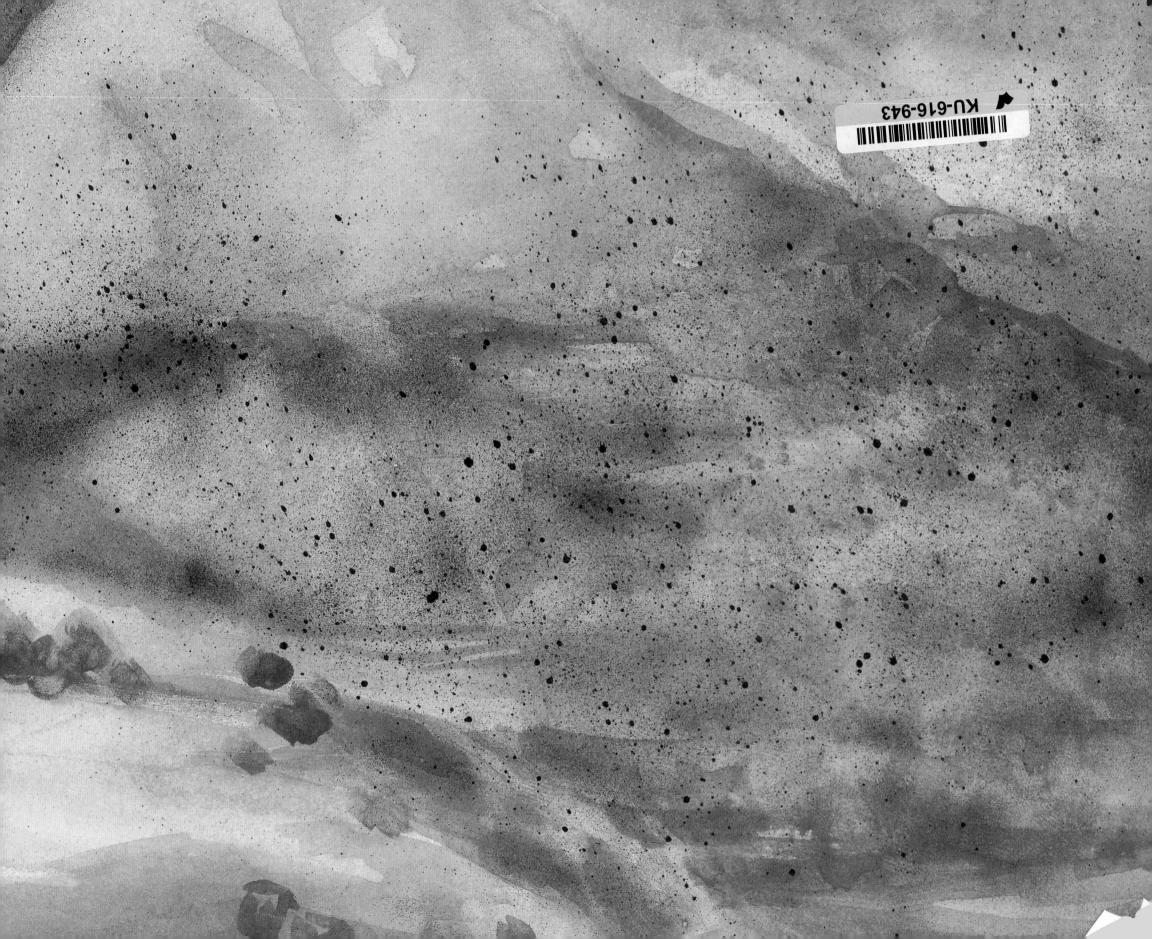

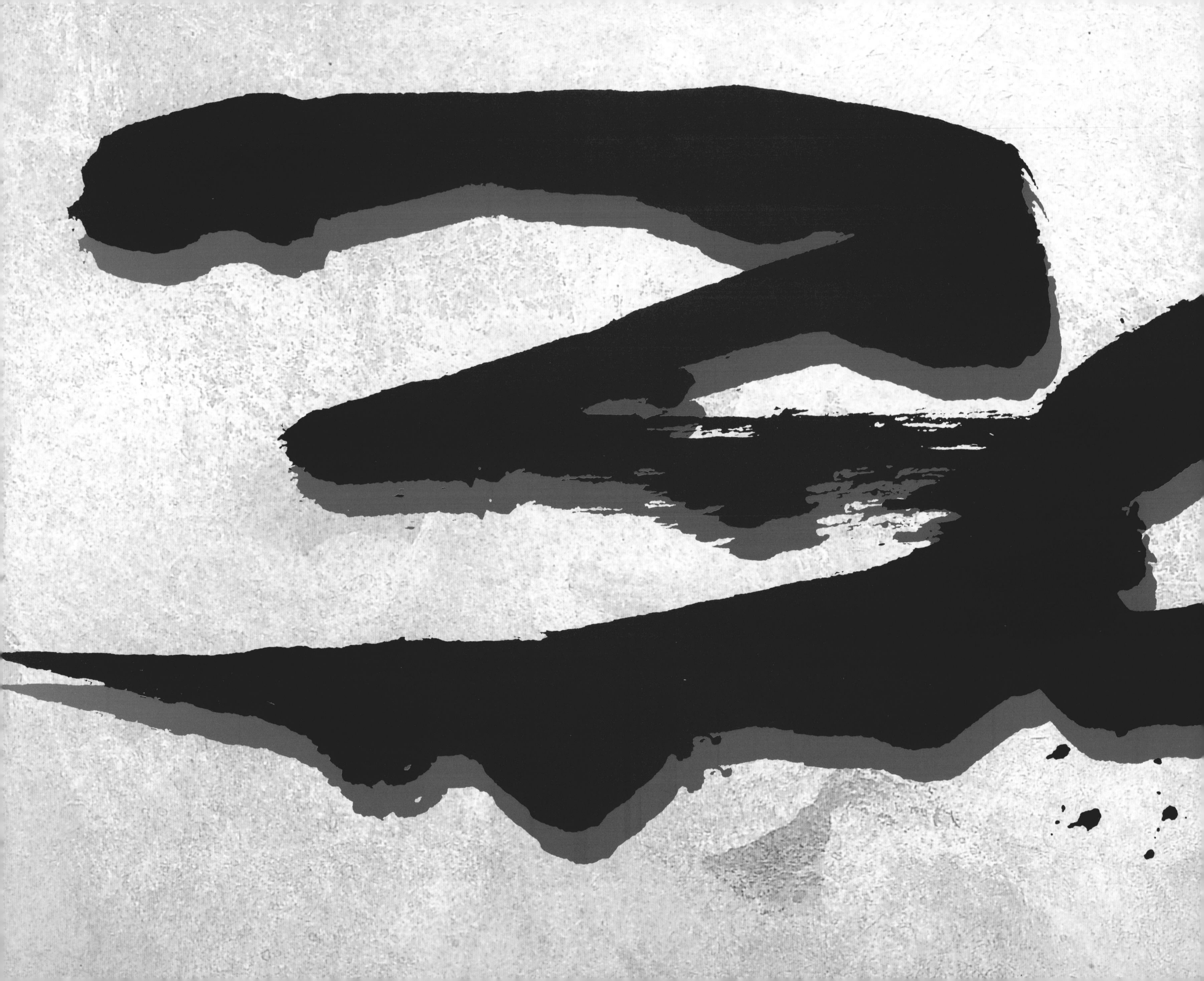

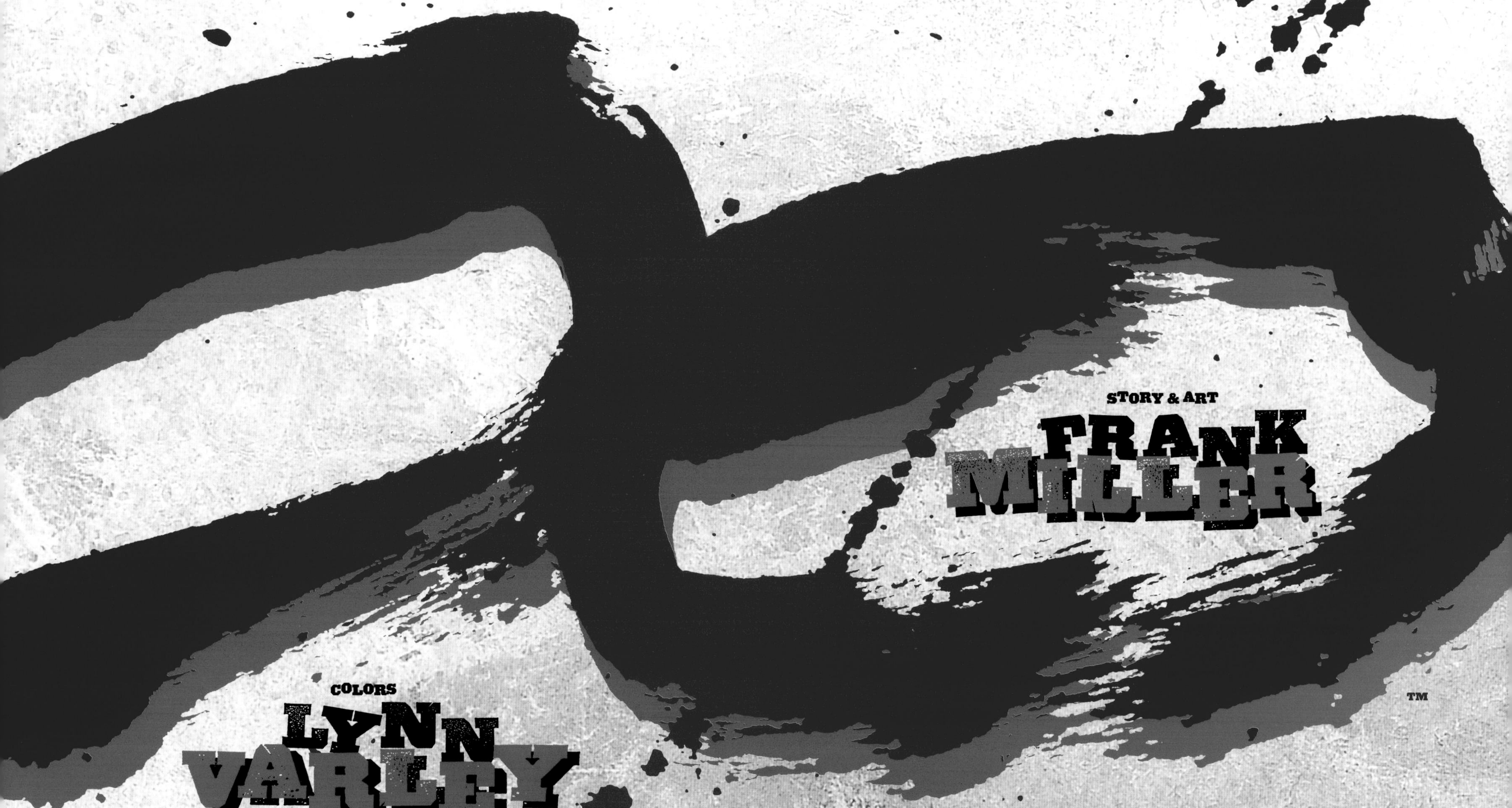

STORY & ART
FRANK MILLER

COLORS
LYNN VARLEY

TM

DARK HORSE BOOKS™

EDITOR
DIANA SCHUTZ

LOGO DESIGN
STEVEN MILLER

BOOK DESIGN
MARK COX

ENDPAPER ART
LYNN VARLEY

CONSULTING EDITOR,
HARDCOVER EDITION
CHRIS WARNER

PUBLISHER
MIKE RICHARDSON

This volume collects issues one through five of the Dark Horse
comic-book series *300*.

Published by
Dark Horse Books
A division of
Dark Horse Comics, Inc.
10956 SE Main Street
Milwaukie, Oregon 97222

darkhorse.com

First edition: August 1999
ISBN-10: 1-56971-402-9
ISBN-13: 978-1-56971-402-7

10 9 8

Printed in China

CHAPTER ONE:
HONOR

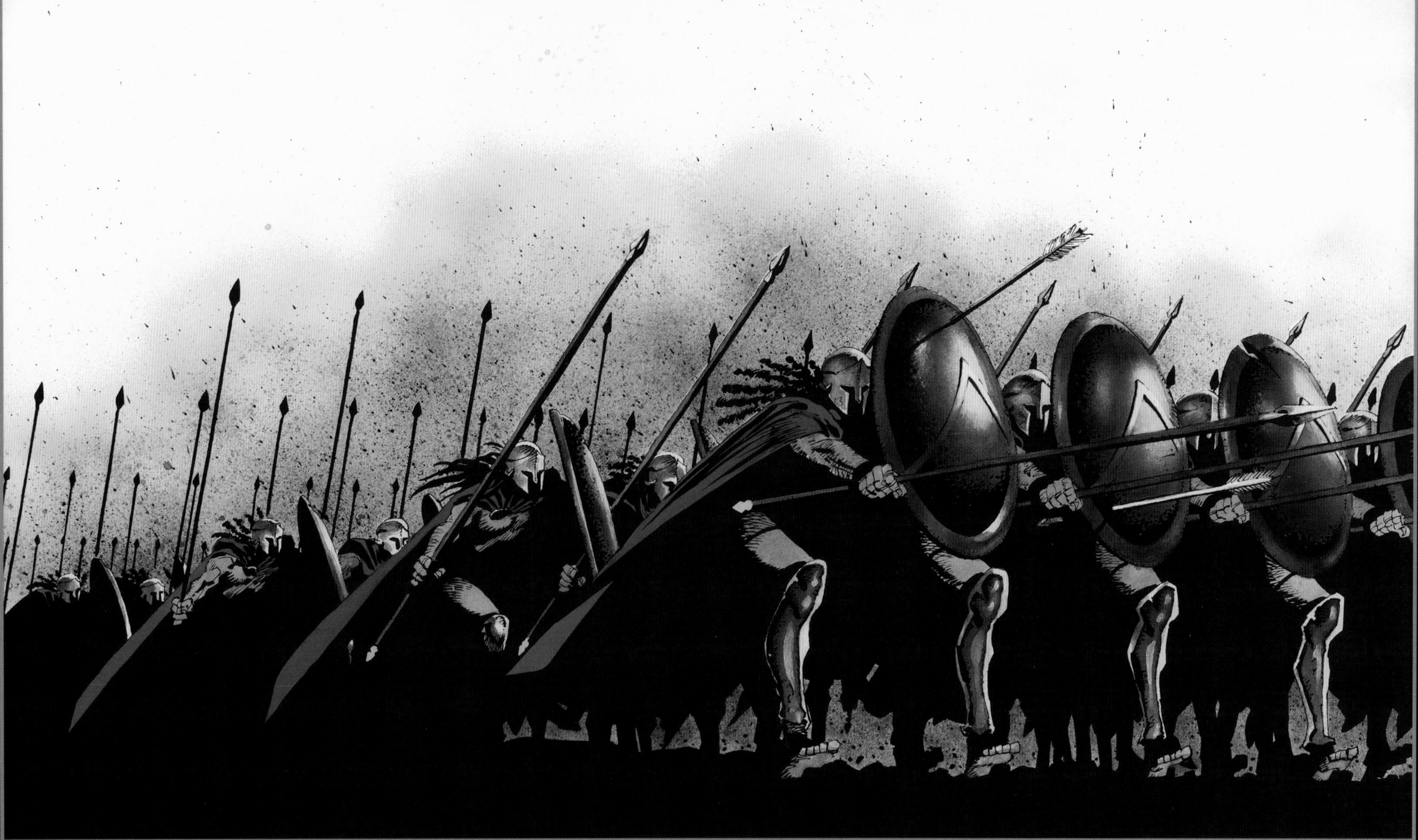

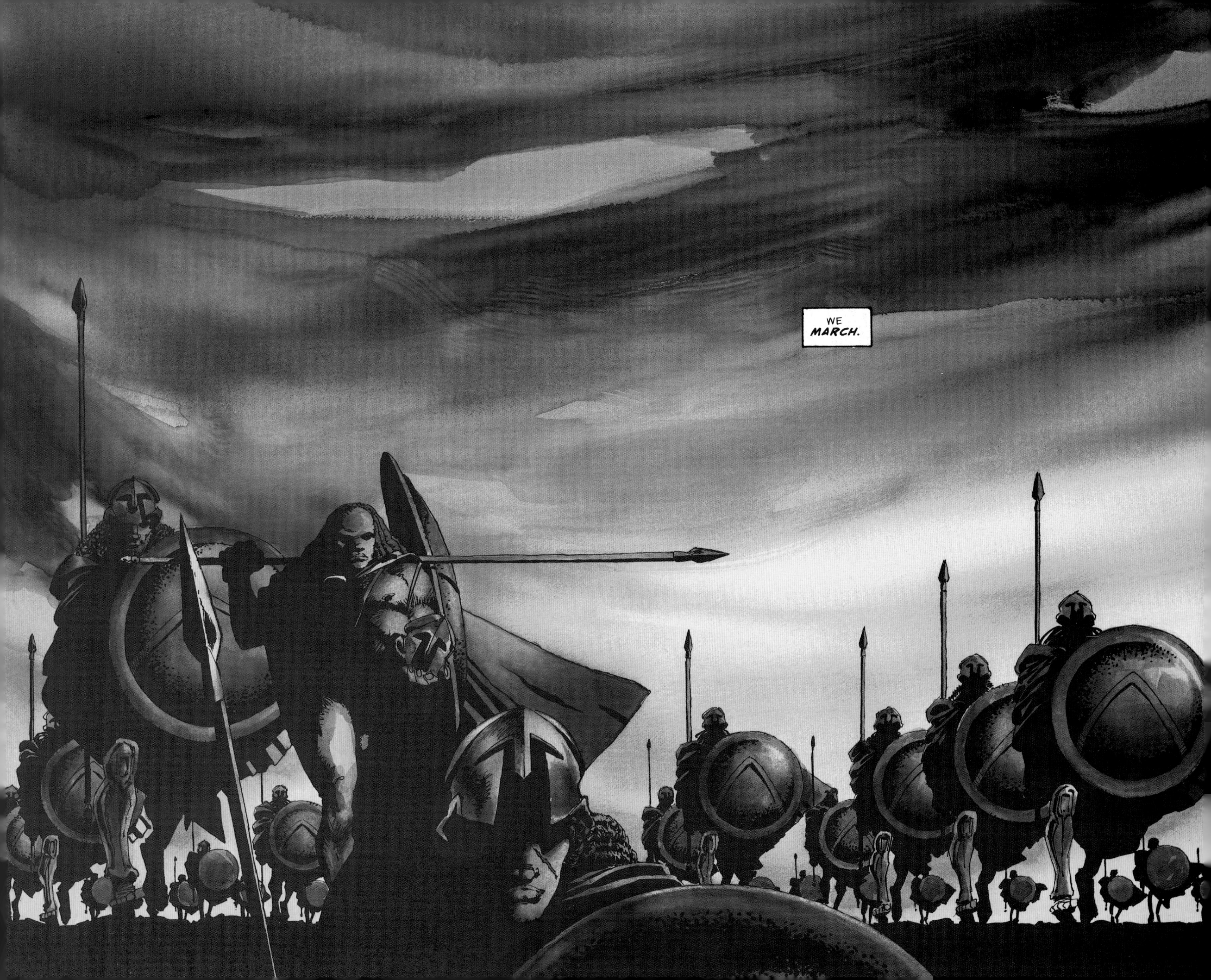
WE MARCH.

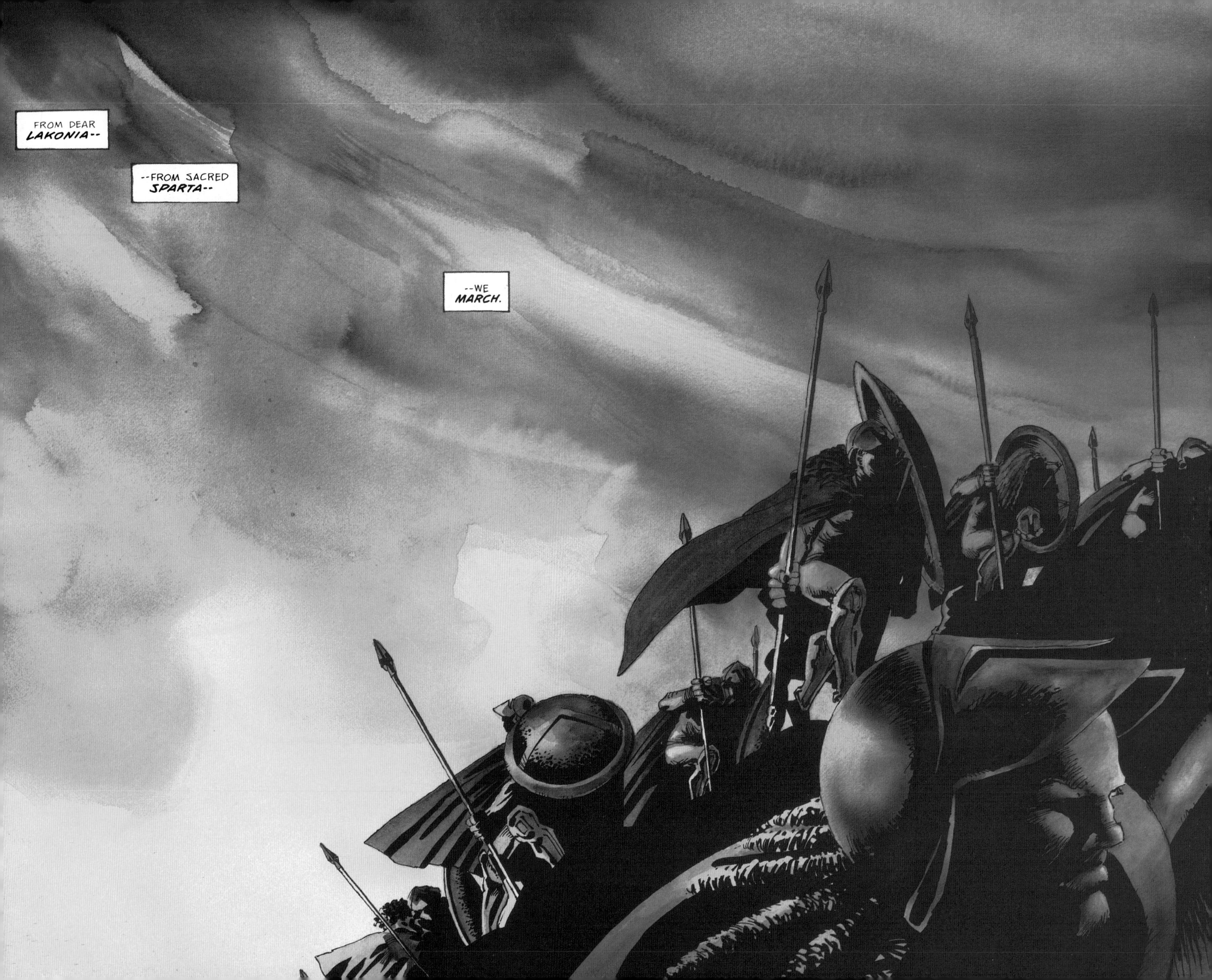
FROM DEAR
LAKONIA--
--FROM SACRED
SPARTA--
--WE
MARCH.

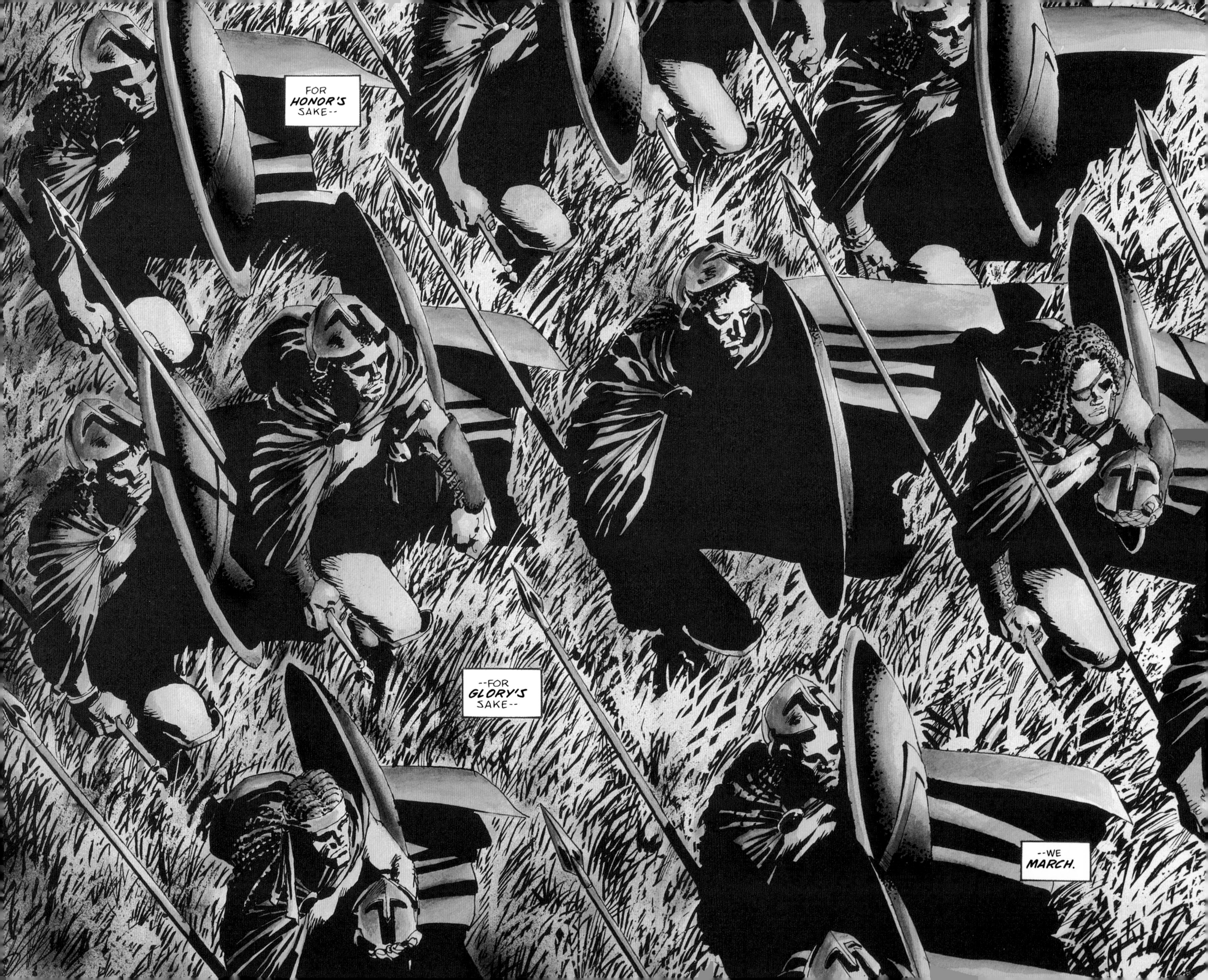
FOR HONOR'S SAKE--
--FOR GLORY'S SAKE--
--WE MARCH.

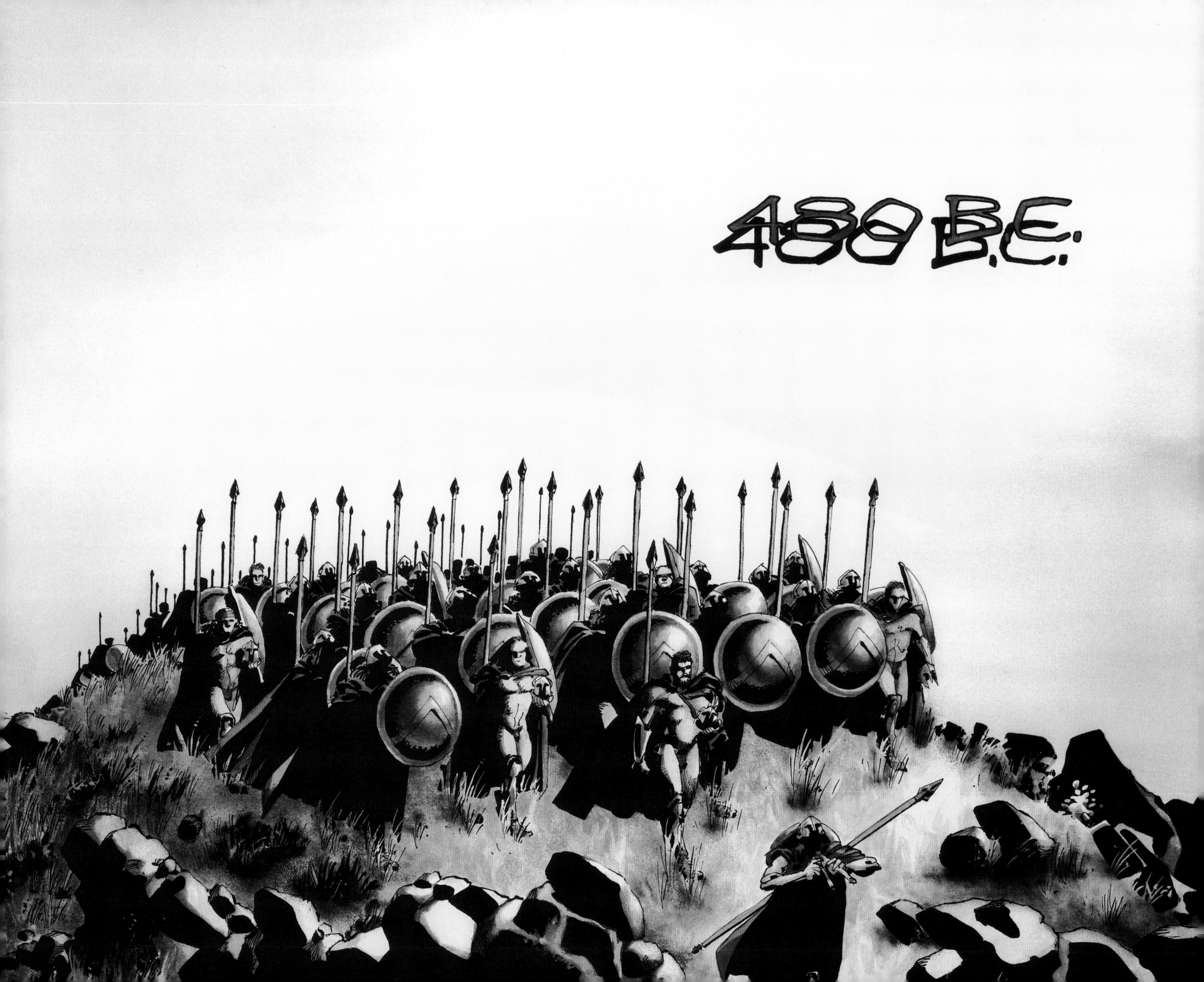
480 B.C.

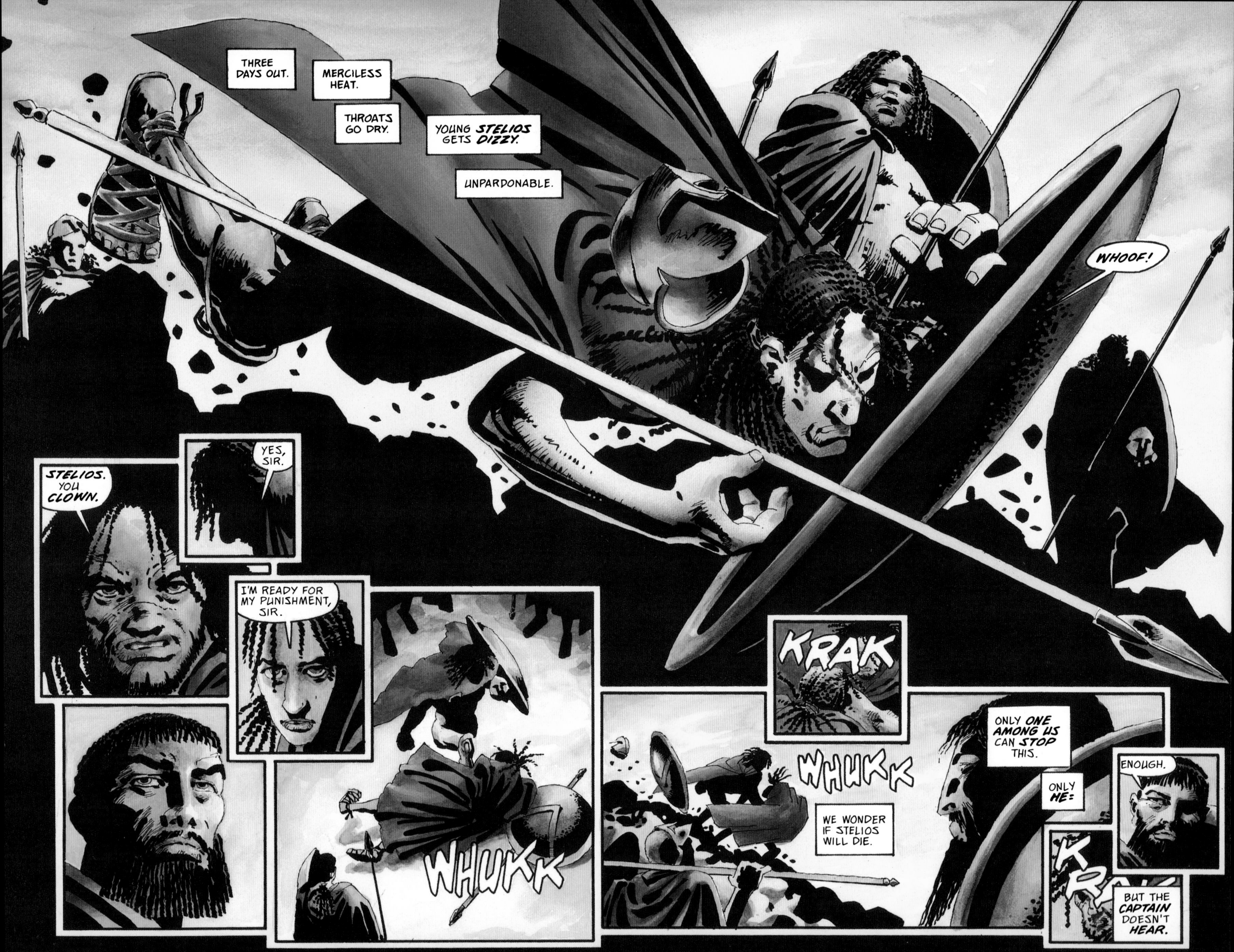
THREE DAYS OUT.
MERCILESS HEAT.
THROATS GO DRY.
YOUNG STELIOS GETS DIZZY.
UNPARDONABLE.
WHOOF!
STELIOS. YOU CLOWN.
YES, SIR.
I'M READY FOR MY PUNISHMENT, SIR.
WHUKK
KRAK
WHUKK
WE WONDER IF STELIOS WILL DIE.
ONLY ONE AMONG US CAN STOP THIS.
ONLY HE:
ENOUGH.
KR
BUT THE CAPTAIN DOESN'T HEAR.

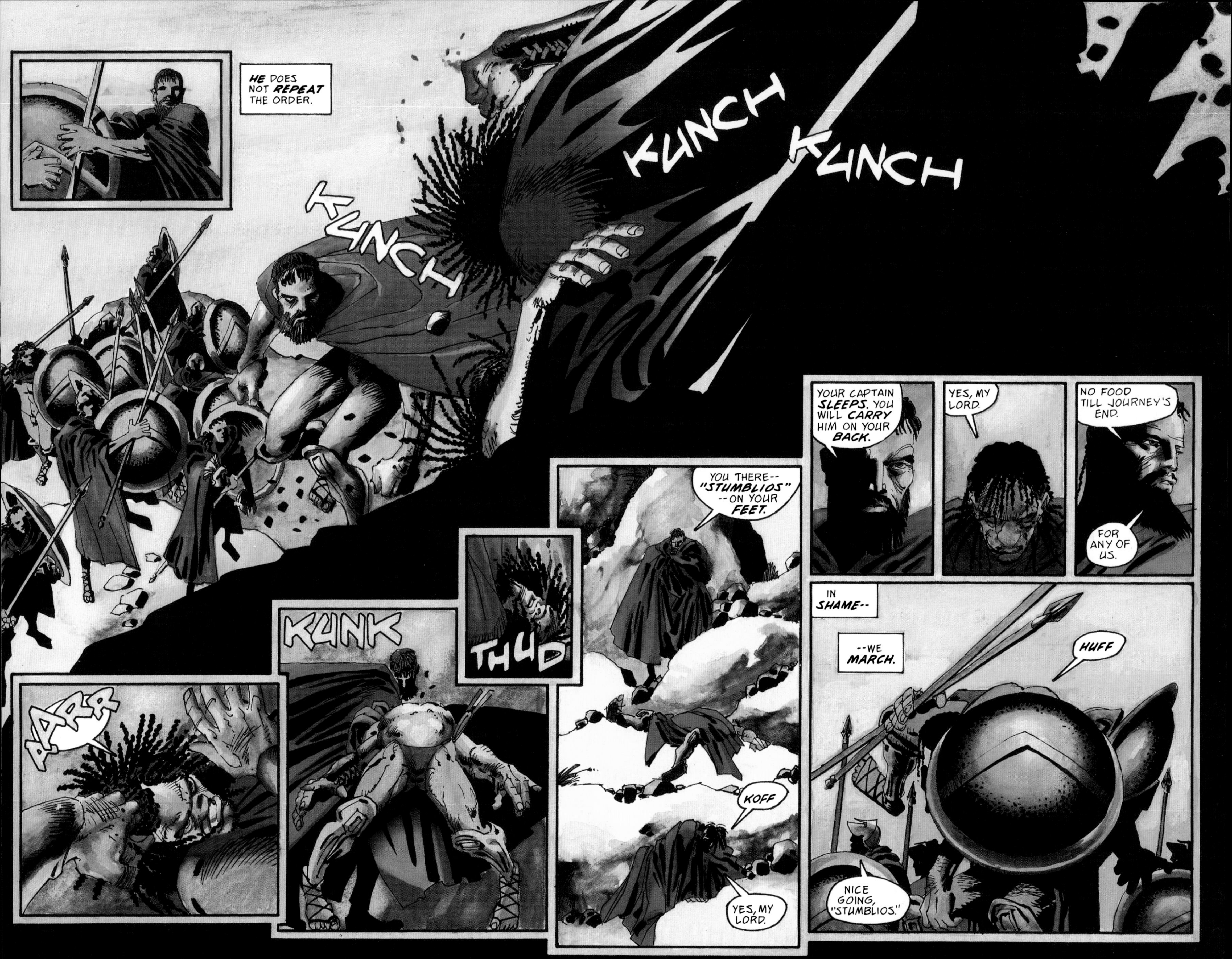
HE DOES NOT REPEAT THE ORDER.
KUNCH
KUNCH KUNCH
AARR
KUNK
THUD
YOU THERE-- "STUMBLIOS" --ON YOUR FEET.
KOFF
YES, MY LORD.
YOUR CAPTAIN SLEEPS. YOU WILL CARRY HIM ON YOUR BACK.
YES, MY LORD.
NO FOOD TILL JOURNEY'S END.
FOR ANY OF US.
IN SHAME--
--WE MARCH.
HUFF
NICE GOING, "STUMBLIOS."

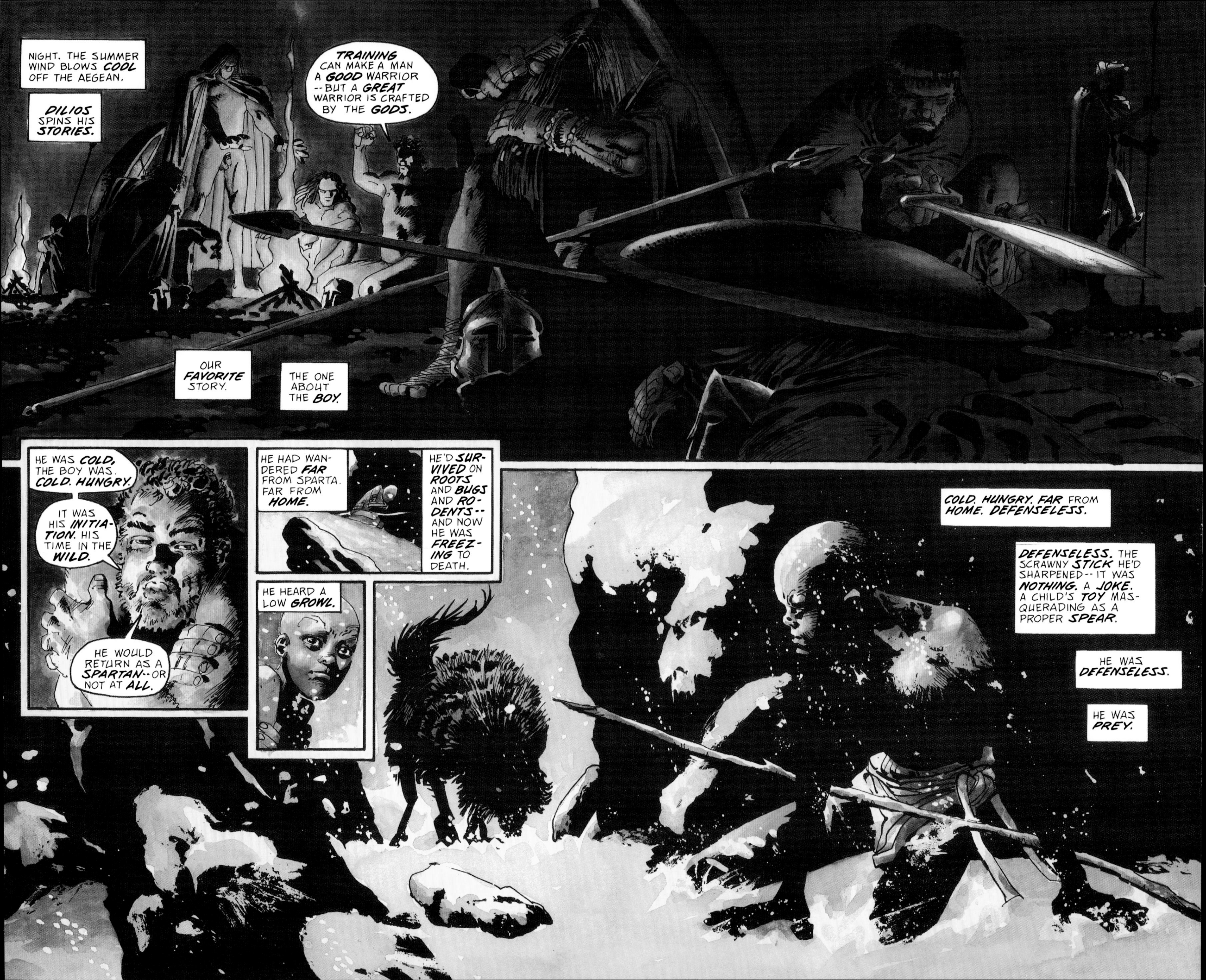
NIGHT. THE SUMMER WIND BLOWS COOL OFF THE AEGEAN.
DILIOS SPINS HIS STORIES.
TRAINING CAN MAKE A MAN A GOOD WARRIOR --BUT A GREAT WARRIOR IS CRAFTED BY THE GODS.
OUR FAVORITE STORY.
THE ONE ABOUT THE BOY.
HE WAS COLD, THE BOY WAS. COLD. HUNGRY.
IT WAS HIS INITIATION. HIS TIME IN THE WILD.
HE WOULD RETURN AS A SPARTAN--OR NOT AT ALL.
HE HAD WANDERED FAR FROM SPARTA. FAR FROM HOME.
HE'D SURVIVED ON ROOTS AND BUGS AND RODENTS--AND NOW HE WAS FREEZING TO DEATH.
HE HEARD A LOW GROWL.
COLD. HUNGRY. FAR FROM HOME. DEFENSELESS.
DEFENSELESS. THE SCRAWNY STICK HE'D SHARPENED--IT WAS NOTHING. A JOKE. A CHILD'S TOY MASQUERADING AS A PROPER SPEAR.
HE WAS DEFENSELESS.
HE WAS PREY.

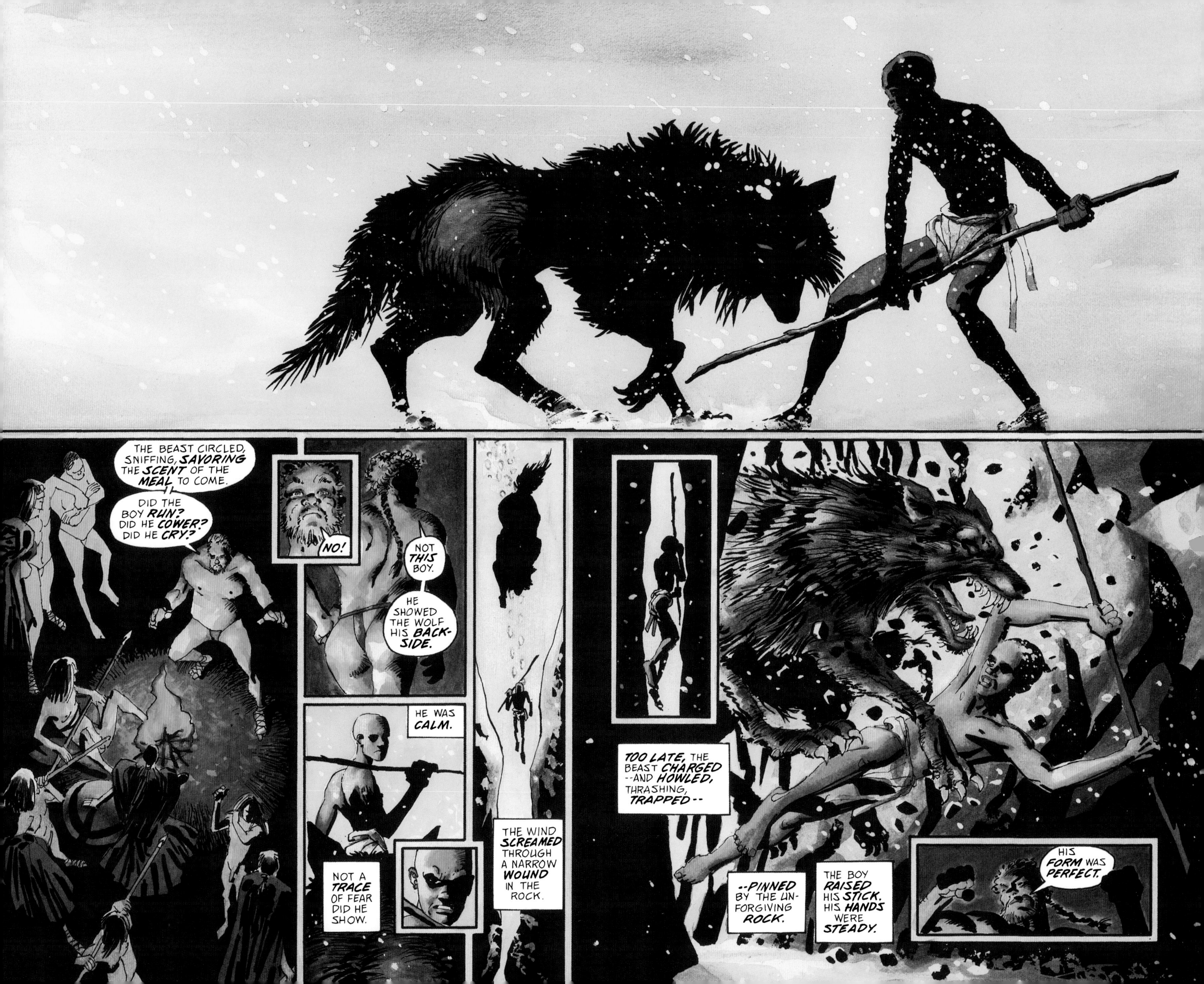
THE BEAST CIRCLED, SNIFFING, SAVORING THE SCENT OF THE MEAL TO COME.
DID THE BOY RUN? DID HE COWER? DID HE CRY?
NO!
NOT THIS BOY.
HE SHOWED THE WOLF HIS BACK-SIDE.
HE WAS CALM.
NOT A TRACE OF FEAR DID HE SHOW.
THE WIND SCREAMED THROUGH A NARROW WOUND IN THE ROCK.
TOO LATE, THE BEAST CHARGED --AND HOWLED, THRASHING, TRAPPED--
--PINNED BY THE UN-FORGIVING ROCK.
THE BOY RAISED HIS STICK. HIS HANDS WERE STEADY.
HIS FORM WAS PERFECT.

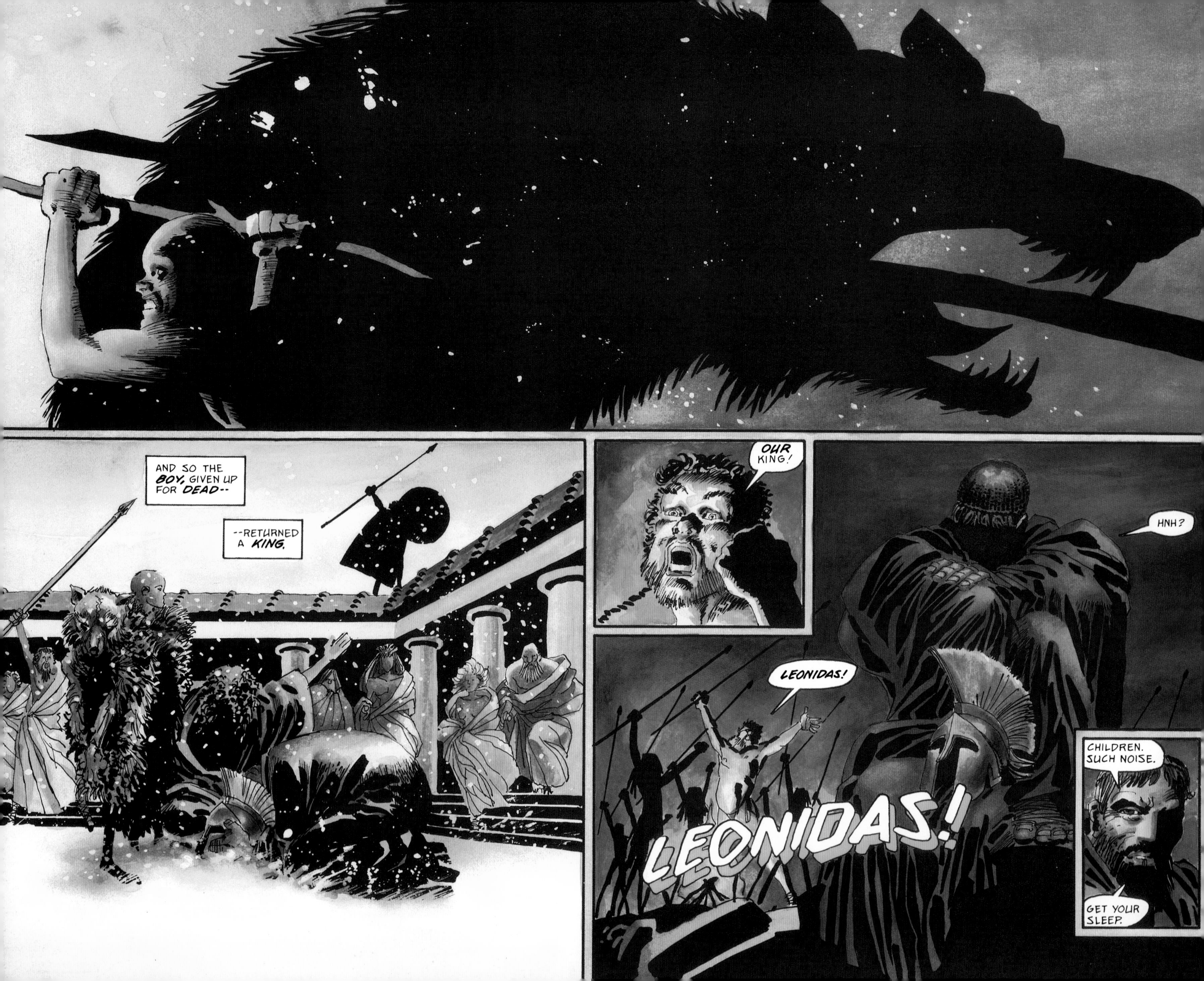
AND SO THE BOY, GIVEN UP FOR DEAD--
--RETURNED A KING.
OUR KING!
HNH?
LEONIDAS!
LEONIDAS!
CHILDREN. SUCH NOISE.
GET YOUR SLEEP.

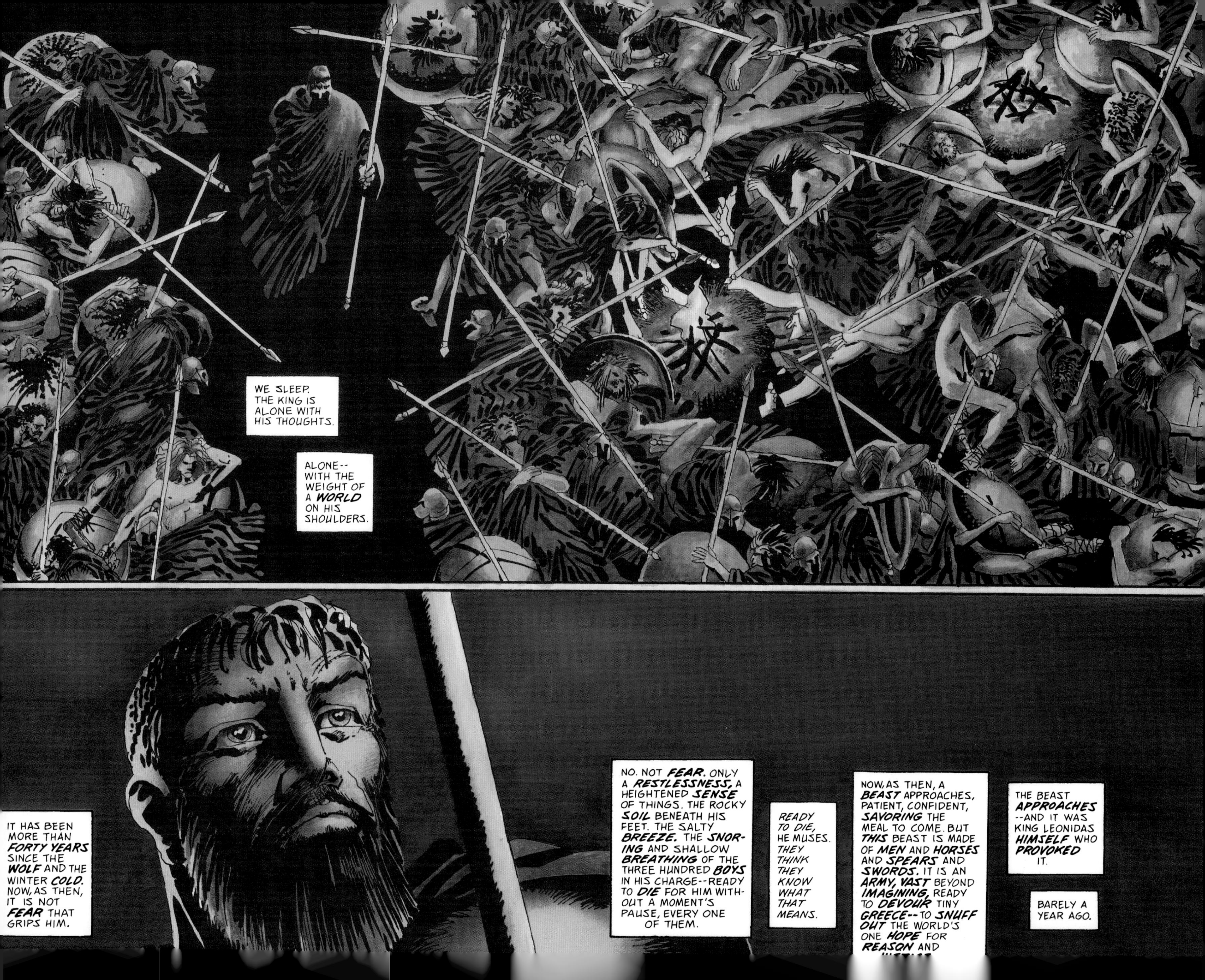
WE SLEEP. THE KING IS ALONE WITH HIS THOUGHTS.
ALONE-- WITH THE WEIGHT OF A WORLD ON HIS SHOULDERS.
IT HAS BEEN MORE THAN FORTY YEARS SINCE THE WOLF AND THE WINTER COLD. NOW, AS THEN, IT IS NOT FEAR THAT GRIPS HIM.
NO. NOT FEAR. ONLY A RESTLESSNESS, A HEIGHTENED SENSE OF THINGS. THE ROCKY SOIL BENEATH HIS FEET. THE SALTY BREEZE. THE SNORING AND SHALLOW BREATHING OF THE THREE HUNDRED BOYS IN HIS CHARGE--READY TO DIE FOR HIM WITHOUT A MOMENT'S PAUSE, EVERY ONE OF THEM.
READY TO DIE, HE MUSES. THEY THINK THEY KNOW WHAT THAT MEANS.
NOW, AS THEN, A BEAST APPROACHES, PATIENT, CONFIDENT, SAVORING THE MEAL TO COME. BUT THIS BEAST IS MADE OF MEN AND HORSES AND SPEARS AND SWORDS. IT IS AN ARMY, VAST BEYOND IMAGINING, READY TO DEVOUR TINY GREECE--TO SNUFF OUT THE WORLD'S ONE HOPE FOR REASON AND
THE BEAST APPROACHES --AND IT WAS KING LEONIDAS HIMSELF WHO PROVOKED IT.
BARELY A YEAR AGO.

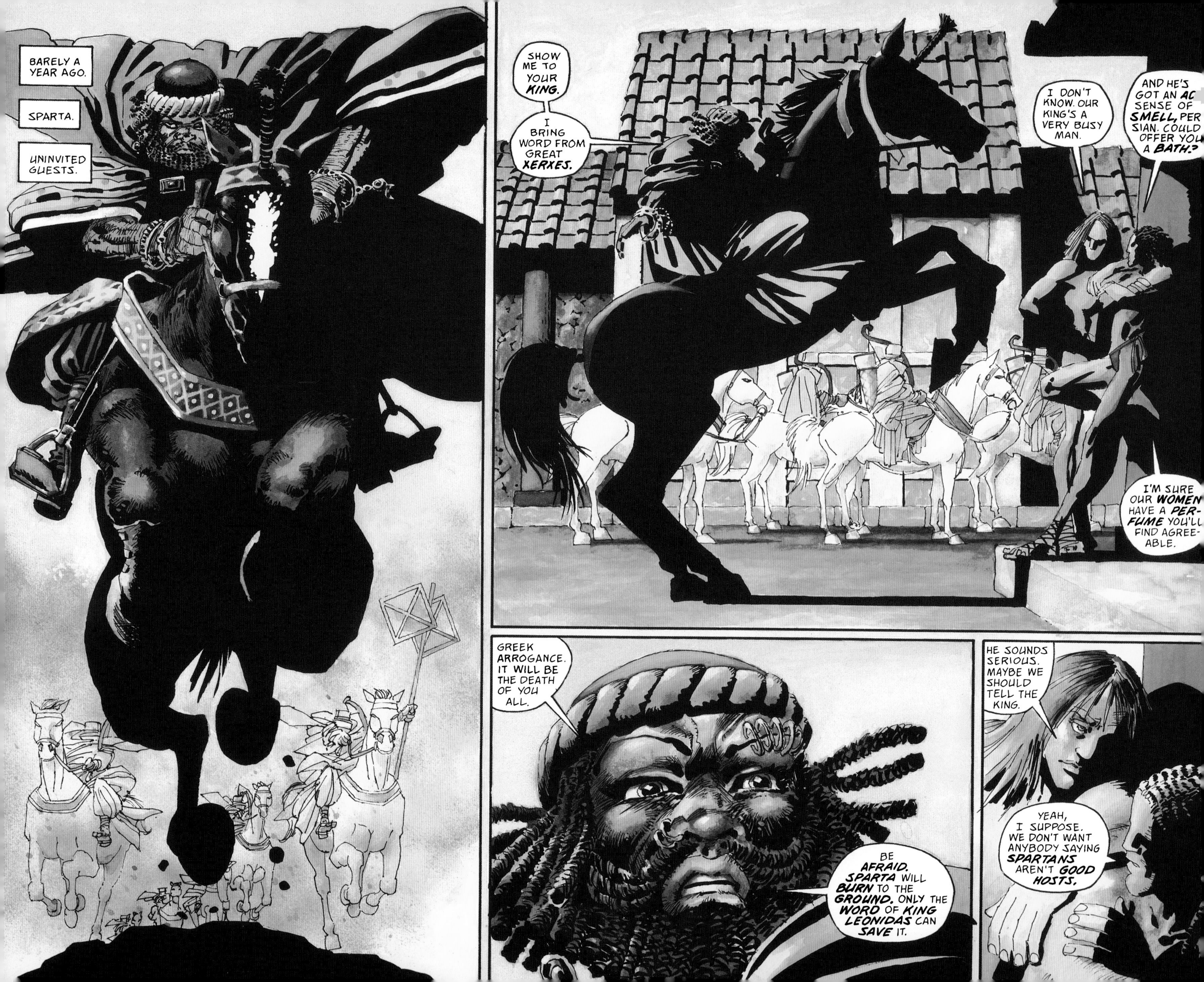

BARELY A YEAR AGO.
SPARTA.
UNINVITED GUESTS.
SHOW ME TO YOUR KING.
I BRING WORD FROM GREAT XERXES.
I DON'T KNOW. OUR KING'S A VERY BUSY MAN.
AND HE'S GOT AN AC SENSE OF SMELL, PER SIAN. COULD OFFER YOU A BATH?
I'M SURE OUR WOMEN HAVE A PER- FUME YOU'LL FIND AGREE- ABLE.
GREEK ARROGANCE. IT WILL BE THE DEATH OF YOU ALL.
BE AFRAID. SPARTA WILL BURN TO THE GROUND. ONLY THE WORD OF KING LEONIDAS CAN SAVE IT.
HE SOUNDS SERIOUS. MAYBE WE SHOULD TELL THE KING.
YEAH, I SUPPOSE. WE DON'T WANT ANYBODY SAYING SPARTANS AREN'T GOOD HOSTS.

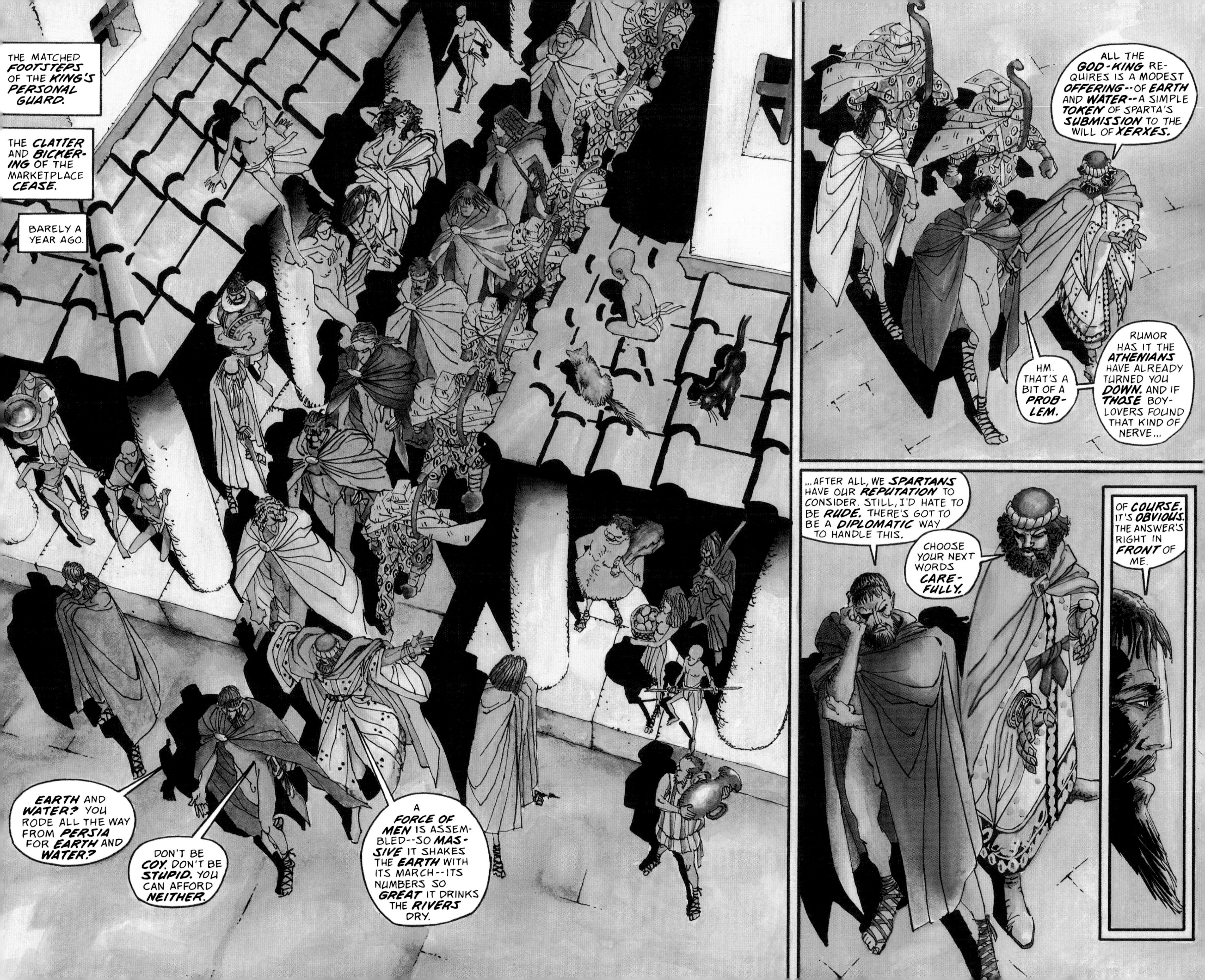
THE MATCHED FOOTSTEPS OF THE KING'S PERSONAL GUARD.
THE CLATTER AND BICKERING OF THE MARKETPLACE CEASE.
BARELY A YEAR AGO.
EARTH AND WATER? YOU RODE ALL THE WAY FROM PERSIA FOR EARTH AND WATER?
DON'T BE COY. DON'T BE STUPID. YOU CAN AFFORD NEITHER.
A FORCE OF MEN IS ASSEMBLED--SO MASSIVE IT SHAKES THE EARTH WITH ITS MARCH--ITS NUMBERS SO GREAT IT DRINKS THE RIVERS DRY.
ALL THE GOD-KING REQUIRES IS A MODEST OFFERING--OF EARTH AND WATER--A SIMPLE TOKEN OF SPARTA'S SUBMISSION TO THE WILL OF XERXES.
HM. THAT'S A BIT OF A PROBLEM.
RUMOR HAS IT THE ATHENIANS HAVE ALREADY TURNED YOU DOWN. AND IF THOSE BOY-LOVERS FOUND THAT KIND OF NERVE...
...AFTER ALL, WE SPARTANS HAVE OUR REPUTATION TO CONSIDER. STILL, I'D HATE TO BE RUDE. THERE'S GOT TO BE A DIPLOMATIC WAY TO HANDLE THIS.
CHOOSE YOUR NEXT WORDS CAREFULLY.
OF COURSE. IT'S OBVIOUS. THE ANSWER'S RIGHT IN FRONT OF ME.

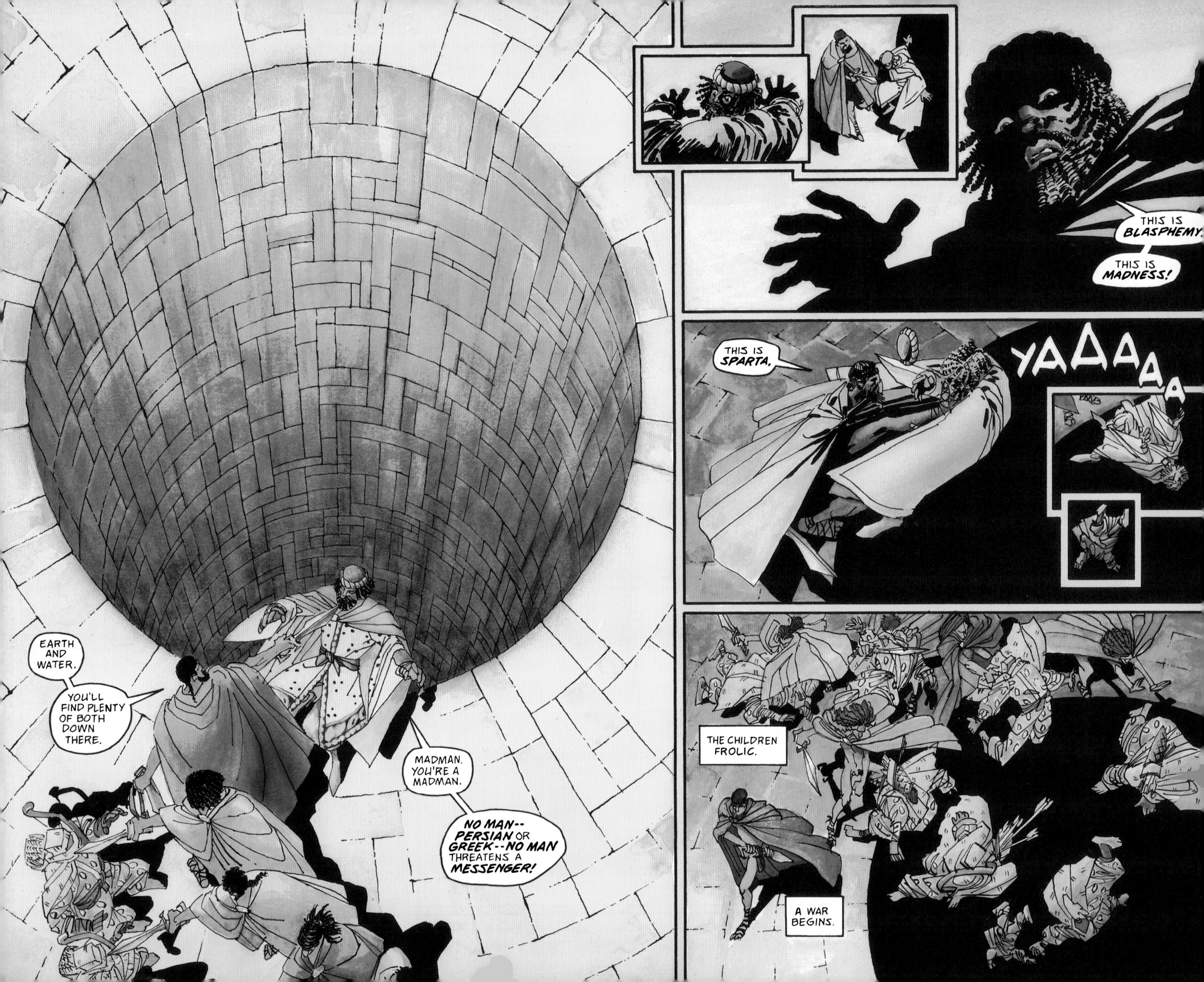
EARTH AND WATER.
YOU'LL FIND PLENTY OF BOTH DOWN THERE.
MADMAN. YOU'RE A MADMAN.
NO MAN-- PERSIAN OR GREEK--NO MAN THREATENS A MESSENGER!
THIS IS BLASPHEMY.
THIS IS MADNESS!
THIS IS SPARTA.
YAAAAA
THE CHILDREN FROLIC.
A WAR BEGINS.

CHAPTER TWO:

DUTY

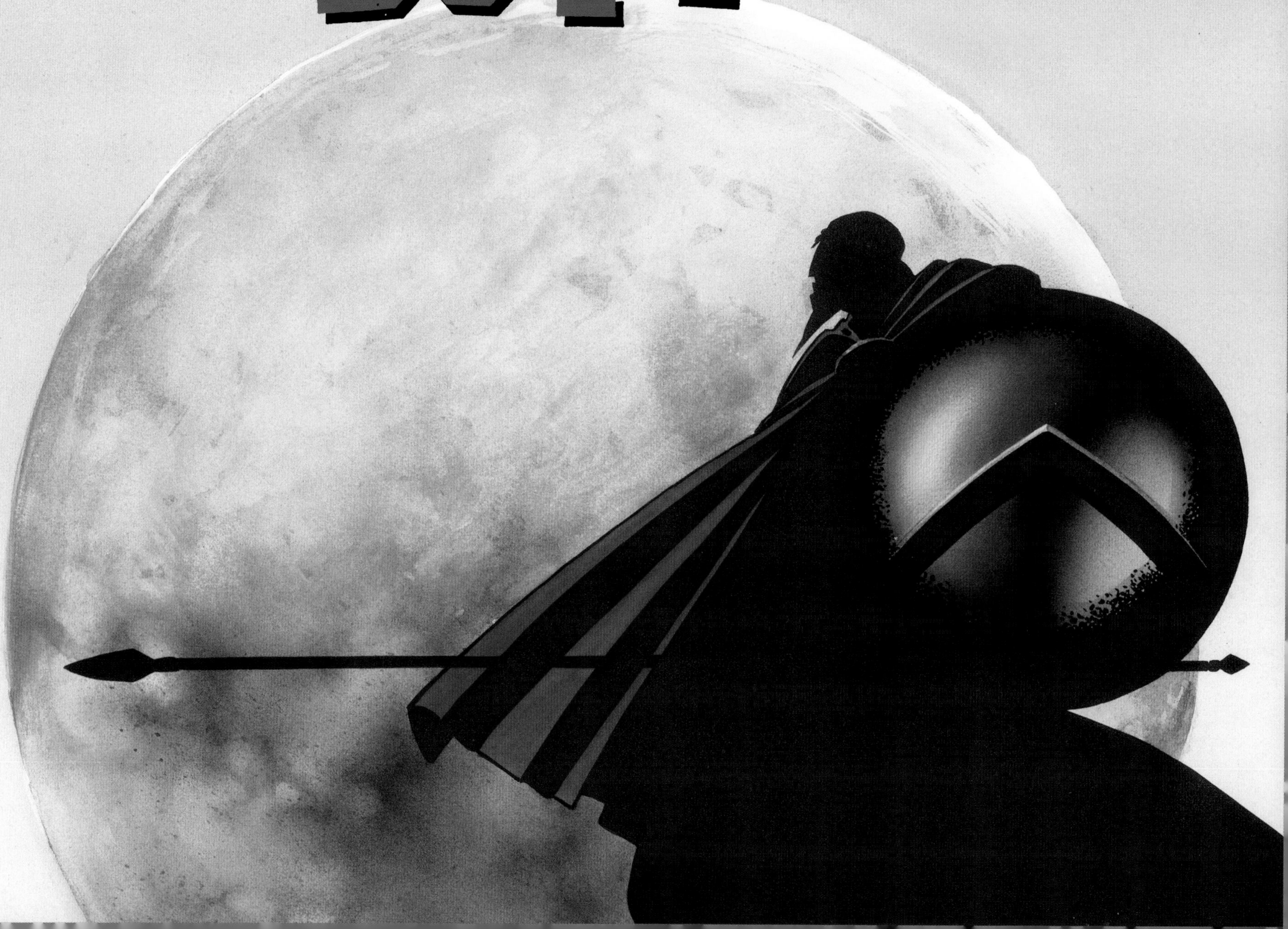

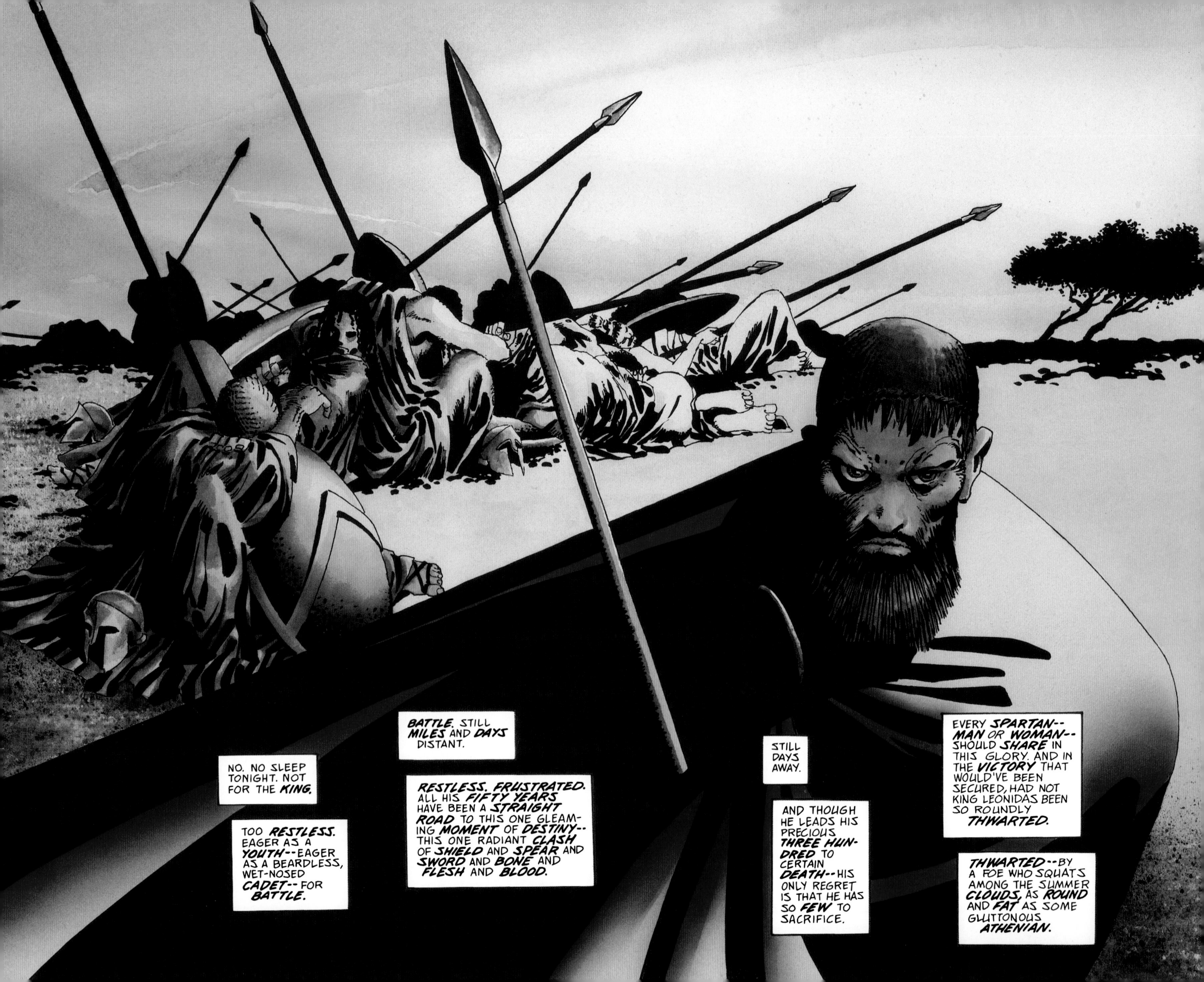
NO. NO SLEEP TONIGHT. NOT FOR THE KING.
TOO RESTLESS. EAGER AS A YOUTH--EAGER AS A BEARDLESS, WET-NOSED CADET-- FOR BATTLE.
BATTLE. STILL MILES AND DAYS DISTANT.
RESTLESS. FRUSTRATED. ALL HIS FIFTY YEARS HAVE BEEN A STRAIGHT ROAD TO THIS ONE GLEAMING MOMENT OF DESTINY-- THIS ONE RADIANT CLASH OF SHIELD AND SPEAR AND SWORD AND BONE AND FLESH AND BLOOD.
STILL DAYS AWAY.
AND THOUGH HE LEADS HIS PRECIOUS THREE HUNDRED TO CERTAIN DEATH--HIS ONLY REGRET IS THAT HE HAS SO FEW TO SACRIFICE.
EVERY SPARTAN-- MAN OR WOMAN-- SHOULD SHARE IN THIS GLORY. AND IN THE VICTORY THAT WOULD'VE BEEN SECURED, HAD NOT KING LEONIDAS BEEN SO ROUNDLY THWARTED.
THWARTED--BY A FOE WHO SQUATS AMONG THE SUMMER CLOUDS, AS ROUND AND FAT AS SOME GLUTTONOUS ATHENIAN.

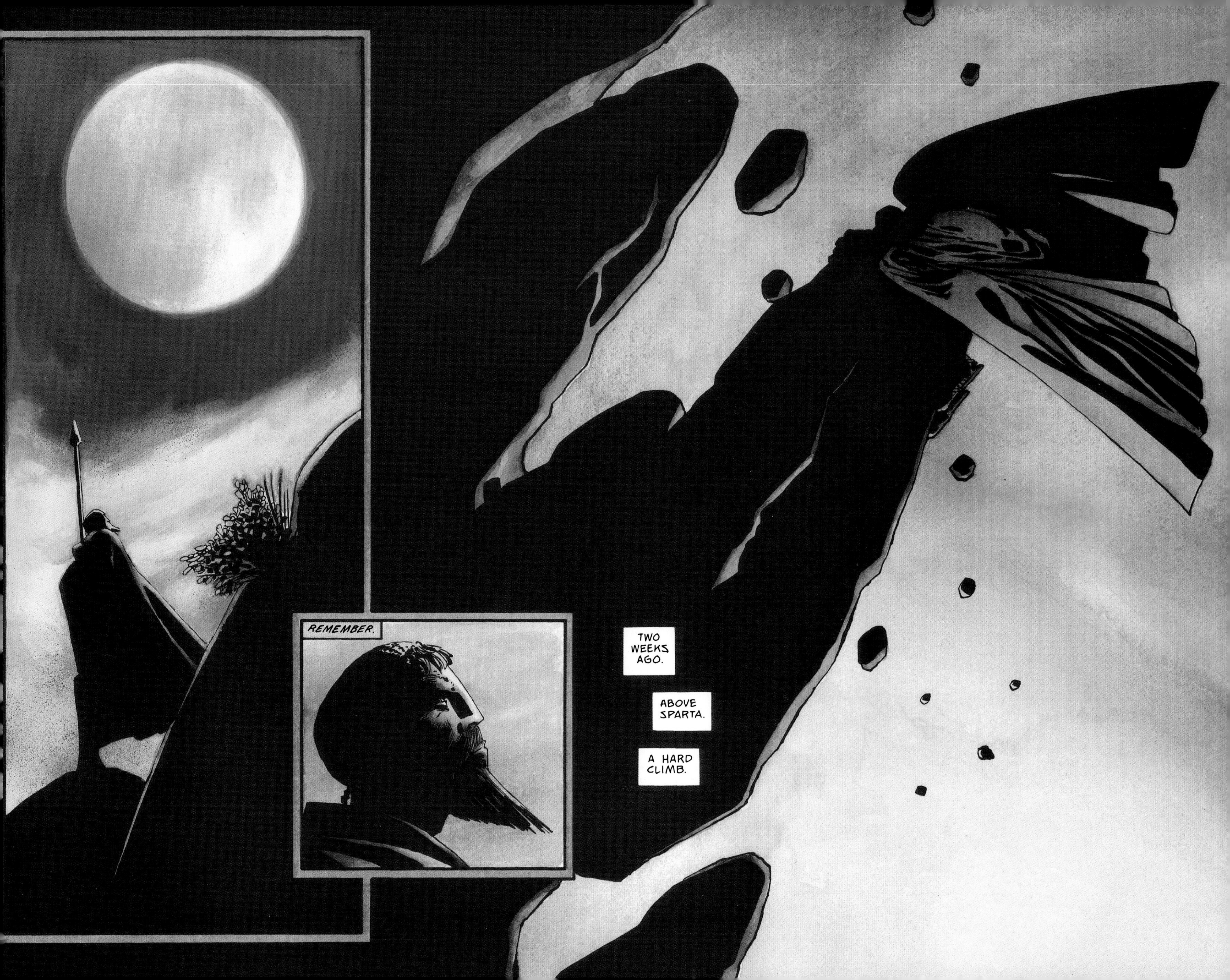
REMEMBER.
TWO WEEKS AGO.
ABOVE SPARTA.
A HARD CLIMB.

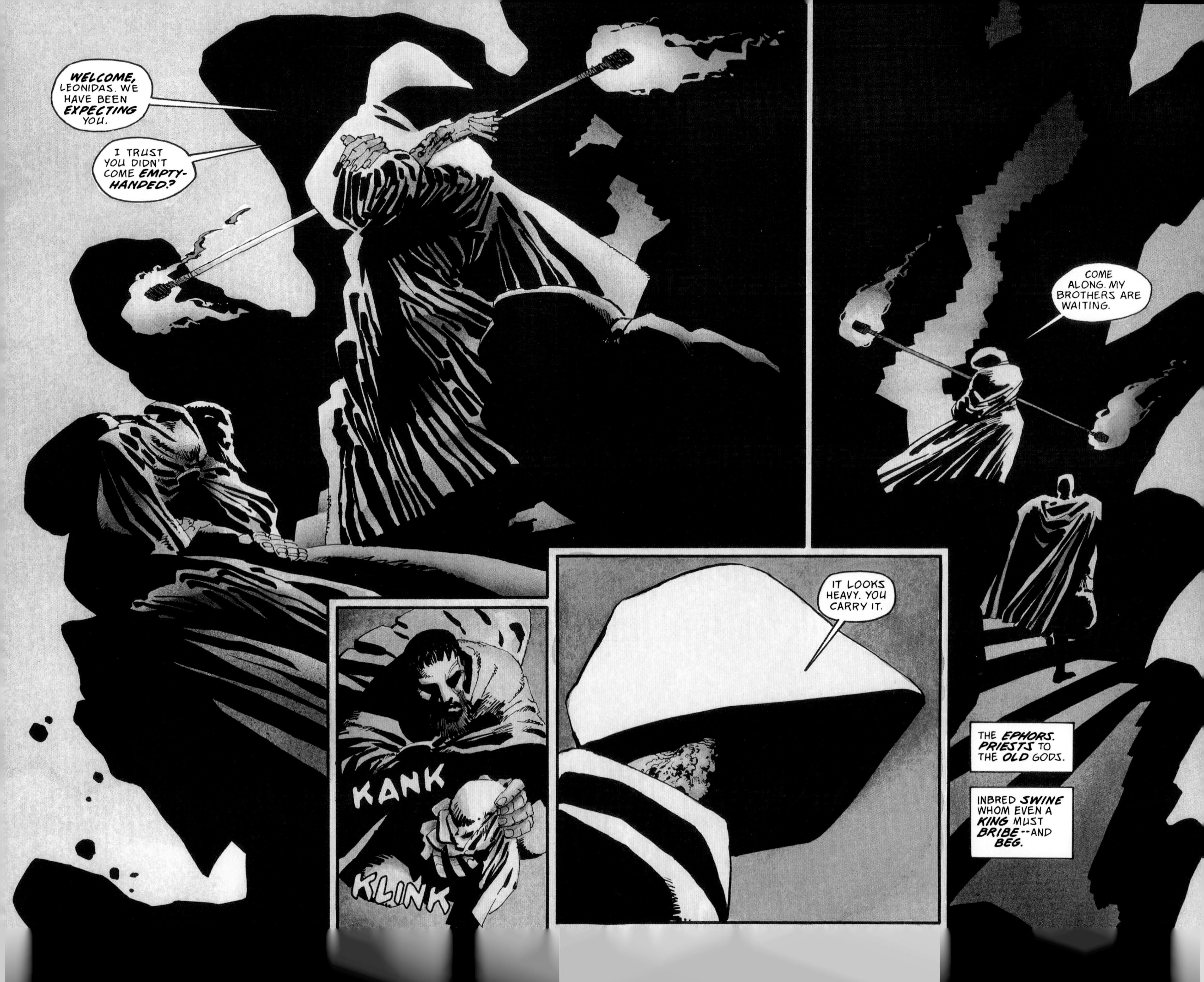
WELCOME, LEONIDAS. WE HAVE BEEN EXPECTING YOU.
I TRUST YOU DIDN'T COME EMPTY-HANDED?
COME ALONG. MY BROTHERS ARE WAITING.
THE EPHORS. PRIESTS TO THE OLD GODS.
INBRED SWINE WHOM EVEN A KING MUST BRIBE--AND BEG.
KANK
KLINK
IT LOOKS HEAVY. YOU CARRY IT.

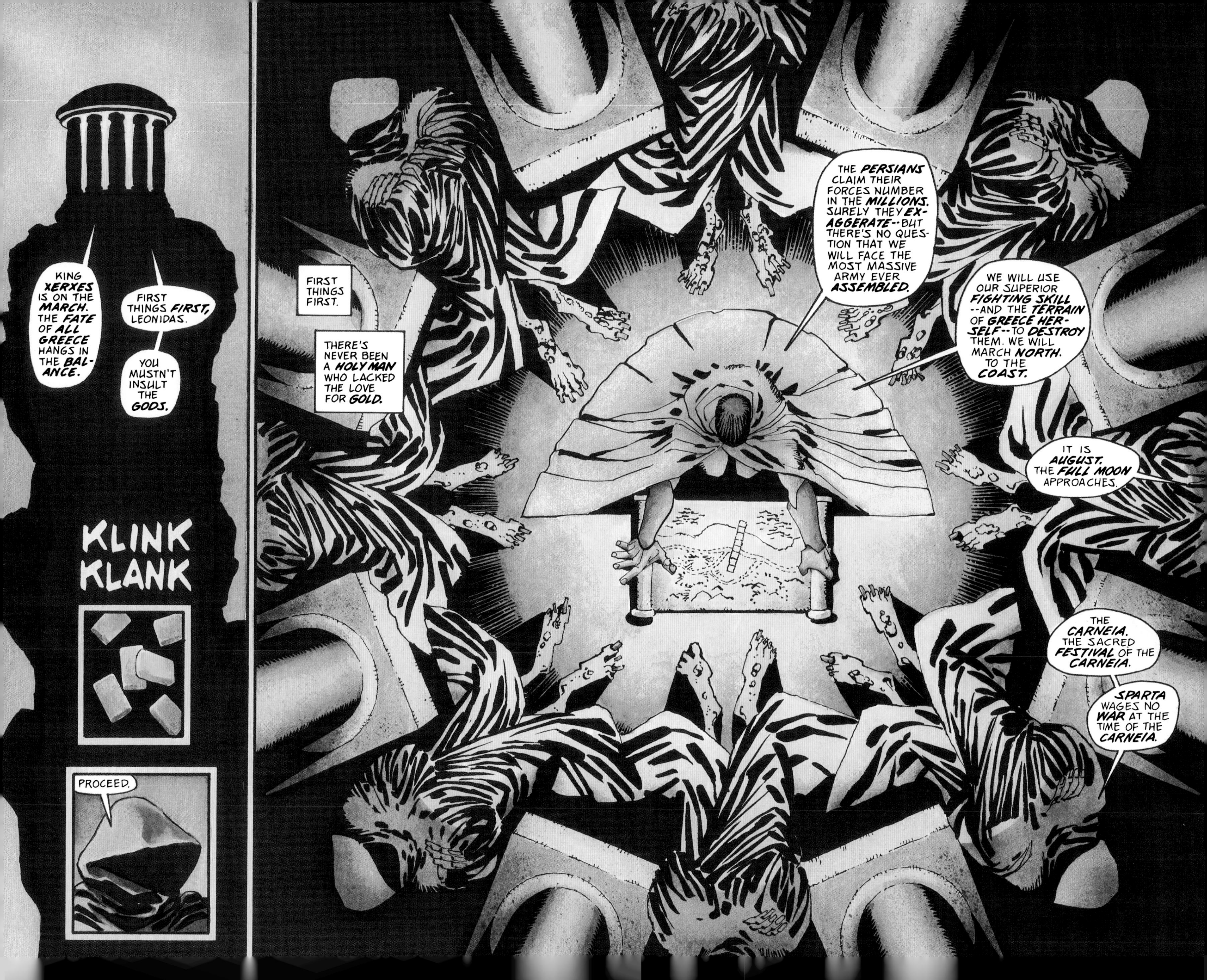
KING XERXES IS ON THE MARCH. THE FATE OF ALL GREECE HANGS IN THE BAL-ANCE.
FIRST THINGS FIRST, LEONIDAS.
YOU MUSTN'T INSULT THE GODS.
KLINK KLANK
PROCEED.
FIRST THINGS FIRST.
THERE'S NEVER BEEN A HOLY MAN WHO LACKED THE LOVE FOR GOLD.
THE PERSIANS CLAIM THEIR FORCES NUMBER IN THE MILLIONS. SURELY THEY EX-AGGERATE--BUT THERE'S NO QUES-TION THAT WE WILL FACE THE MOST MASSIVE ARMY EVER ASSEMBLED.
WE WILL USE OUR SUPERIOR FIGHTING SKILL --AND THE TERRAIN OF GREECE HER-SELF--TO DESTROY THEM. WE WILL MARCH NORTH. TO THE COAST.
IT IS AUGUST. THE FULL MOON APPROACHES.
THE CARNEIA. THE SACRED FESTIVAL OF THE CARNEIA.
SPARTA WAGES NO WAR AT THE TIME OF THE CARNEIA.

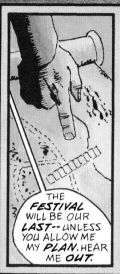

THE FESTIVAL WILL BE OUR LAST--UNLESS YOU ALLOW ME MY PLAN. HEAR ME OUT.

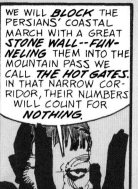

WE WILL BLOCK THE PERSIANS' COASTAL MARCH WITH A GREAT STONE WALL--FUNNELING THEM INTO THE MOUNTAIN PASS WE CALL THE HOT GATES. IN THAT NARROW CORRIDOR, THEIR NUMBERS WILL COUNT FOR NOTHING.

LIKE AN ANGRY SEA HEAVING WAVE AFTER WAVE AGAINST AN UNYIELDING CLIFF, THEY WILL SHATTER AT EACH ADVANCE. XERXES' LOSSES WILL BE SO GREAT--HIS MEN SO DEMORALIZED--HE WILL HAVE NO CHOICE BUT TO ABANDON HIS CAMPAIGN.

BUT--THE CARNEIA...

...WE MUST CONSULT THE ORACLE.

I'D PREFER YOU TRUSTED YOUR REASON.

YOUR BLASPHEMIES HAVE COST US QUITE ENOUGH ALREADY. DON'T COMPOUND THEM.

WE WILL CONSULT THE ORACLE.

COME ALONG. ENJOY THE SHOW.

INBRED SWINE. DISEASED OLD MYSTICS.

WORTHLESS REMNANTS.

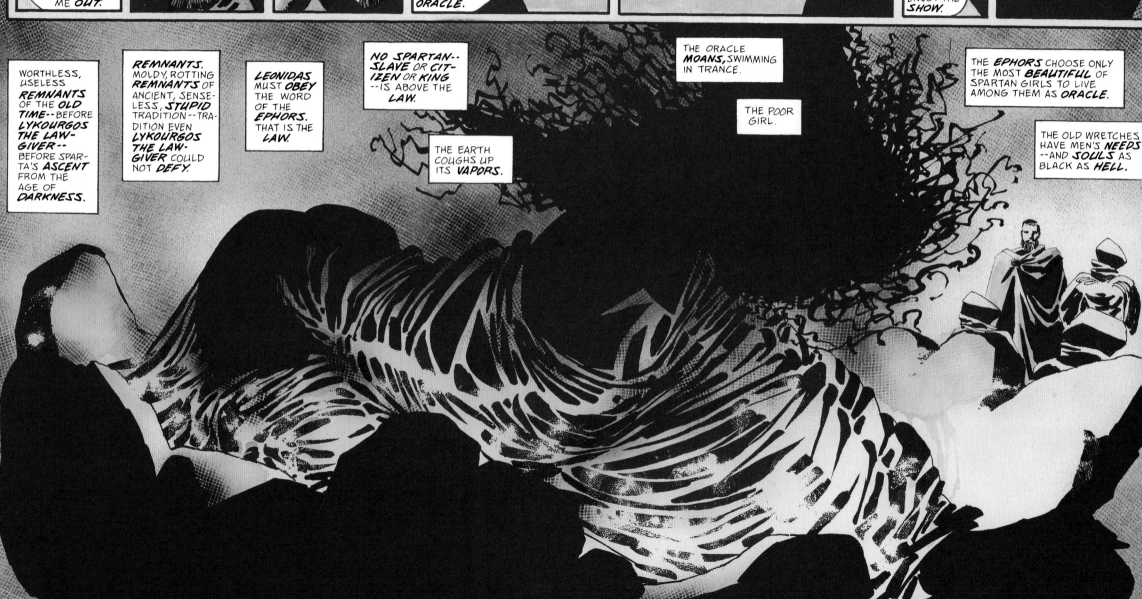

WORTHLESS, USELESS REMNANTS OF THE OLD TIME--BEFORE LYKOURGOS THE LAWGIVER--BEFORE SPARTA'S ASCENT FROM THE AGE OF DARKNESS.

REMNANTS. MOLDY, ROTTING REMNANTS OF ANCIENT, SENSELESS, STUPID TRADITION--TRADITION EVEN LYKOURGOS THE LAWGIVER COULD NOT DEFY.

LEONIDAS MUST OBEY THE WORD OF THE EPHORS. THAT IS THE LAW.

NO SPARTAN--SLAVE OR CITIZEN OR KING--IS ABOVE THE LAW.

THE EARTH COUGHS UP ITS VAPORS.

THE ORACLE MOANS, SWIMMING IN TRANCE.

THE POOR GIRL.

THE EPHORS CHOOSE ONLY THE MOST BEAUTIFUL OF SPARTAN GIRLS TO LIVE AMONG THEM AS ORACLE.

THE OLD WRETCHES HAVE MEN'S NEEDS--AND SOULS AS BLACK AS HELL.

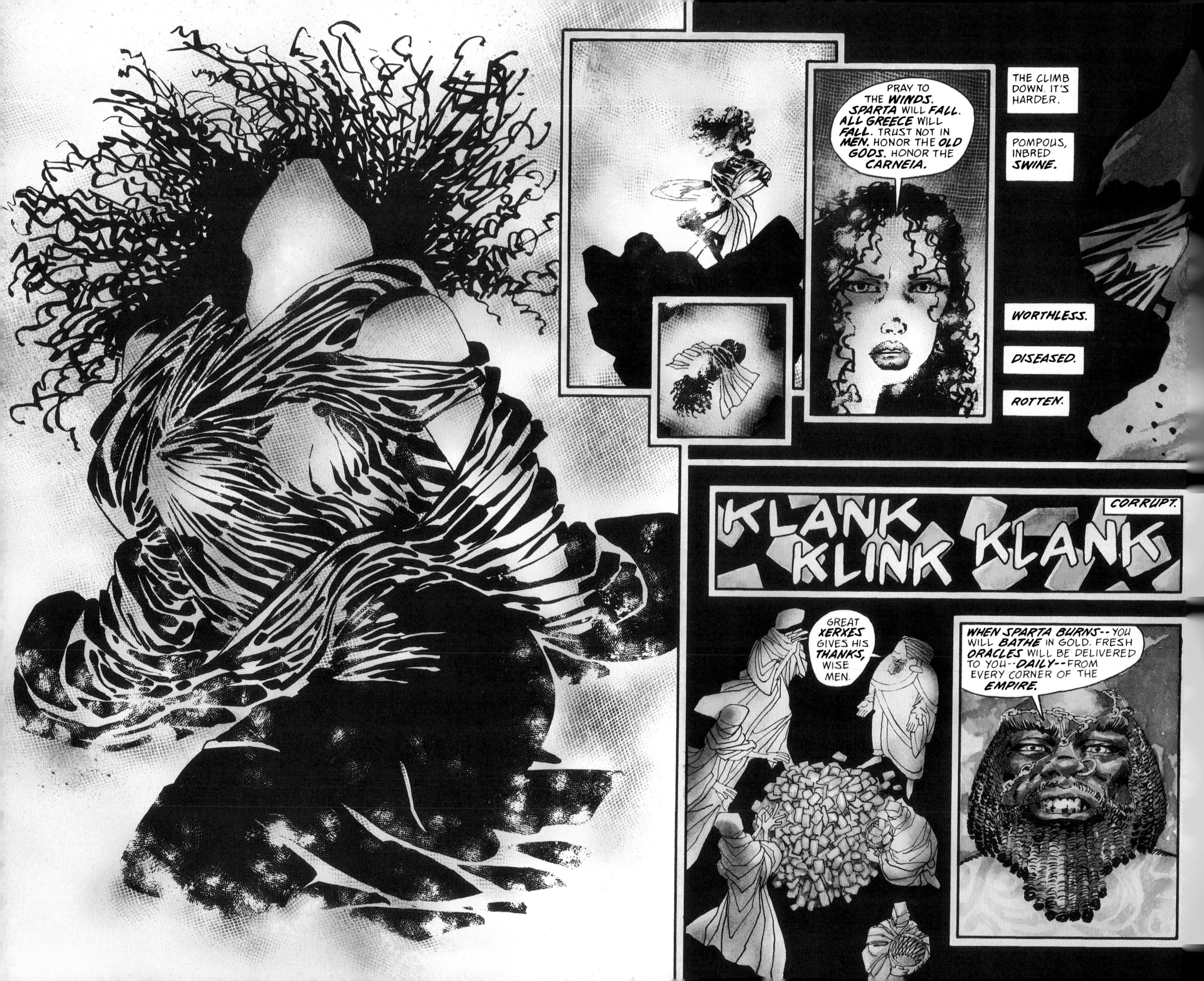
PRAY TO THE WINDS. SPARTA WILL FALL. ALL GREECE WILL FALL. TRUST NOT IN MEN. HONOR THE OLD GODS. HONOR THE CARNEIA.
THE CLIMB DOWN. IT'S HARDER.
POMPOUS, INBRED SWINE.
WORTHLESS.
DISEASED.
ROTTEN.
CORRUPT.
KLANK KLINK KLANK KLANK
GREAT XERXES GIVES HIS THANKS, WISE MEN.
WHEN SPARTA BURNS-- YOU WILL BATHE IN GOLD. FRESH ORACLES WILL BE DELIVERED TO YOU--DAILY--FROM EVERY CORNER OF THE EMPIRE.

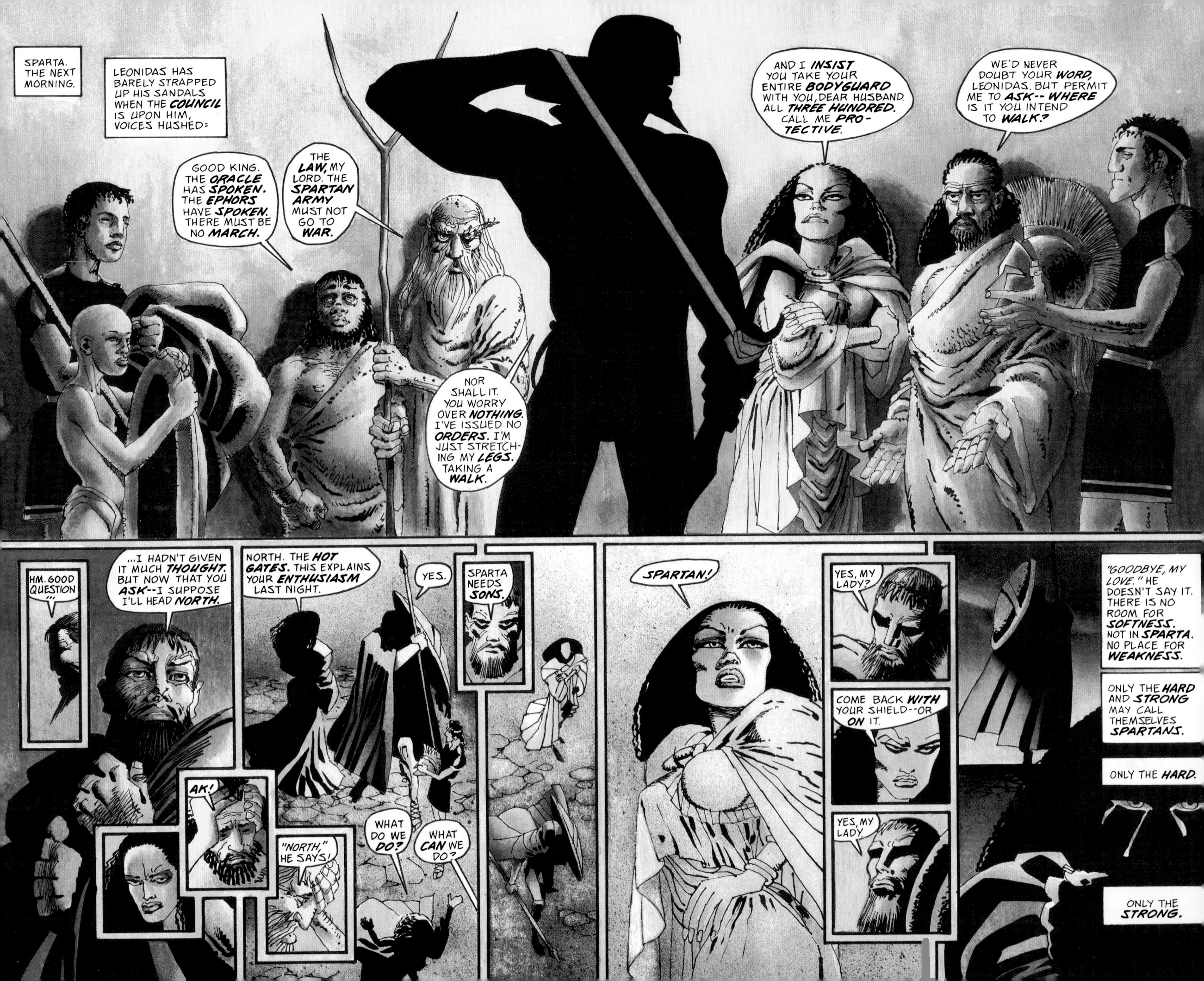
SPARTA. THE NEXT MORNING.
LEONIDAS HAS BARELY STRAPPED UP HIS SANDALS WHEN THE COUNCIL IS UPON HIM, VOICES HUSHED=
GOOD KING. THE ORACLE HAS SPOKEN. THE EPHORS HAVE SPOKEN. THERE MUST BE NO MARCH.
THE LAW, MY LORD. THE SPARTAN ARMY MUST NOT GO TO WAR.
NOR SHALL IT. YOU WORRY OVER NOTHING. I'VE ISSUED NO ORDERS. I'M JUST STRETCHING MY LEGS. TAKING A WALK.
AND I INSIST YOU TAKE YOUR ENTIRE BODYGUARD WITH YOU, DEAR HUSBAND. ALL THREE HUNDRED. CALL ME PROTECTIVE.
WE'D NEVER DOUBT YOUR WORD, LEONIDAS. BUT PERMIT ME TO ASK-- WHERE IS IT YOU INTEND TO WALK?
HM. GOOD QUESTION...
...I HADN'T GIVEN IT MUCH THOUGHT. BUT NOW THAT YOU ASK--I SUPPOSE I'LL HEAD NORTH.
AK!
NORTH. THE HOT GATES. THIS EXPLAINS YOUR ENTHUSIASM LAST NIGHT.
YES.
SPARTA NEEDS SONS.
"NORTH," HE SAYS!
WHAT DO WE DO?
WHAT CAN WE DO?
SPARTAN!
YES, MY LADY?
COME BACK WITH YOUR SHIELD--OR ON IT.
YES, MY LADY.
"GOODBYE, MY LOVE." HE DOESN'T SAY IT. THERE IS NO ROOM FOR SOFTNESS. NOT IN SPARTA. NO PLACE FOR WEAKNESS.
ONLY THE HARD AND STRONG MAY CALL THEMSELVES SPARTANS.
ONLY THE HARD.
ONLY THE STRONG.

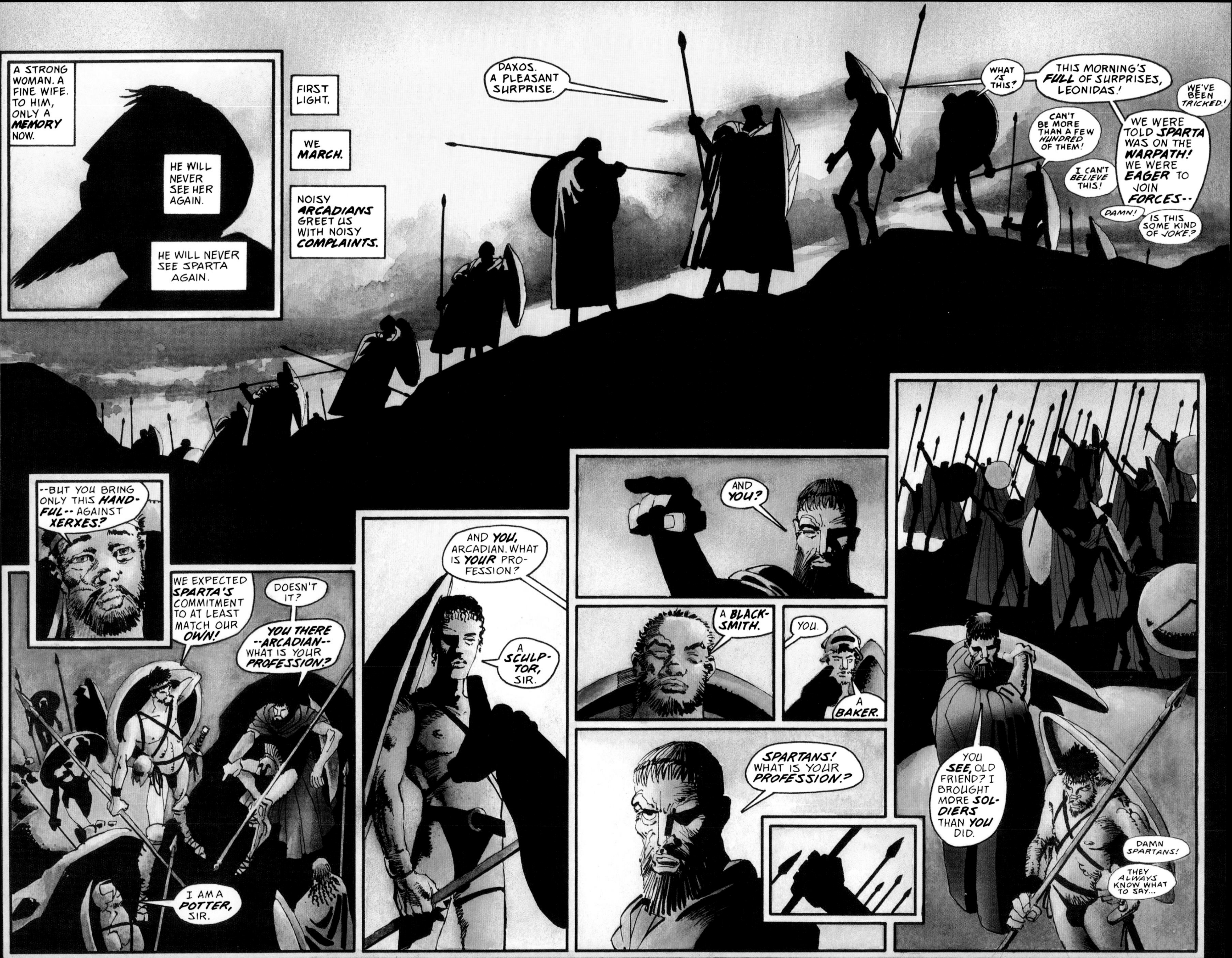
A STRONG WOMAN. A FINE WIFE. TO HIM, ONLY A MEMORY NOW.
HE WILL NEVER SEE HER AGAIN.
HE WILL NEVER SEE SPARTA AGAIN.
FIRST LIGHT.
WE MARCH.
NOISY ARCADIANS GREET US WITH NOISY COMPLAINTS.
DAXOS. A PLEASANT SURPRISE.
WHAT IS THIS?
THIS MORNING'S FULL OF SURPRISES, LEONIDAS!
WE'VE BEEN TRICKED!
CAN'T BE MORE THAN A FEW HUNDRED OF THEM!
WE WERE TOLD SPARTA WAS ON THE WARPATH! WE WERE EAGER TO JOIN FORCES--
I CAN'T BELIEVE THIS!
DAMN!
IS THIS SOME KIND OF JOKE?
--BUT YOU BRING ONLY THIS HANDFUL-- AGAINST XERXES?
WE EXPECTED SPARTA'S COMMITMENT TO AT LEAST MATCH OUR OWN!
DOESN'T IT?
YOU THERE --ARCADIAN-- WHAT IS YOUR PROFESSION?
I AM A POTTER, SIR.
AND YOU, ARCADIAN. WHAT IS YOUR PROFESSION?
A SCULPTOR, SIR.
AND YOU?
A BLACKSMITH.
YOU.
A BAKER.
SPARTANS! WHAT IS YOUR PROFESSION?
YOU SEE, OLD FRIEND? I BROUGHT MORE SOLDIERS THAN YOU DID.
DAMN SPARTANS!
THEY ALWAYS KNOW WHAT TO SAY...

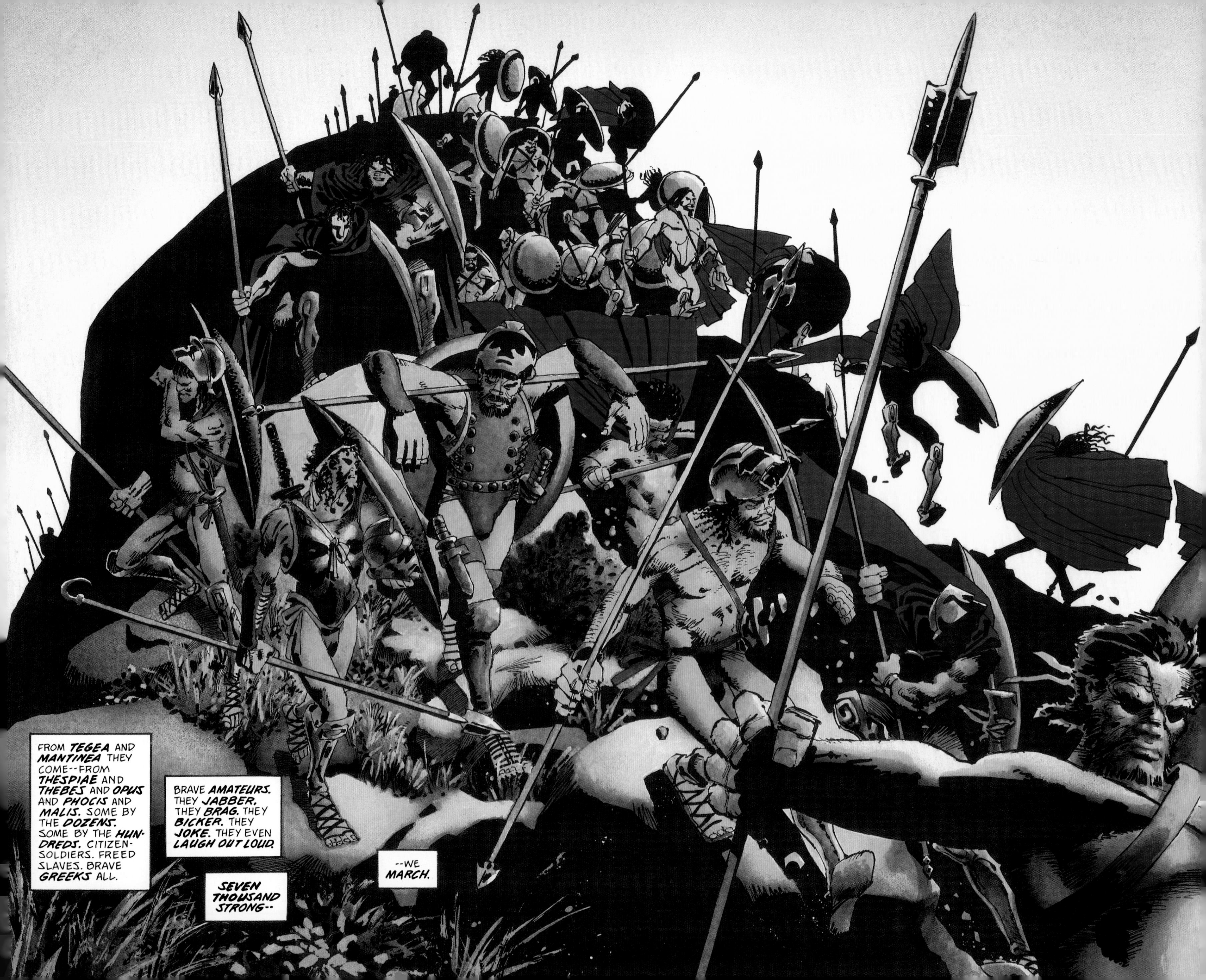
FROM TEGEA AND MANTINEA THEY COME--FROM THESPIAE AND THEBES AND OPUS AND PHOCIS AND MALIS. SOME BY THE DOZENS. SOME BY THE HUNDREDS. CITIZEN-SOLDIERS. FREED SLAVES. BRAVE GREEKS ALL.
SEVEN THOUSAND STRONG--
BRAVE AMATEURS. THEY JABBER. THEY BRAG. THEY BICKER. THEY JOKE. THEY EVEN LAUGH OUT LOUD.
--WE MARCH.

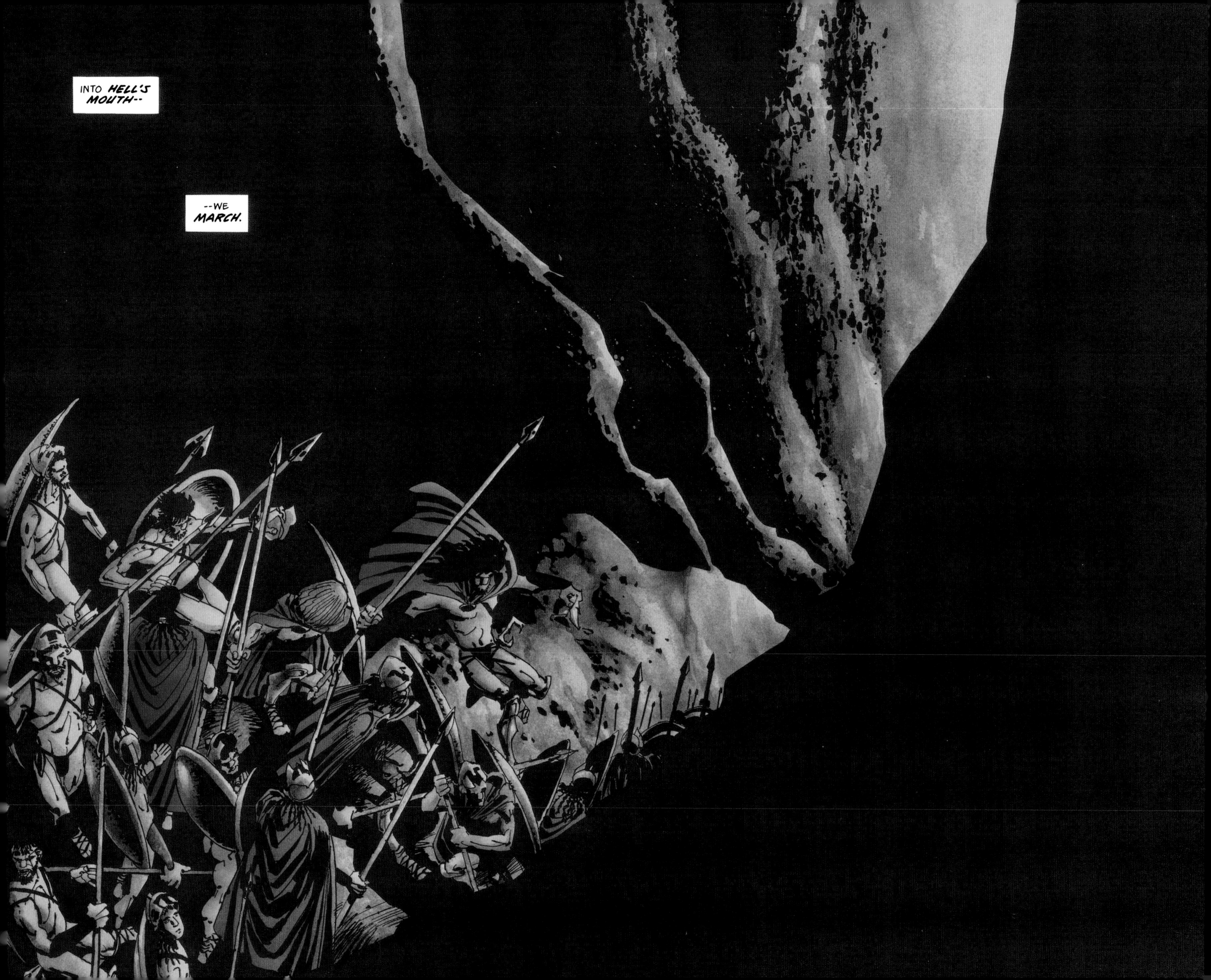
INTO HELL'S MOUTH--
--WE MARCH.

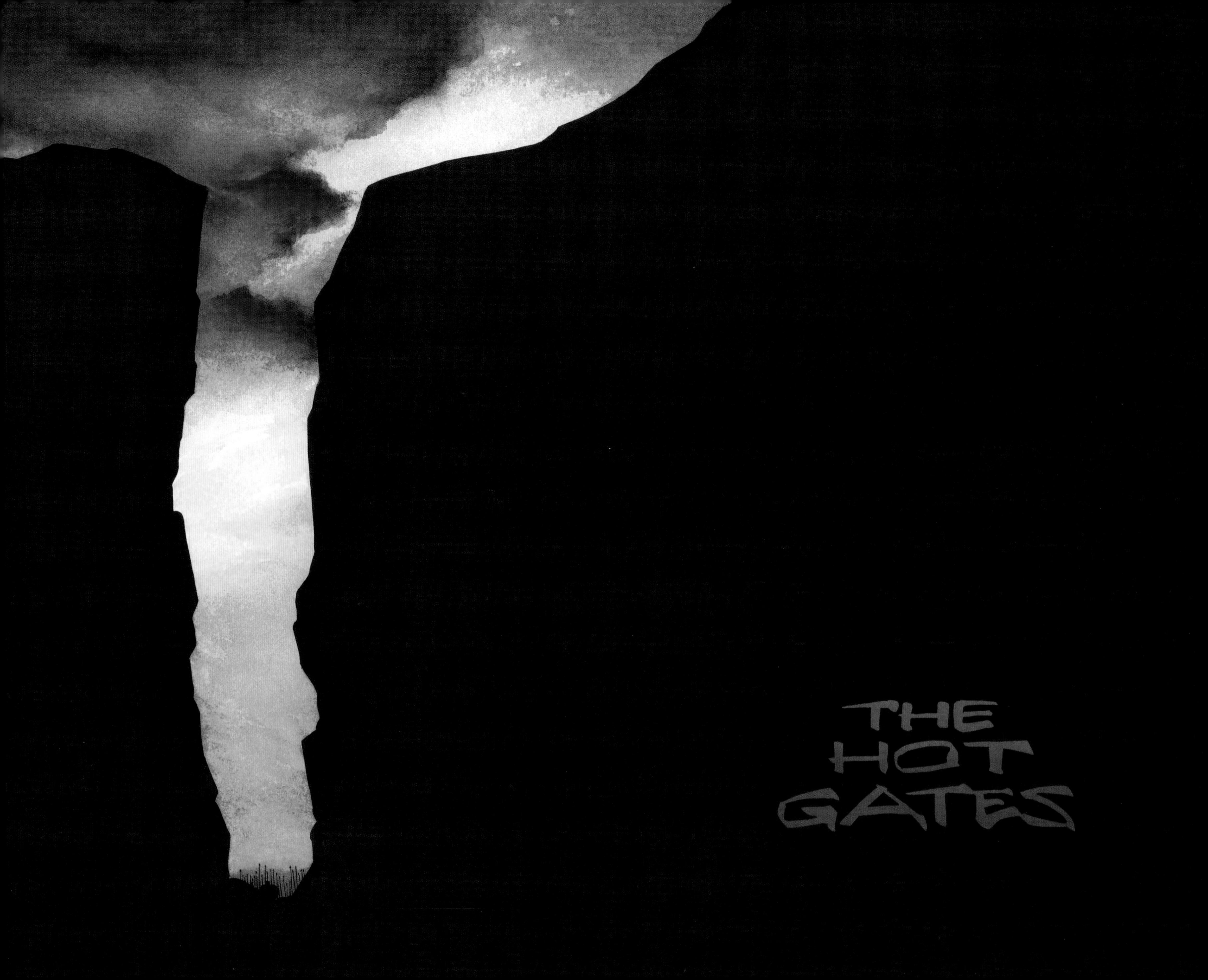
THE HOT GATES

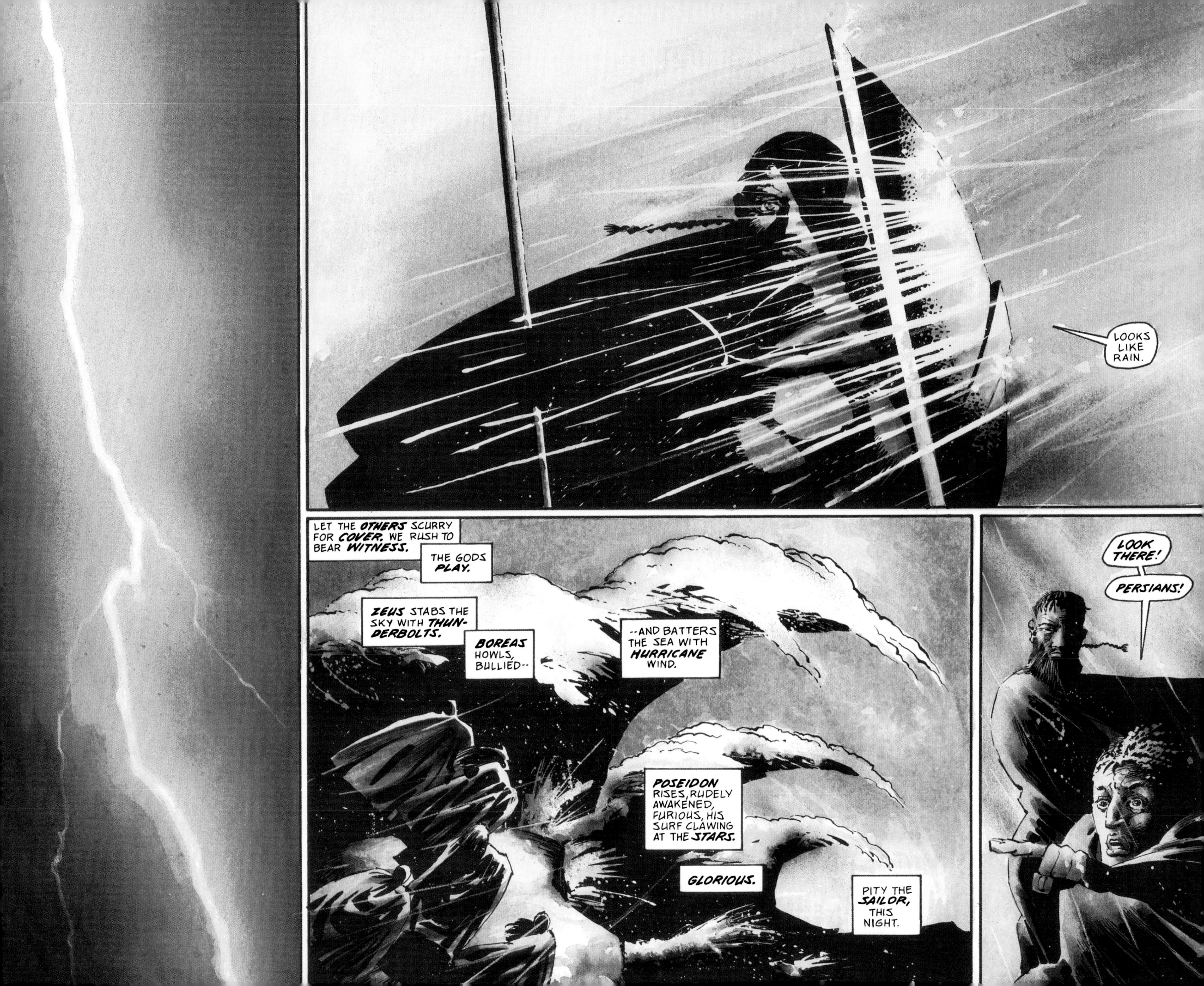
LOOKS LIKE RAIN.
LET THE OTHERS SCURRY FOR COVER. WE RUSH TO BEAR WITNESS.
THE GODS PLAY.
ZEUS STABS THE SKY WITH THUNDERBOLTS.
BOREAS HOWLS, BULLIED--
--AND BATTERS THE SEA WITH HURRICANE WIND.
POSEIDON RISES, RUDELY AWAKENED, FURIOUS, HIS SURF CLAWING AT THE STARS.
GLORIOUS.
PITY THE SAILOR, THIS NIGHT.
LOOK THERE!
PERSIANS!

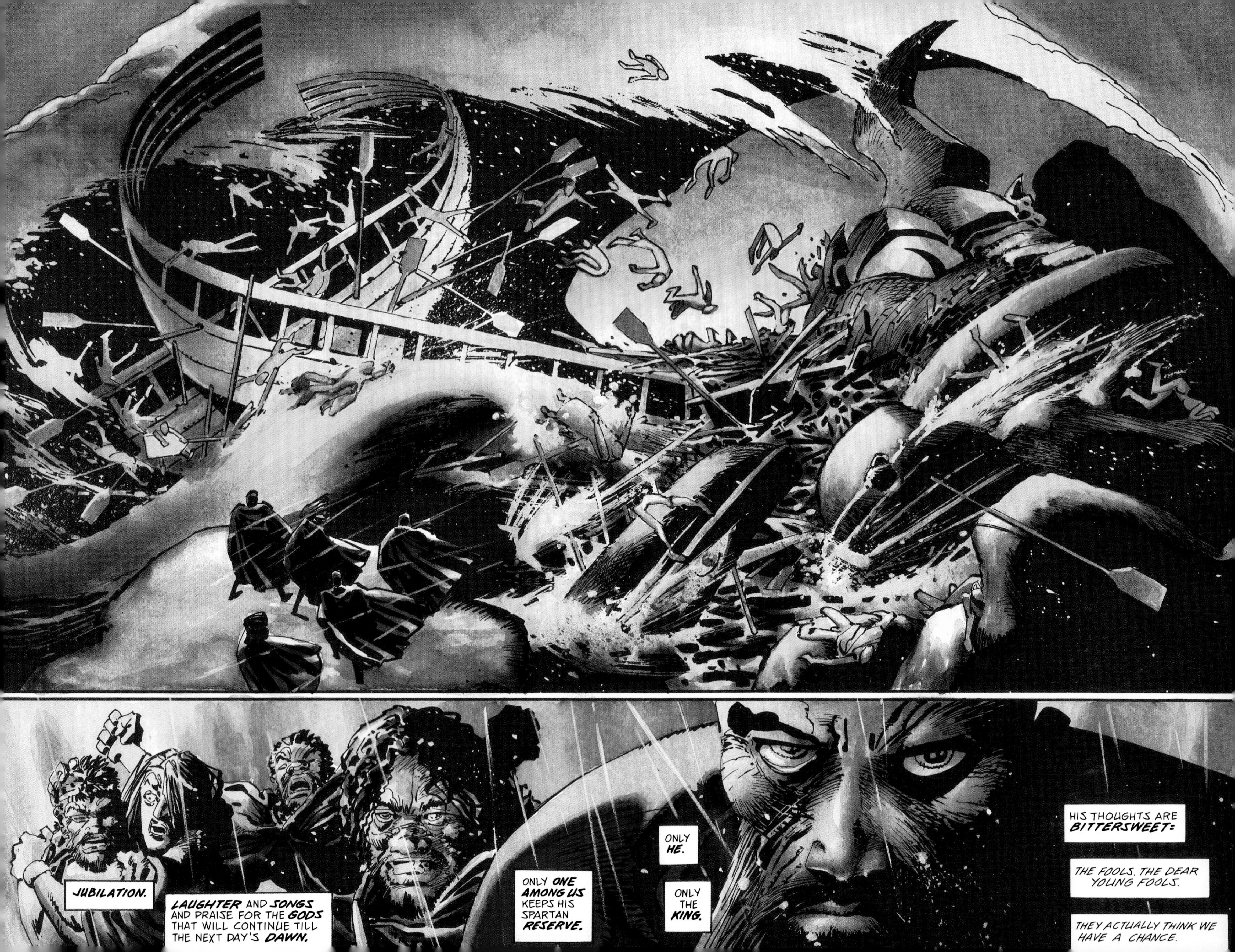
JUBILATION.
LAUGHTER AND SONGS AND PRAISE FOR THE GODS THAT WILL CONTINUE TILL THE NEXT DAY'S DAWN.
ONLY ONE AMONG US KEEPS HIS SPARTAN RESERVE.
ONLY HE.
ONLY THE KING.
HIS THOUGHTS ARE BITTERSWEET:
THE FOOLS. THE DEAR YOUNG FOOLS.
THEY ACTUALLY THINK WE HAVE A CHANCE.

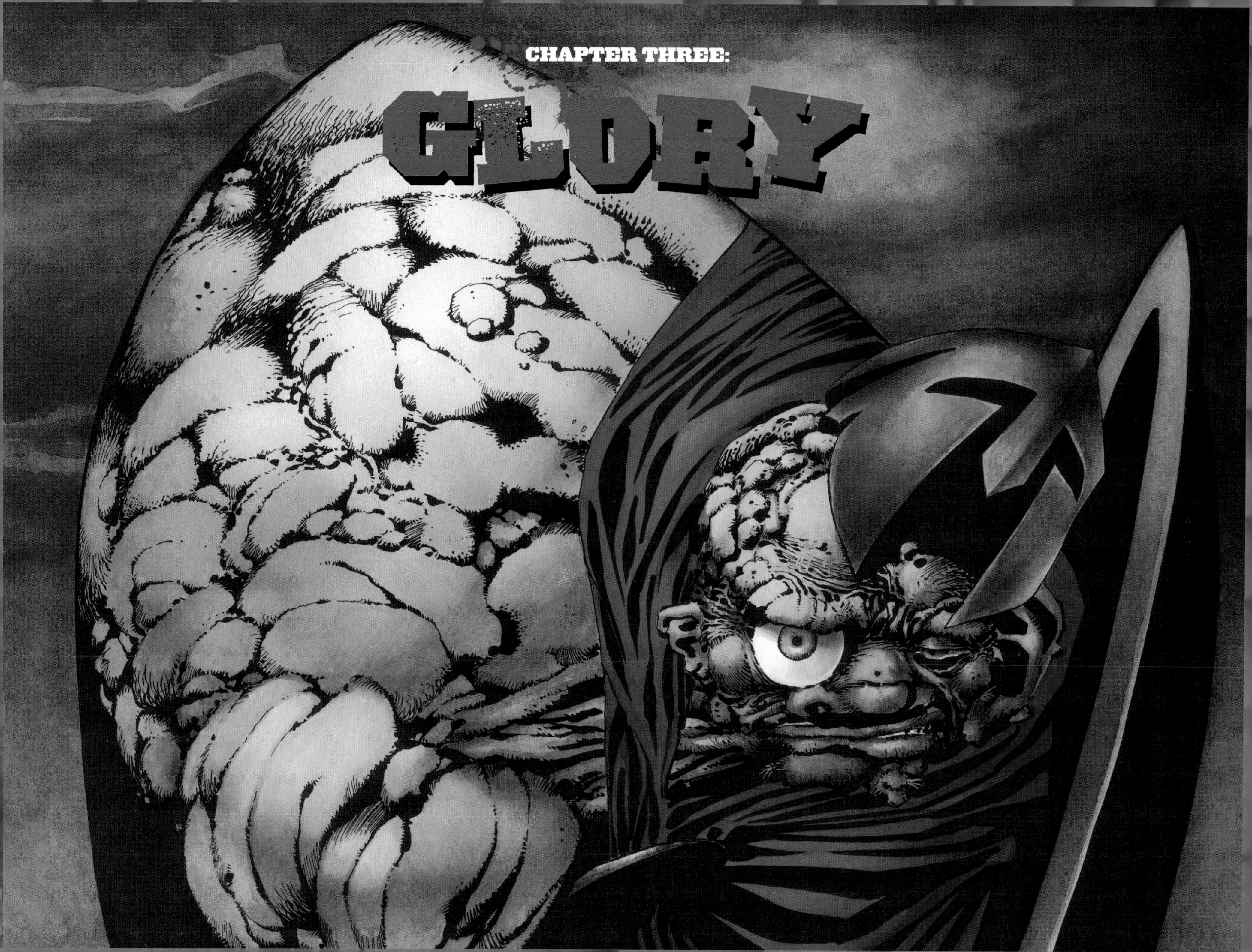
CHAPTER THREE:
GLORY

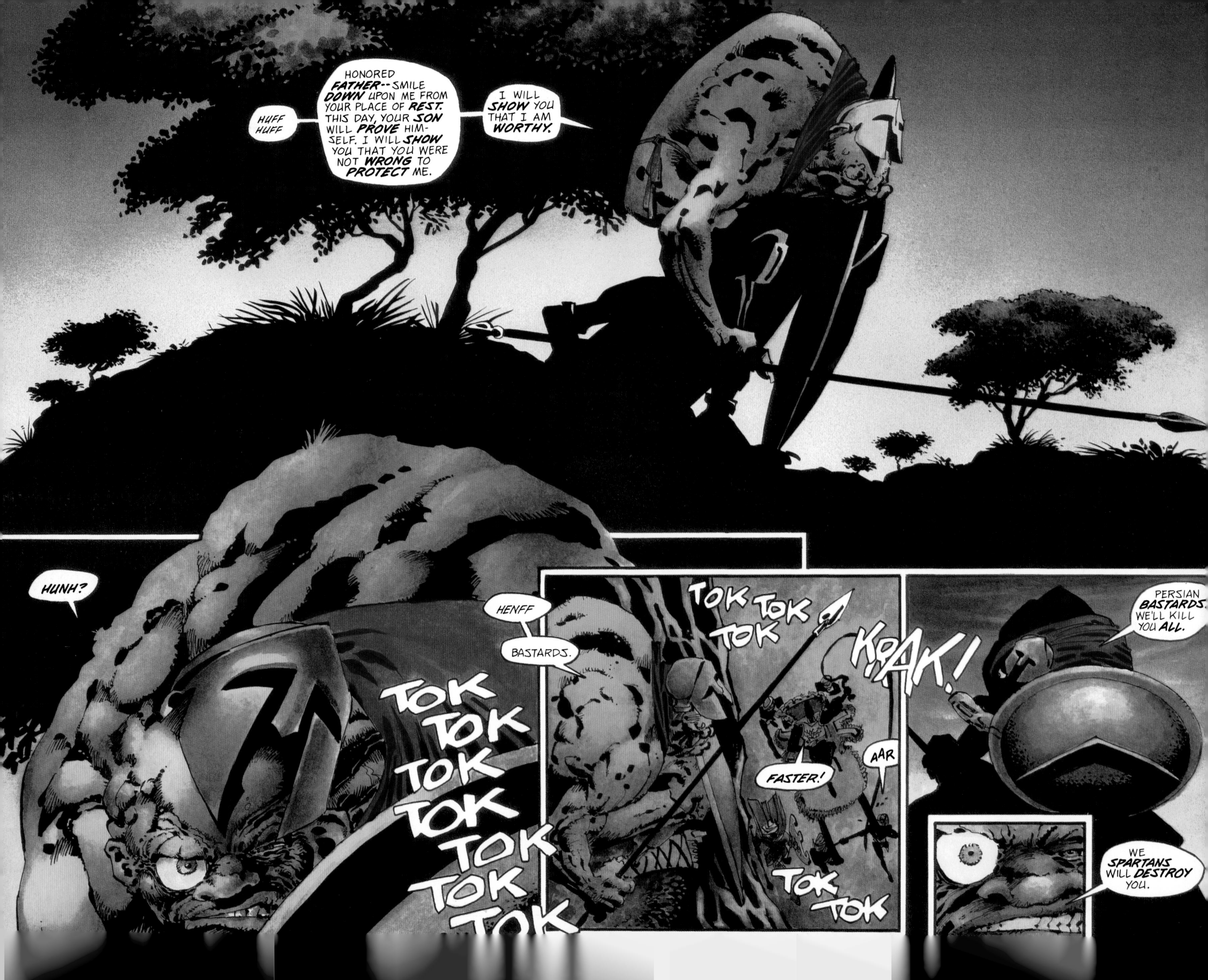
HUFF HUFF
HONORED FATHER-- SMILE DOWN UPON ME FROM YOUR PLACE OF REST. THIS DAY, YOUR SON WILL PROVE HIMSELF. I WILL SHOW YOU THAT YOU WERE NOT WRONG TO PROTECT ME.
I WILL SHOW YOU THAT I AM WORTHY.
HUNH?
TOK TOK TOK TOK TOK TOK TOK
HENFF
BASTARDS.
TOK TOK TOK
KRAK!
FASTER!
AAR
TOK TOK
PERSIAN BASTARDS. WE'LL KILL YOU ALL.
WE SPARTANS WILL DESTROY YOU.

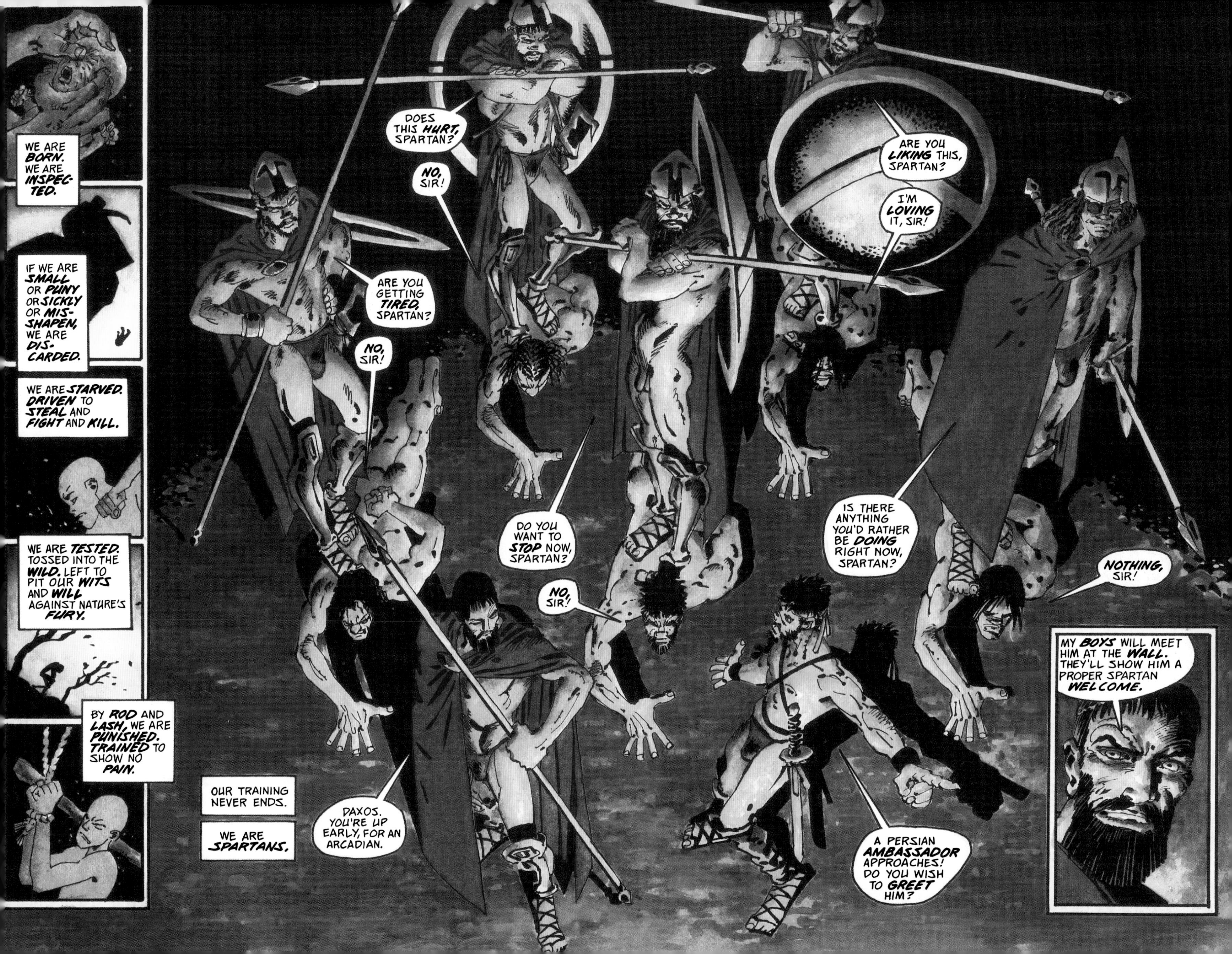
WE ARE BORN. WE ARE INSPECTED.
IF WE ARE SMALL OR PUNY OR SICKLY OR MISSHAPEN, WE ARE DISCARDED.
WE ARE STARVED. DRIVEN TO STEAL AND FIGHT AND KILL.
WE ARE TESTED. TOSSED INTO THE WILD. LEFT TO PIT OUR WITS AND WILL AGAINST NATURE'S FURY.
BY ROD AND LASH, WE ARE PUNISHED. TRAINED TO SHOW NO PAIN.
DOES THIS HURT, SPARTAN?
NO, SIR!
ARE YOU LIKING THIS, SPARTAN?
I'M LOVING IT, SIR!
ARE YOU GETTING TIRED, SPARTAN?
NO, SIR!
DO YOU WANT TO STOP NOW, SPARTAN?
NO, SIR!
IS THERE ANYTHING YOU'D RATHER BE DOING RIGHT NOW, SPARTAN?
NOTHING, SIR!
OUR TRAINING NEVER ENDS.
WE ARE SPARTANS.
DAXOS. YOU'RE UP EARLY, FOR AN ARCADIAN.
A PERSIAN AMBASSADOR APPROACHES! DO YOU WISH TO GREET HIM?
MY BOYS WILL MEET HIM AT THE WALL. THEY'LL SHOW HIM A PROPER SPARTAN WELCOME.

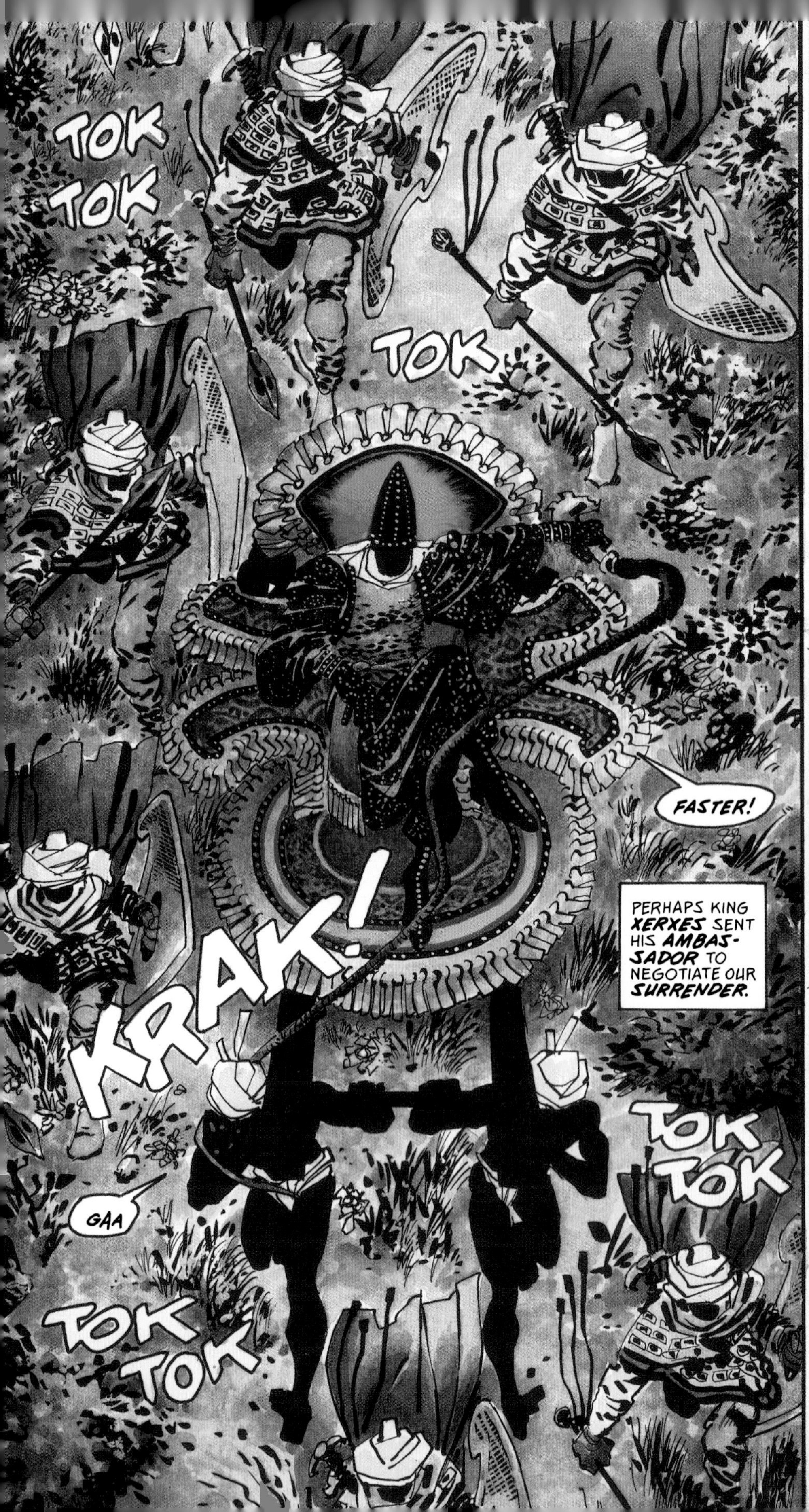
TOK
TOK
TOK
TOK
FASTER!
PERHAPS KING **XERXES** SENT HIS **AMBASSADOR** TO NEGOTIATE OUR **SURRENDER.**
KRAK!
TOK TOK
GAA
TOK TOK

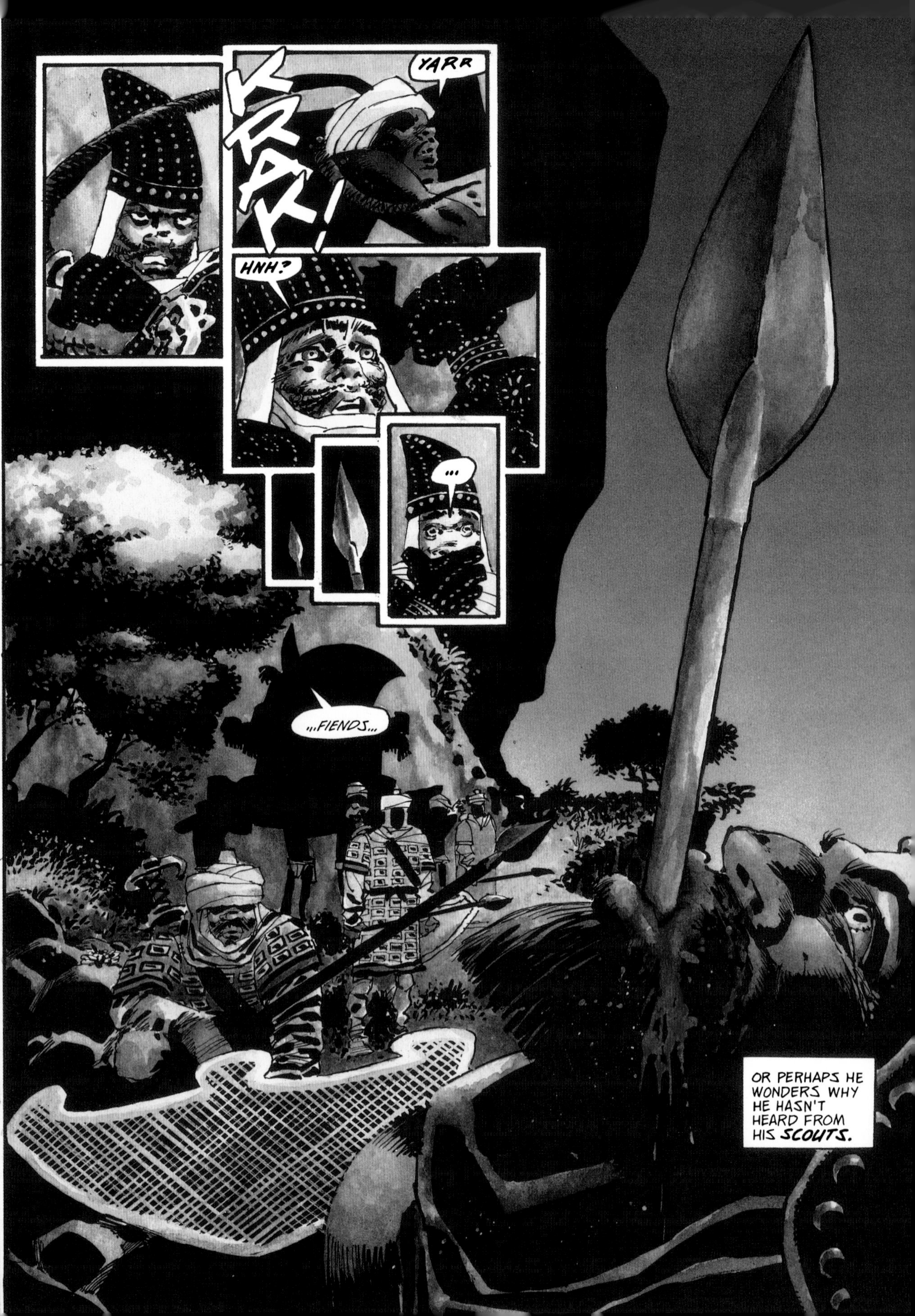
KRAK!
YARR
HNH?
...
...FIENDS...
OR PERHAPS HE WONDERS WHY HE HASN'T HEARD FROM HIS **SCOUTS.**

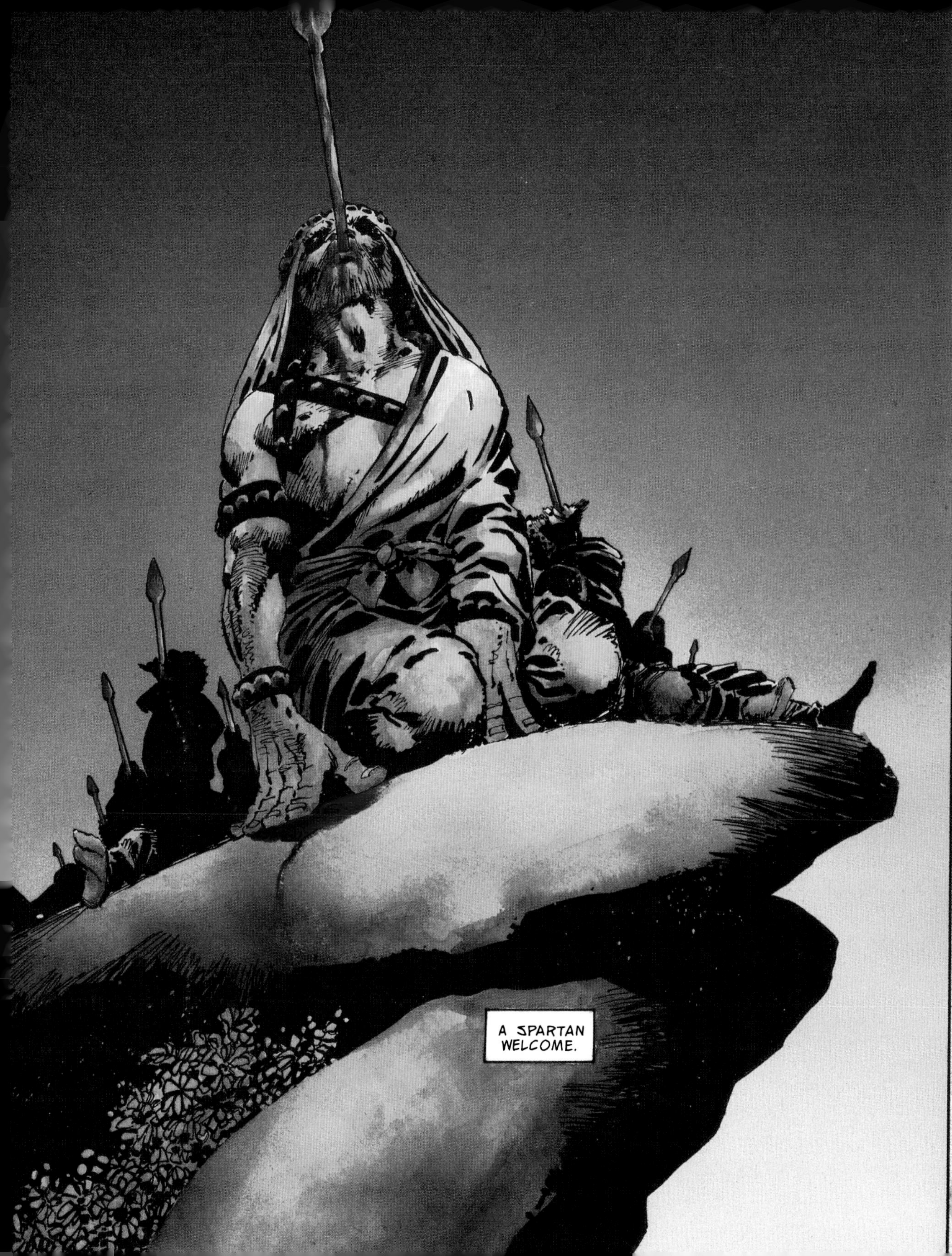
A SPARTAN WELCOME.

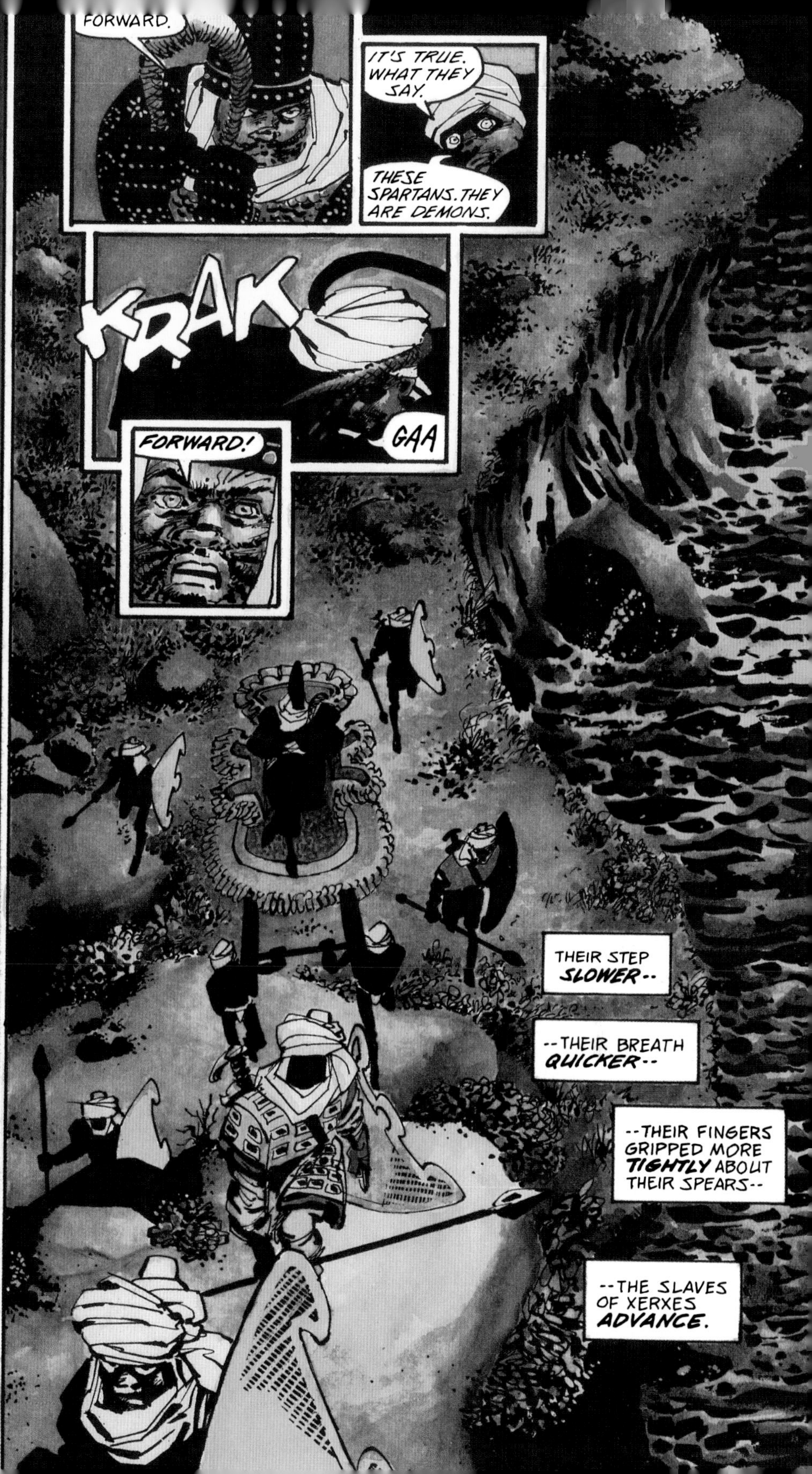
FORWARD.
IT'S TRUE. WHAT THEY SAY.
THESE SPARTANS. THEY ARE DEMONS.
KRAK
GAA
FORWARD!
THEIR STEP SLOWER--
--THEIR BREATH QUICKER--
--THEIR FINGERS GRIPPED MORE TIGHTLY ABOUT THEIR SPEARS--
--THE SLAVES OF XERXES ADVANCE.

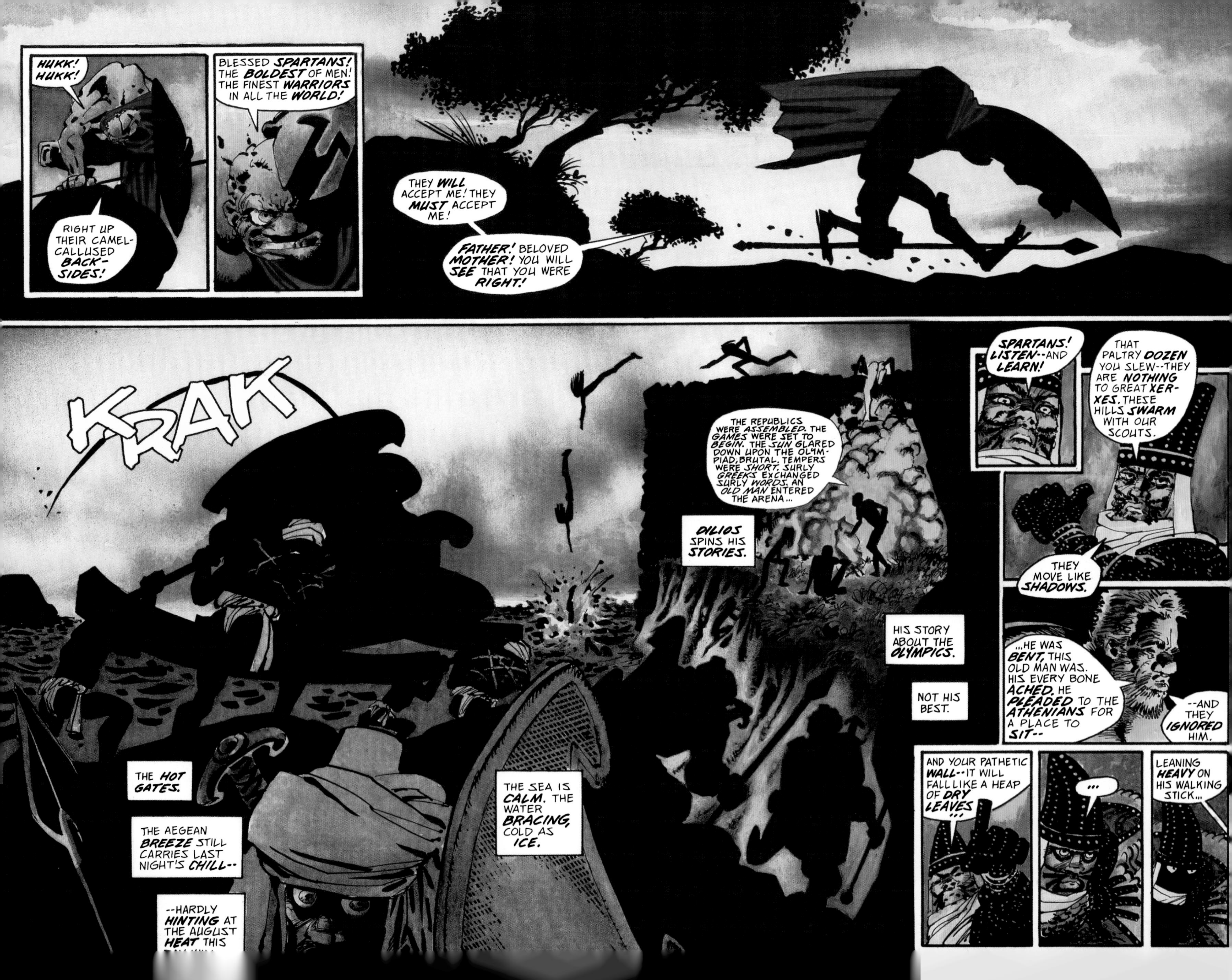
HUKK! HUKK!
RIGHT UP THEIR CAMEL-CALLUSED BACK-SIDES!
BLESSED SPARTANS! THE BOLDEST OF MEN! THE FINEST WARRIORS IN ALL THE WORLD!
THEY WILL ACCEPT ME! THEY MUST ACCEPT ME!
FATHER! BELOVED MOTHER! YOU WILL SEE THAT YOU WERE RIGHT!
KRAK
THE HOT GATES.
THE AEGEAN BREEZE STILL CARRIES LAST NIGHT'S CHILL--
--HARDLY HINTING AT THE AUGUST HEAT THIS
THE SEA IS CALM. THE WATER BRACING, COLD AS ICE.
DILIOS SPINS HIS STORIES.
THE REPUBLICS WERE ASSEMBLED. THE GAMES WERE SET TO BEGIN. THE SUN GLARED DOWN UPON THE OLYM-PIAD, BRUTAL. TEMPERS WERE SHORT. SURLY GREEKS EXCHANGED SURLY WORDS. AN OLD MAN ENTERED THE ARENA...
HIS STORY ABOUT THE OLYMPICS.
NOT HIS BEST.
SPARTANS! LISTEN--AND LEARN!
THAT PALTRY DOZEN YOU SLEW--THEY ARE NOTHING TO GREAT XER-XES. THESE HILLS SWARM WITH OUR SCOUTS.
THEY MOVE LIKE SHADOWS.
...HE WAS BENT, THIS OLD MAN WAS. HIS EVERY BONE ACHED. HE PLEADED TO THE ATHENIANS FOR A PLACE TO SIT--
--AND THEY IGNORED HIM.
AND YOUR PATHETIC WALL--IT WILL FALL LIKE A HEAP OF DRY LEAVES...
...
LEANING HEAVY ON HIS WALKING STICK...

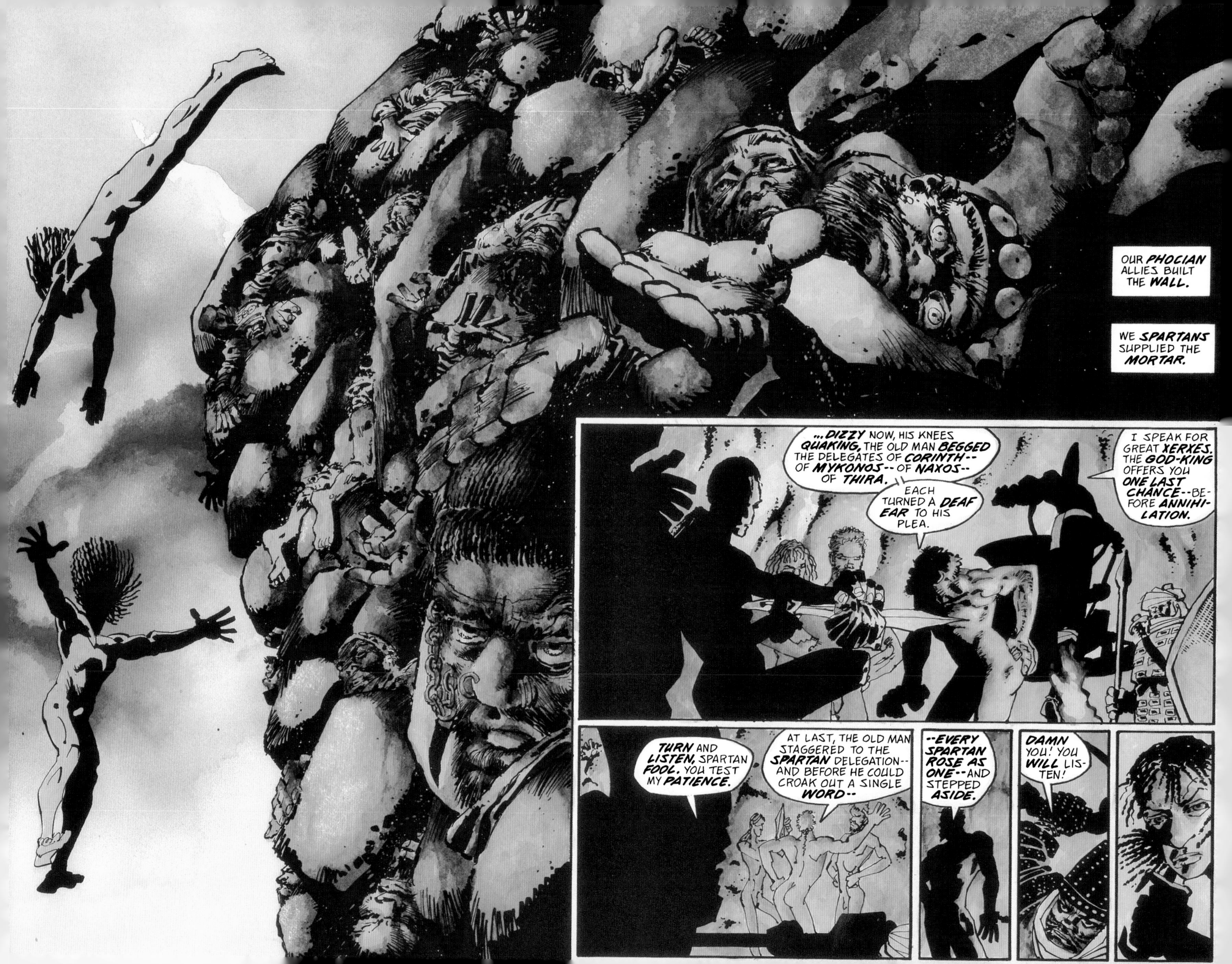
OUR PHOCIAN ALLIES BUILT THE WALL.
WE SPARTANS SUPPLIED THE MORTAR.
...DIZZY NOW, HIS KNEES QUAKING, THE OLD MAN BEGGED THE DELEGATES OF CORINTH-- OF MYKONOS-- OF NAXOS-- OF THIRA.
EACH TURNED A DEAF EAR TO HIS PLEA.
I SPEAK FOR GREAT XERXES. THE GOD-KING OFFERS YOU ONE LAST CHANCE--BEFORE ANNIHILATION.
TURN AND LISTEN, SPARTAN FOOL. YOU TEST MY PATIENCE.
AT LAST, THE OLD MAN STAGGERED TO THE SPARTAN DELEGATION-- AND BEFORE HE COULD CROAK OUT A SINGLE WORD--
--EVERY SPARTAN ROSE AS ONE--AND STEPPED ASIDE.
DAMN YOU! YOU WILL LISTEN!

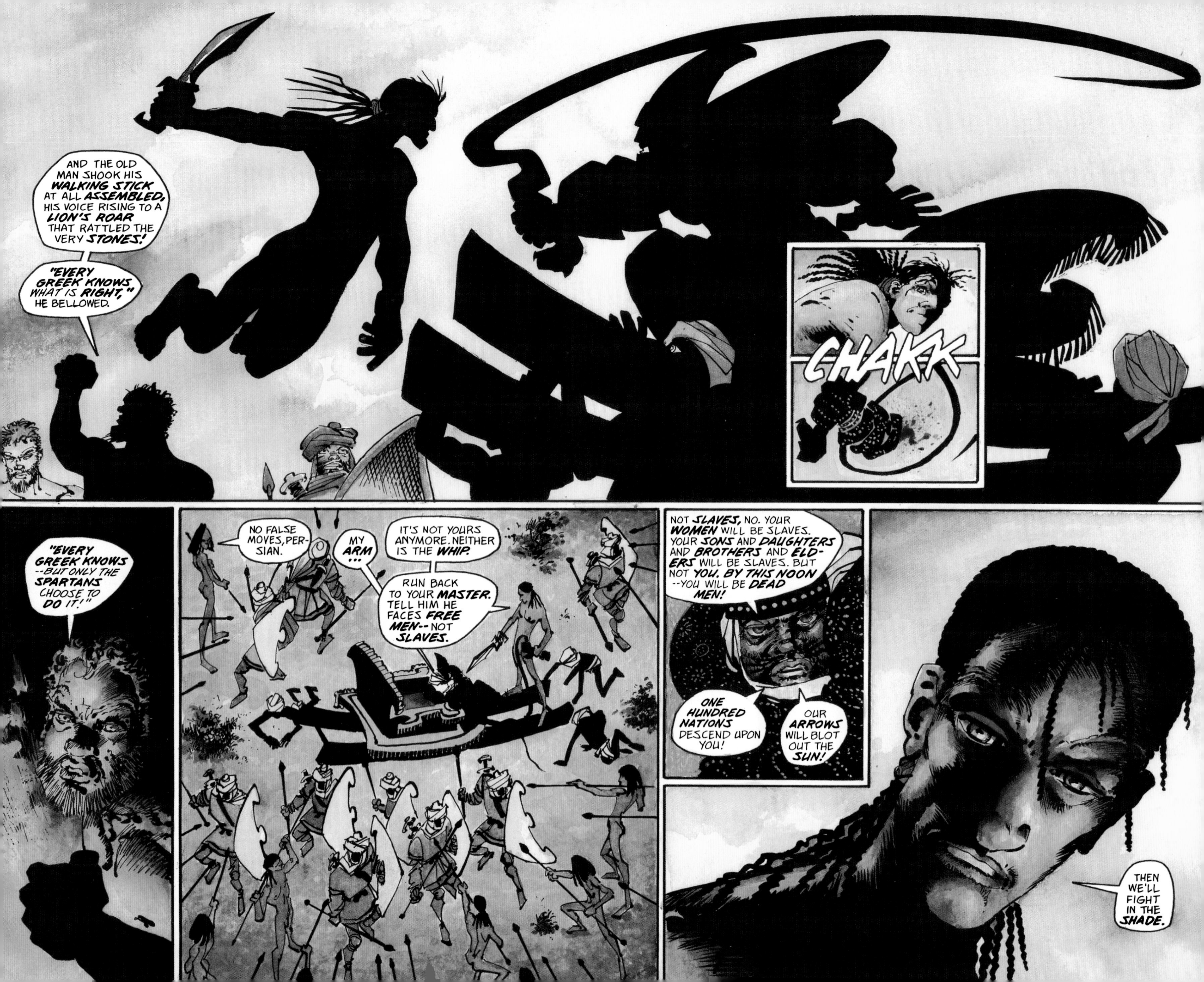

AND THE OLD MAN SHOOK HIS WALKING STICK AT ALL ASSEMBLED, HIS VOICE RISING TO A LION'S ROAR THAT RATTLED THE VERY STONES!
"EVERY GREEK KNOWS WHAT IS RIGHT," HE BELLOWED.
CHAKK
"EVERY GREEK KNOWS --BUT ONLY THE SPARTANS CHOOSE TO DO IT!"
NO FALSE MOVES, PERSIAN.
MY ARM ...
IT'S NOT YOURS ANYMORE. NEITHER IS THE WHIP.
RUN BACK TO YOUR MASTER. TELL HIM HE FACES FREE MEN-- NOT SLAVES.
NOT SLAVES, NO. YOUR WOMEN WILL BE SLAVES. YOUR SONS AND DAUGHTERS AND BROTHERS AND ELDERS WILL BE SLAVES. BUT NOT YOU. BY THIS NOON --YOU WILL BE DEAD MEN!
ONE HUNDRED NATIONS DESCEND UPON YOU!
OUR ARROWS WILL BLOT OUT THE SUN!
THEN WE'LL FIGHT IN THE SHADE.

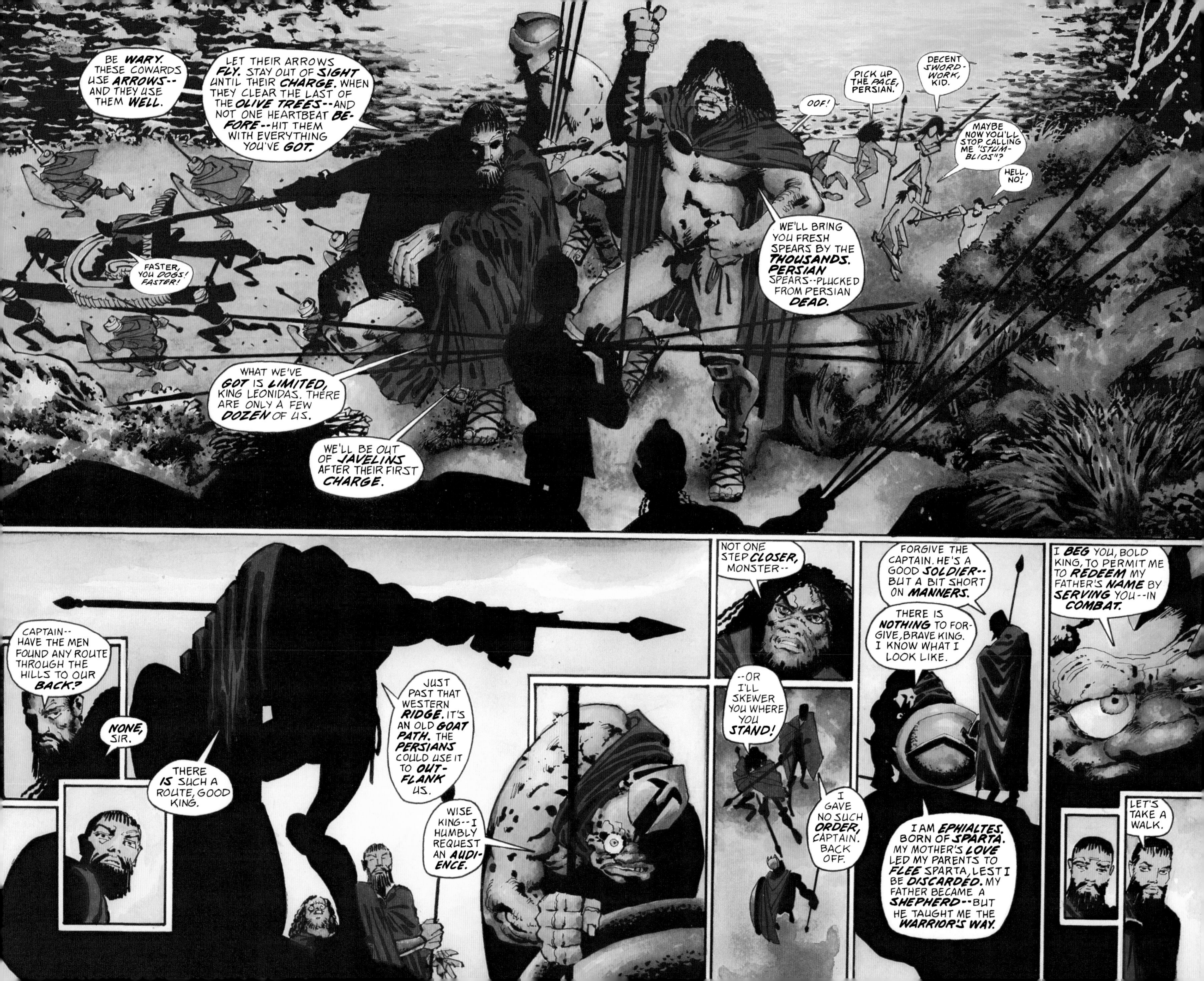
BE WARY. THESE COWARDS USE ARROWS-- AND THEY USE THEM WELL.
LET THEIR ARROWS FLY. STAY OUT OF SIGHT UNTIL THEIR CHARGE. WHEN THEY CLEAR THE LAST OF THE OLIVE TREES--AND NOT ONE HEARTBEAT BEFORE--HIT THEM WITH EVERYTHING YOU'VE GOT.
OOF!
PICK UP THE PACE, PERSIAN.
DECENT SWORD-WORK, KID.
MAYBE NOW YOU'LL STOP CALLING ME "STUMBLIOS"?
HELL, NO!
FASTER, YOU DOGS! FASTER!
WE'LL BRING YOU FRESH SPEARS BY THE THOUSANDS. PERSIAN SPEARS--PLUCKED FROM PERSIAN DEAD.
WHAT WE'VE GOT IS LIMITED, KING LEONIDAS. THERE ARE ONLY A FEW DOZEN OF US.
WE'LL BE OUT OF JAVELINS AFTER THEIR FIRST CHARGE.
CAPTAIN-- HAVE THE MEN FOUND ANY ROUTE THROUGH THE HILLS TO OUR BACK?
NONE, SIR.
THERE IS SUCH A ROUTE, GOOD KING.
JUST PAST THAT WESTERN RIDGE. IT'S AN OLD GOAT PATH. THE PERSIANS COULD USE IT TO OUTFLANK US.
WISE KING--I HUMBLY REQUEST AN AUDIENCE.
NOT ONE STEP CLOSER, MONSTER--
--OR I'LL SKEWER YOU WHERE YOU STAND!
I GAVE NO SUCH ORDER, CAPTAIN. BACK OFF.
FORGIVE THE CAPTAIN. HE'S A GOOD SOLDIER-- BUT A BIT SHORT ON MANNERS.
THERE IS NOTHING TO FORGIVE, BRAVE KING. I KNOW WHAT I LOOK LIKE.
I AM EPHIALTES. BORN OF SPARTA. MY MOTHER'S LOVE LED MY PARENTS TO FLEE SPARTA, LEST I BE DISCARDED. MY FATHER BECAME A SHEPHERD--BUT HE TAUGHT ME THE WARRIOR'S WAY.
I BEG YOU, BOLD KING, TO PERMIT ME TO REDEEM MY FATHER'S NAME BY SERVING YOU--IN COMBAT.
LET'S TAKE A WALK.

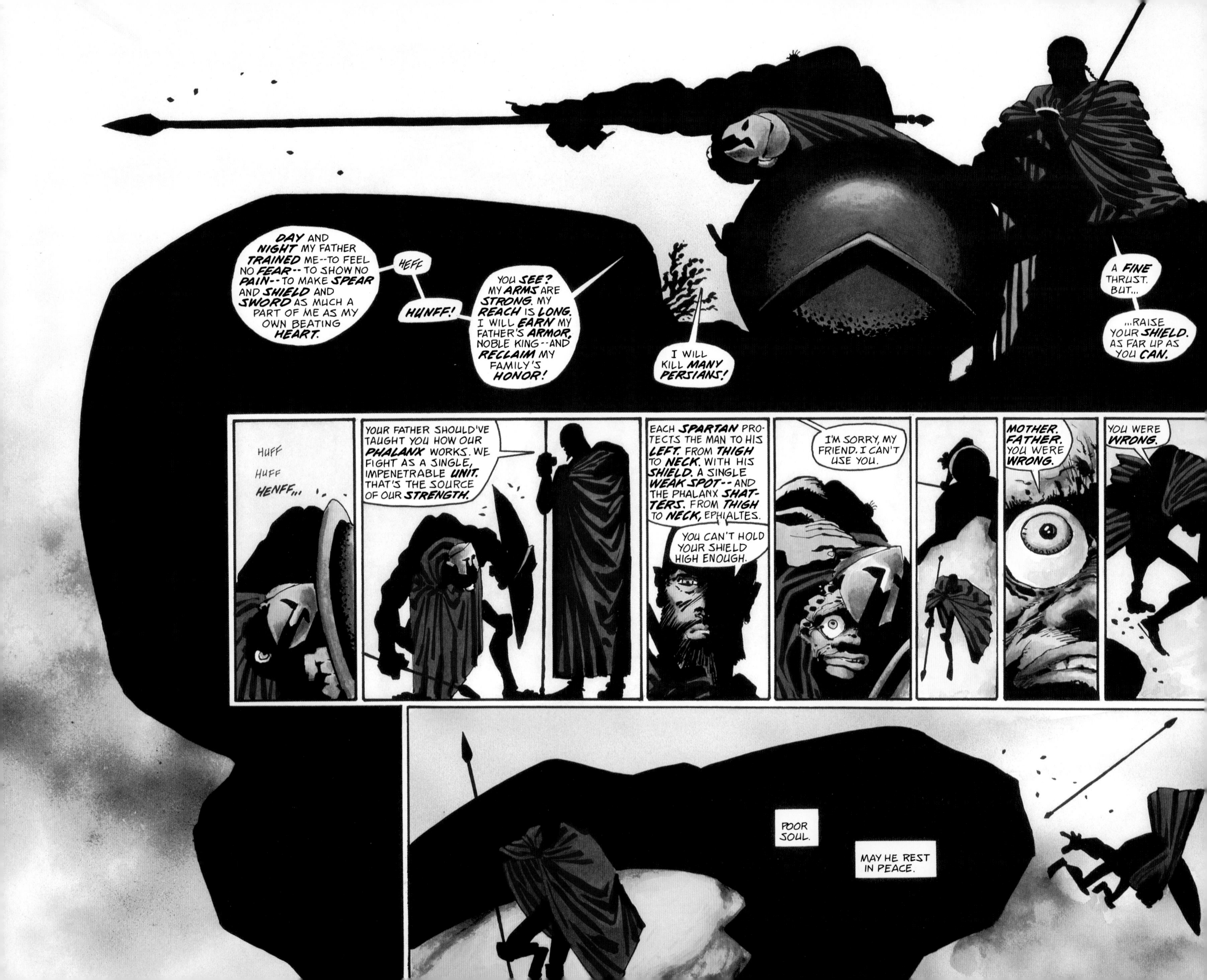
DAY AND NIGHT MY FATHER TRAINED ME--TO FEEL NO FEAR--TO SHOW NO PAIN--TO MAKE SPEAR AND SHIELD AND SWORD AS MUCH A PART OF ME AS MY OWN BEATING HEART.
HEFF
HUNFF!
YOU SEE? MY ARMS ARE STRONG. MY REACH IS LONG. I WILL EARN MY FATHER'S ARMOR, NOBLE KING--AND RECLAIM MY FAMILY'S HONOR!
I WILL KILL MANY PERSIANS!
A FINE THRUST. BUT...
...RAISE YOUR SHIELD. AS FAR UP AS YOU CAN.
HUFF
HUFF
HENFF...
YOUR FATHER SHOULD'VE TAUGHT YOU HOW OUR PHALANX WORKS. WE FIGHT AS A SINGLE, IMPENETRABLE UNIT. THAT'S THE SOURCE OF OUR STRENGTH.
EACH SPARTAN PROTECTS THE MAN TO HIS LEFT. FROM THIGH TO NECK. WITH HIS SHIELD. A SINGLE WEAK SPOT--AND THE PHALANX SHATTERS. FROM THIGH TO NECK, EPHIALTES.
YOU CAN'T HOLD YOUR SHIELD HIGH ENOUGH.
I'M SORRY, MY FRIEND. I CAN'T USE YOU.
MOTHER. FATHER. YOU WERE WRONG.
YOU WERE WRONG.
POOR SOUL.
MAY HE REST IN PEACE.

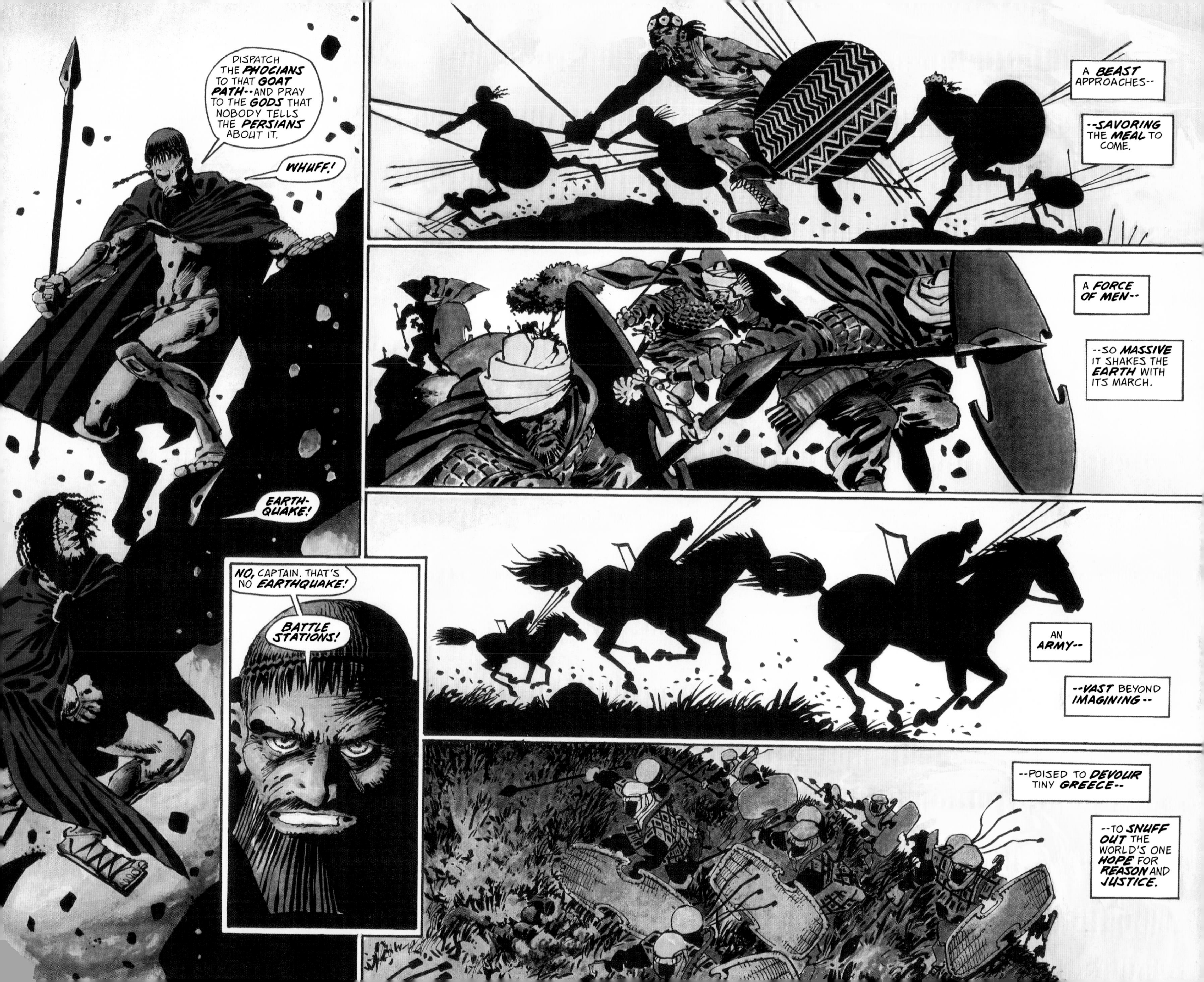

DISPATCH THE PHOCIANS TO THAT GOAT PATH--AND PRAY TO THE GODS THAT NOBODY TELLS THE PERSIANS ABOUT IT.
WHUFF!
EARTH-QUAKE!
NO, CAPTAIN. THAT'S NO EARTHQUAKE!
BATTLE STATIONS!
A BEAST APPROACHES--
--SAVORING THE MEAL TO COME.
A FORCE OF MEN--
--SO MASSIVE IT SHAKES THE EARTH WITH ITS MARCH.
AN ARMY--
--VAST BEYOND IMAGINING--
--POISED TO DEVOUR TINY GREECE--
--TO SNUFF OUT THE WORLD'S ONE HOPE FOR REASON AND JUSTICE.

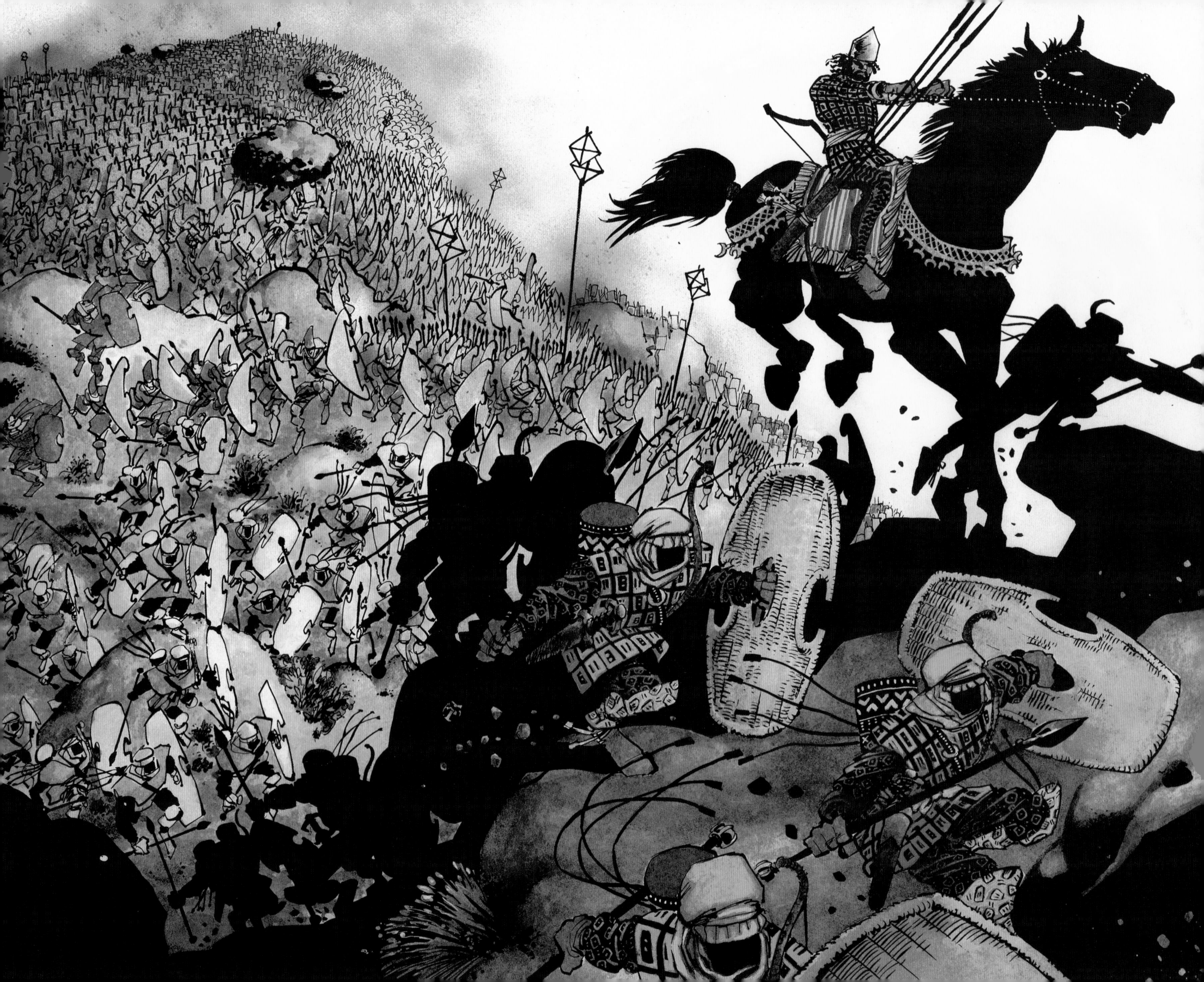

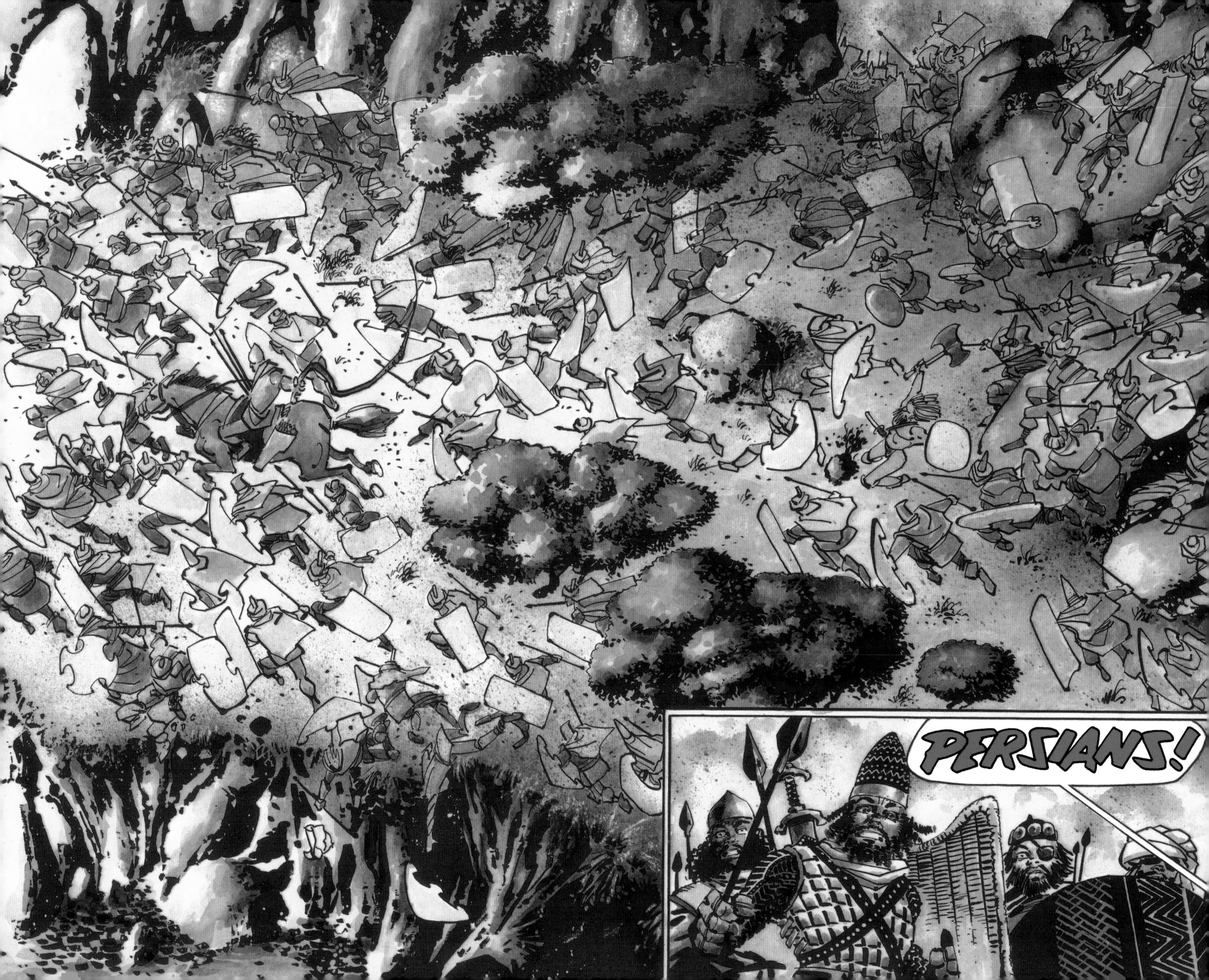
PERSIANS!

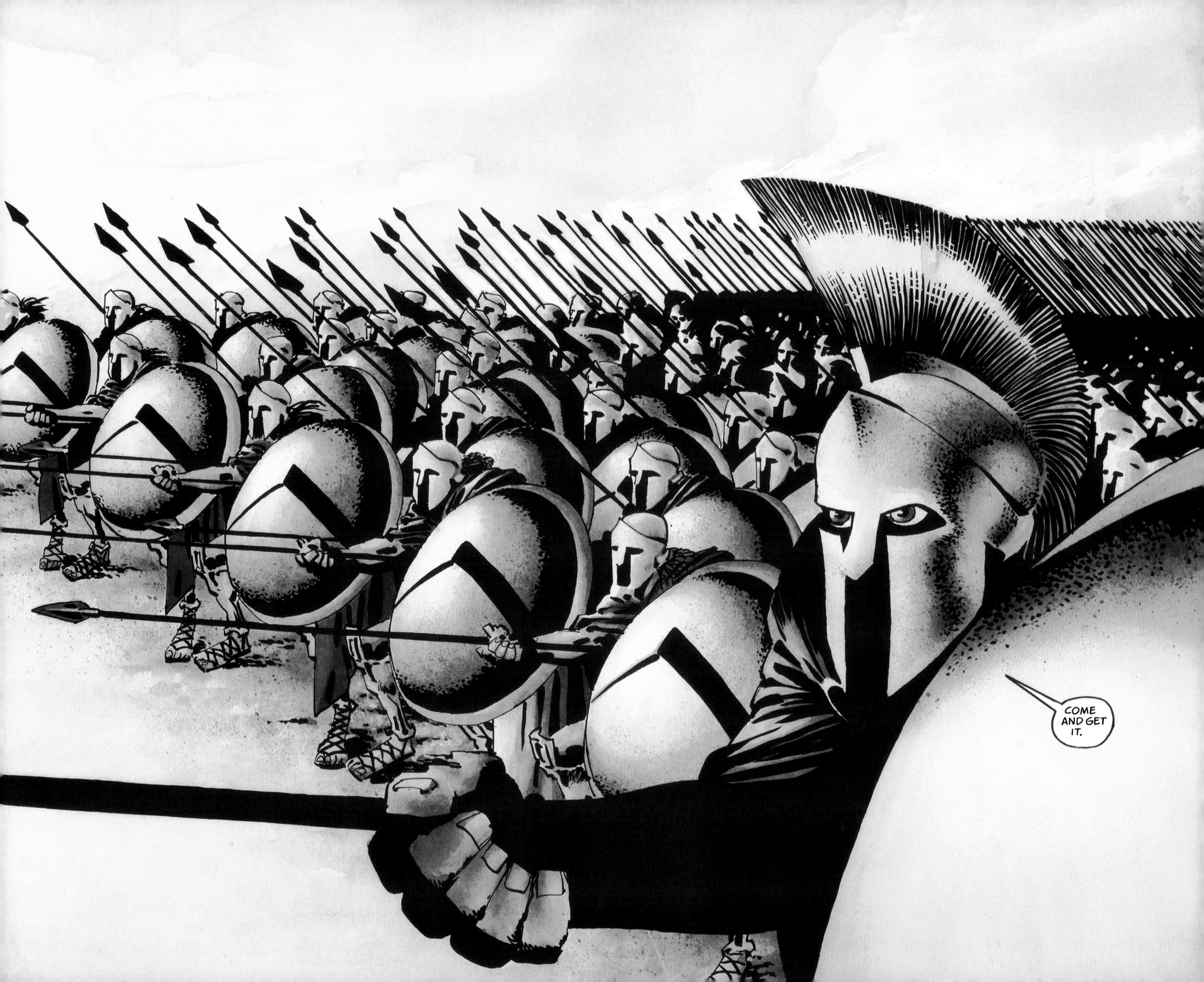
COME AND GET IT.

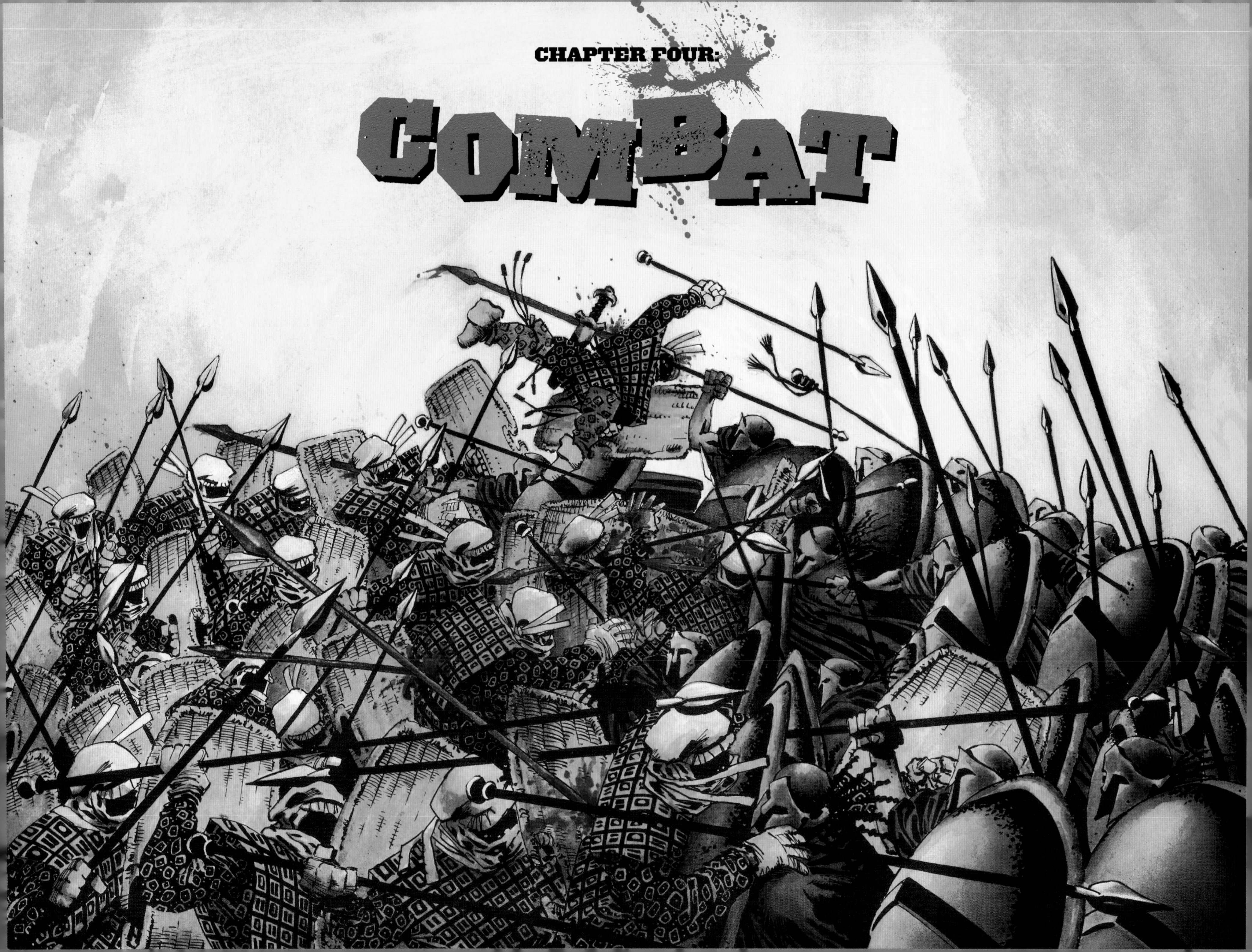
CHAPTER FOUR:
COMBAT

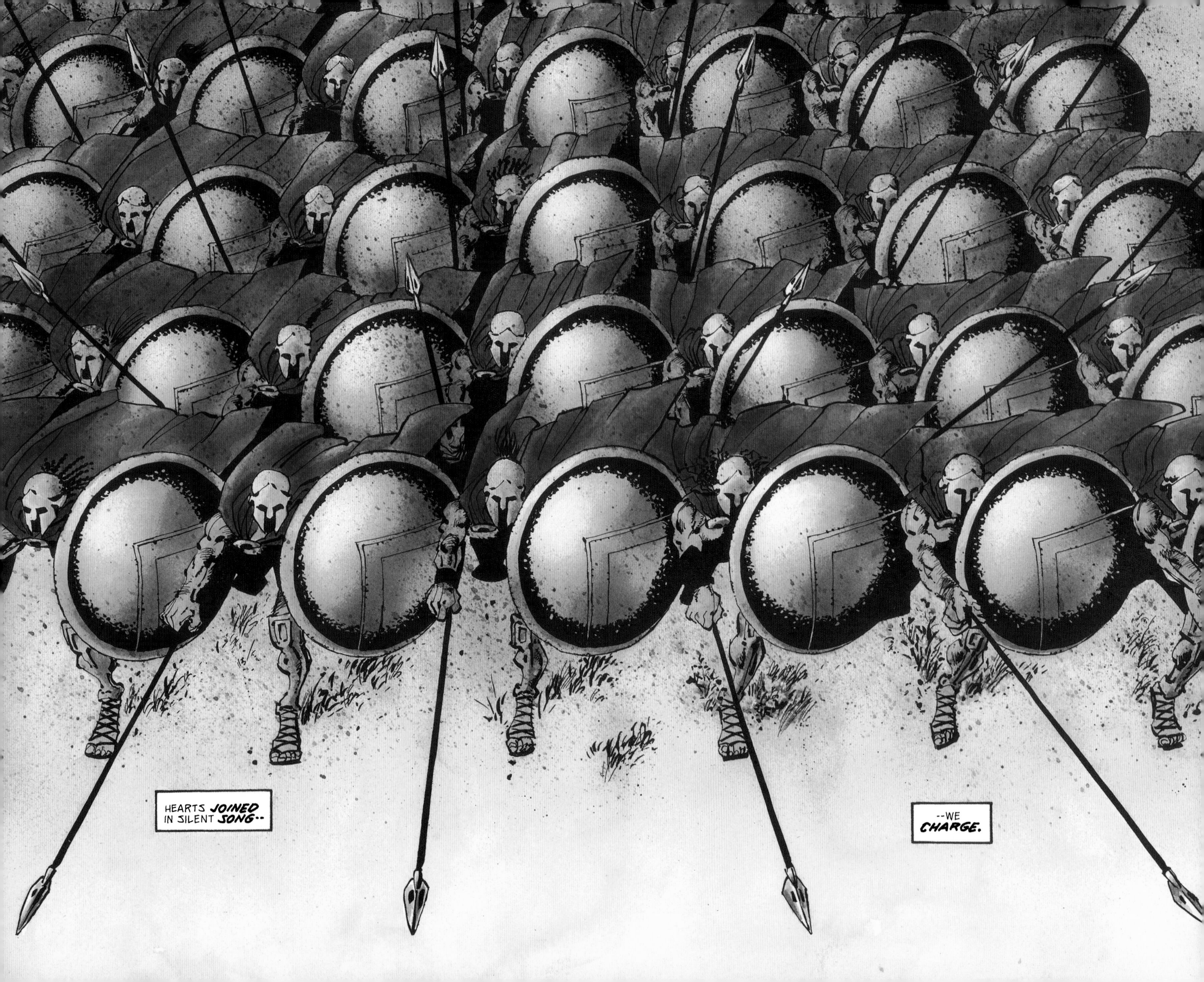
HEARTS JOINED IN SILENT SONG--
--WE CHARGE.

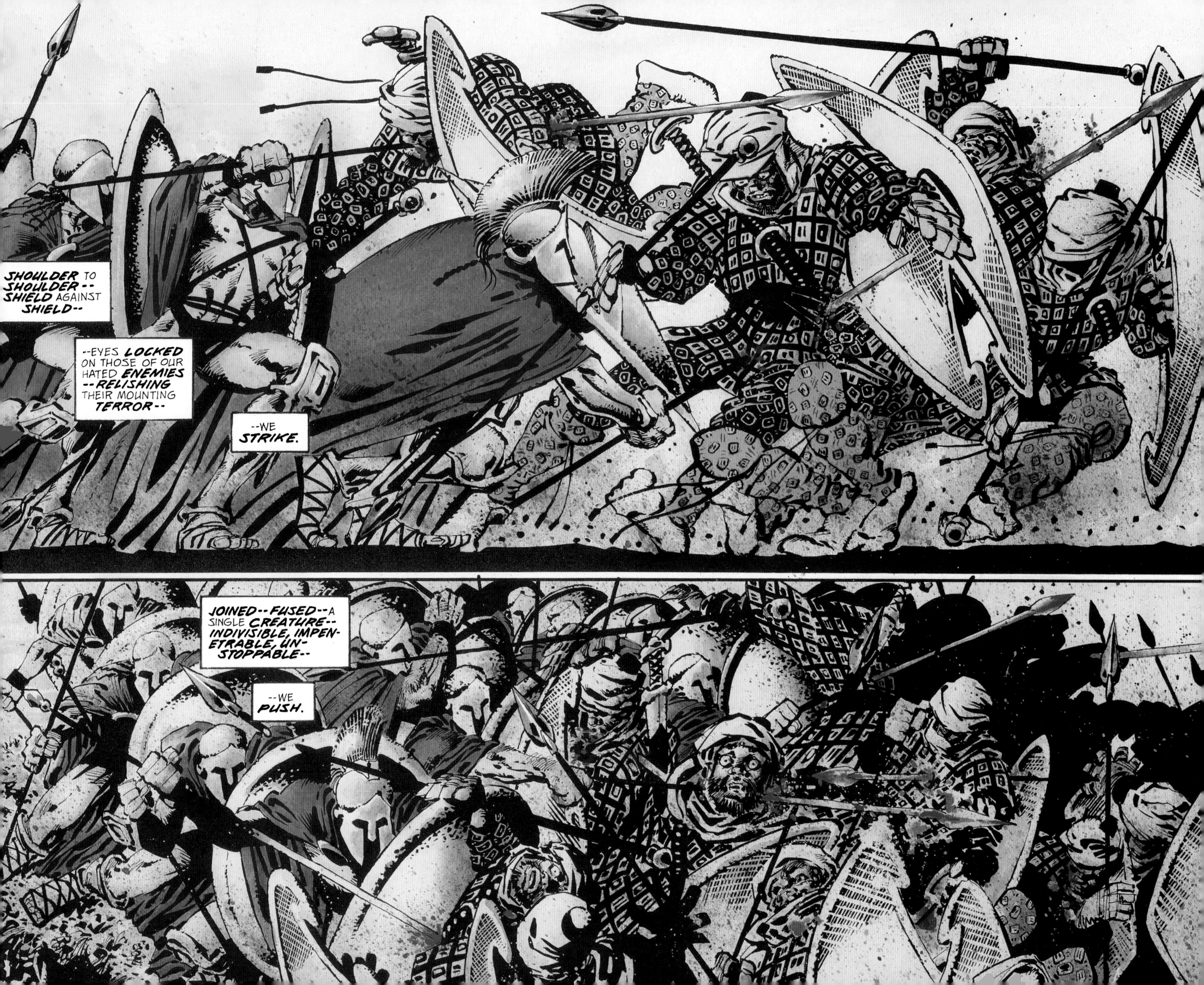
SHOULDER TO SHOULDER-- SHIELD AGAINST SHIELD--
--EYES LOCKED ON THOSE OF OUR HATED ENEMIES --RELISHING THEIR MOUNTING TERROR--
--WE STRIKE.
JOINED--FUSED--A SINGLE CREATURE-- INDIVISIBLE, IMPENETRABLE, UNSTOPPABLE--
--WE PUSH.

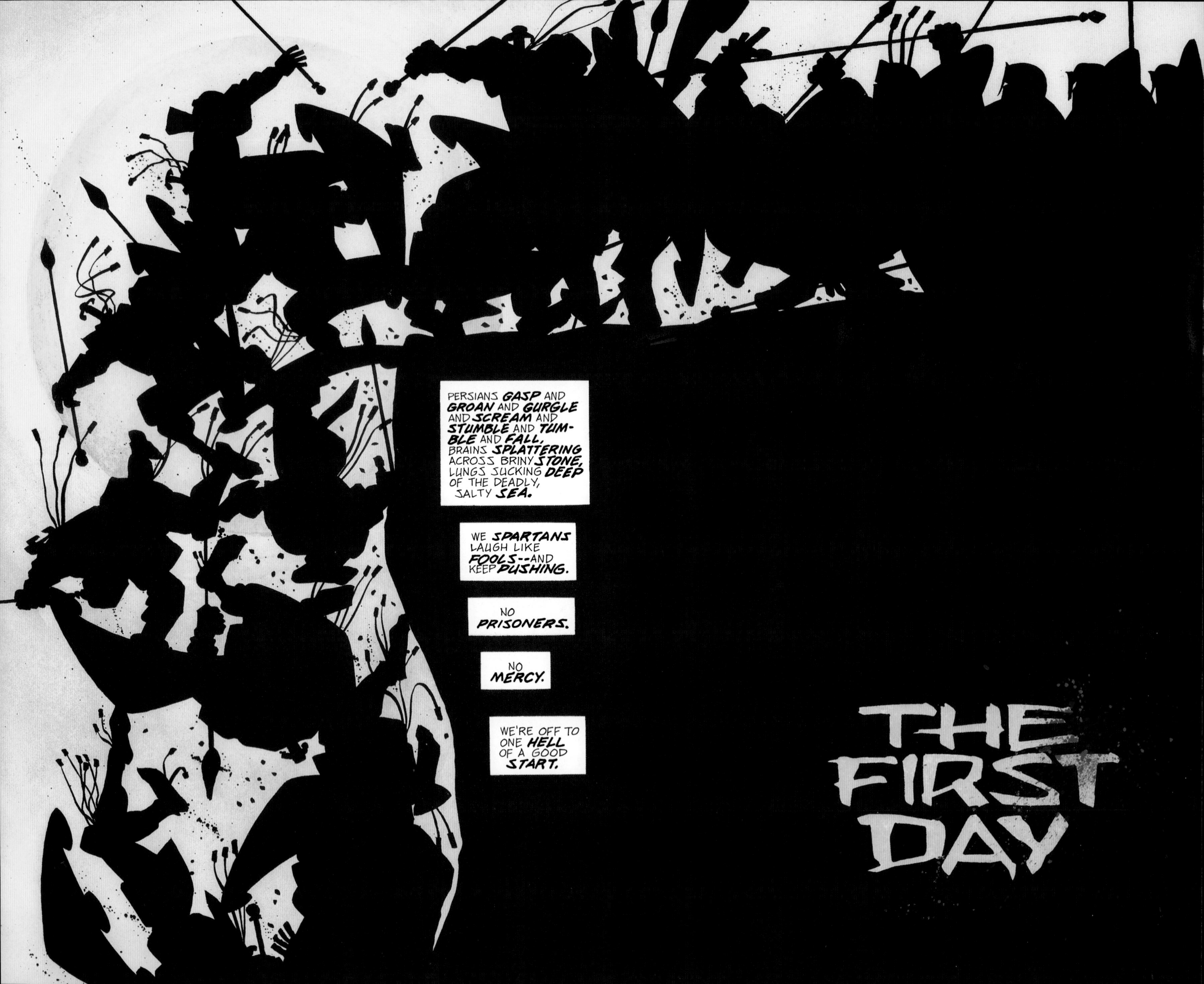
PERSIANS GASP AND GROAN AND GURGLE AND SCREAM AND STUMBLE AND TUMBLE AND FALL, BRAINS SPLATTERING ACROSS BRINY STONE, LUNGS SUCKING DEEP OF THE DEADLY, SALTY SEA.
WE SPARTANS LAUGH LIKE FOOLS--AND KEEP PUSHING.
NO PRISONERS.
NO MERCY.
WE'RE OFF TO ONE HELL OF A GOOD START.
THE FIRST DAY

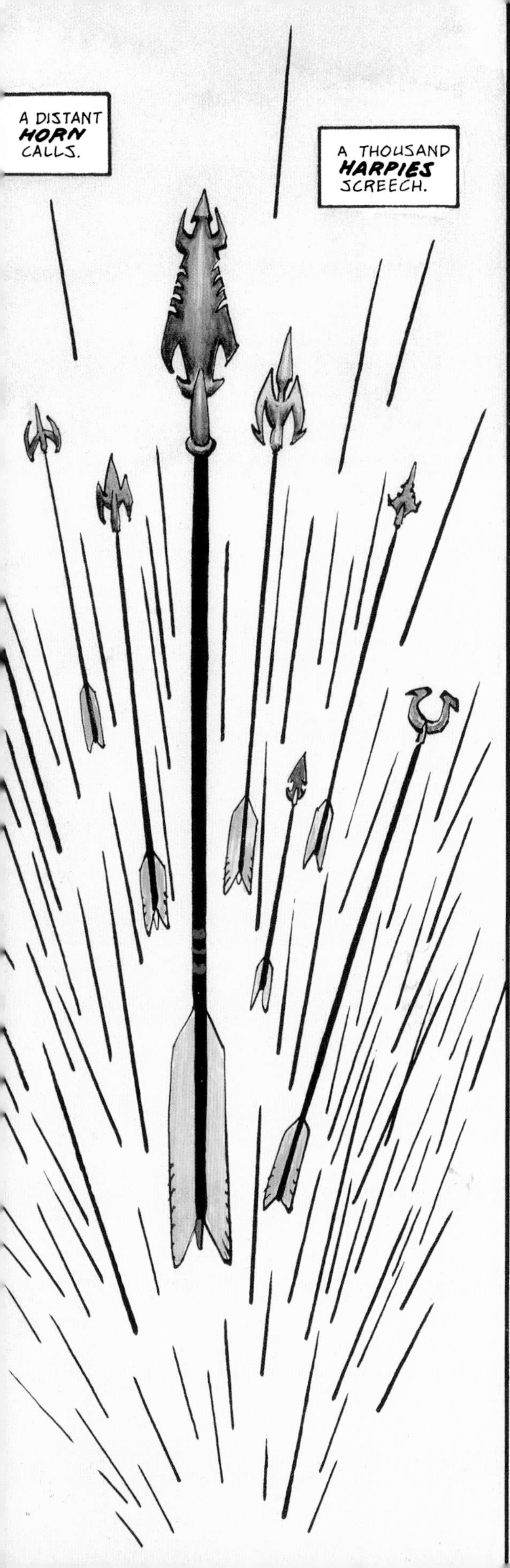
A DISTANT HORN CALLS.
A THOUSAND HARPIES SCREECH.

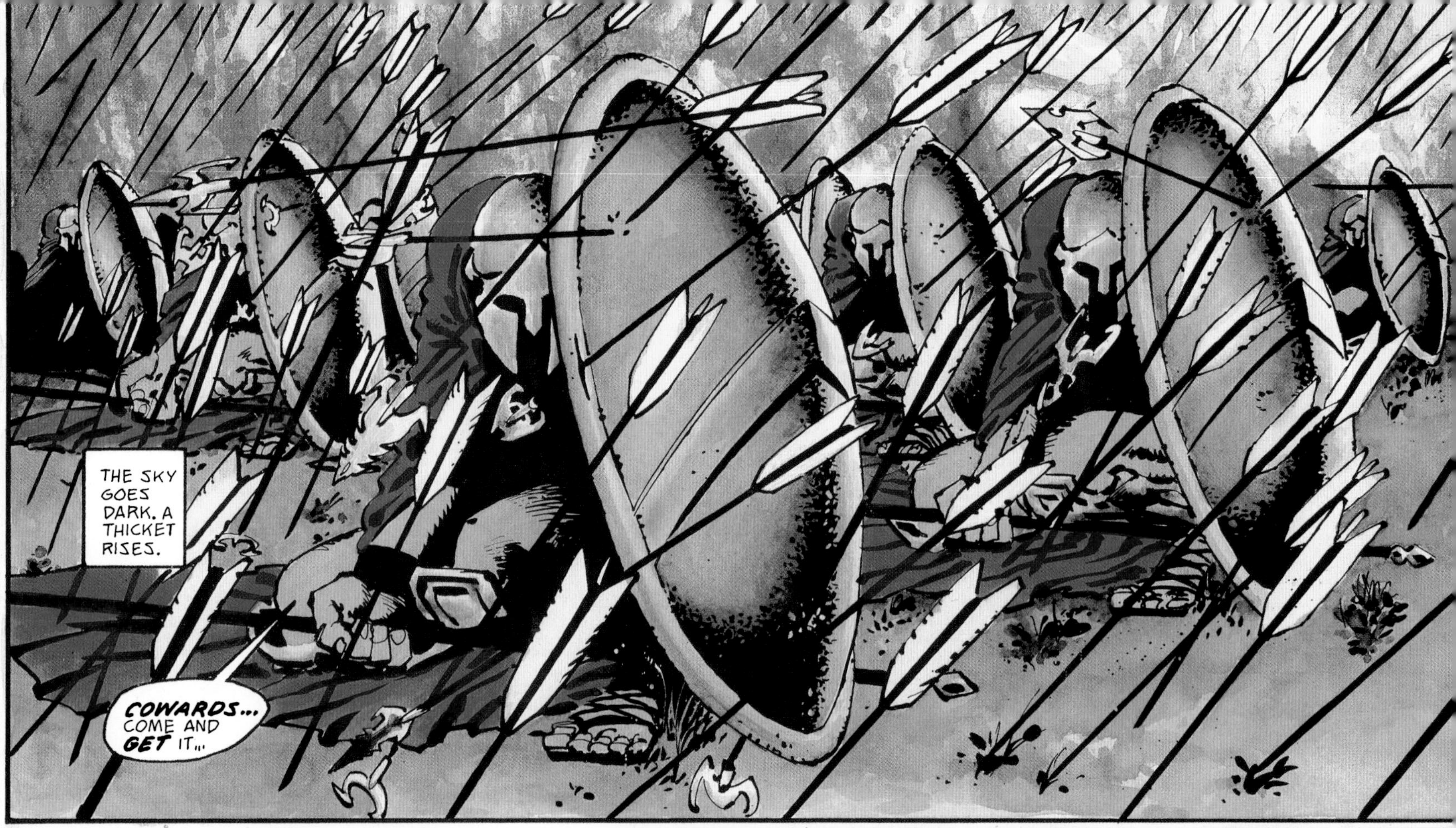
THE SKY GOES DARK. A THICKET RISES.
COWARDS... COME AND GET IT...

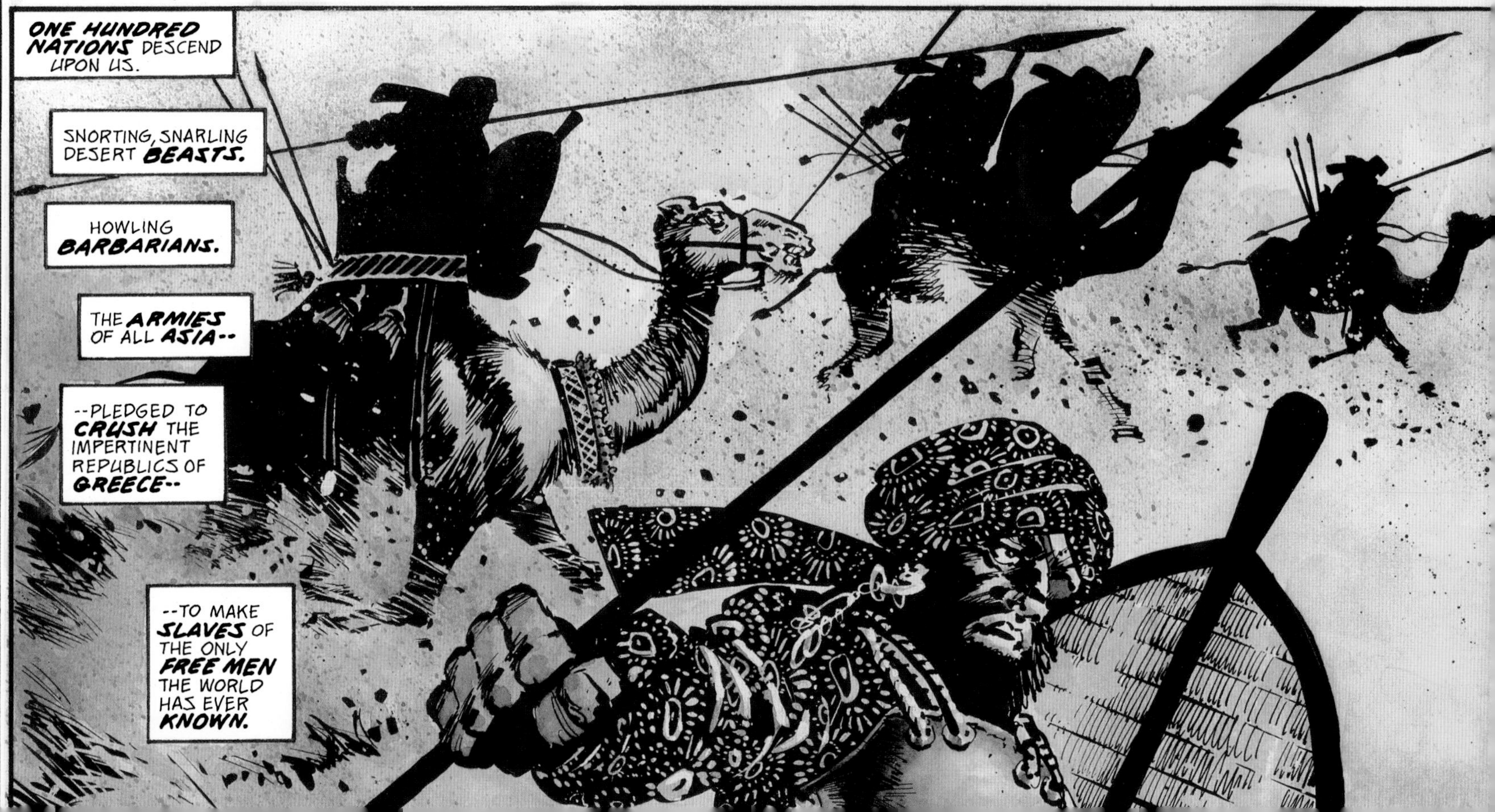
ONE HUNDRED NATIONS DESCEND UPON US.
SNORTING, SNARLING DESERT BEASTS.
HOWLING BARBARIANS.
THE ARMIES OF ALL ASIA--
--PLEDGED TO CRUSH THE IMPERTINENT REPUBLICS OF GREECE--
--TO MAKE SLAVES OF THE ONLY FREE MEN THE WORLD HAS EVER KNOWN.

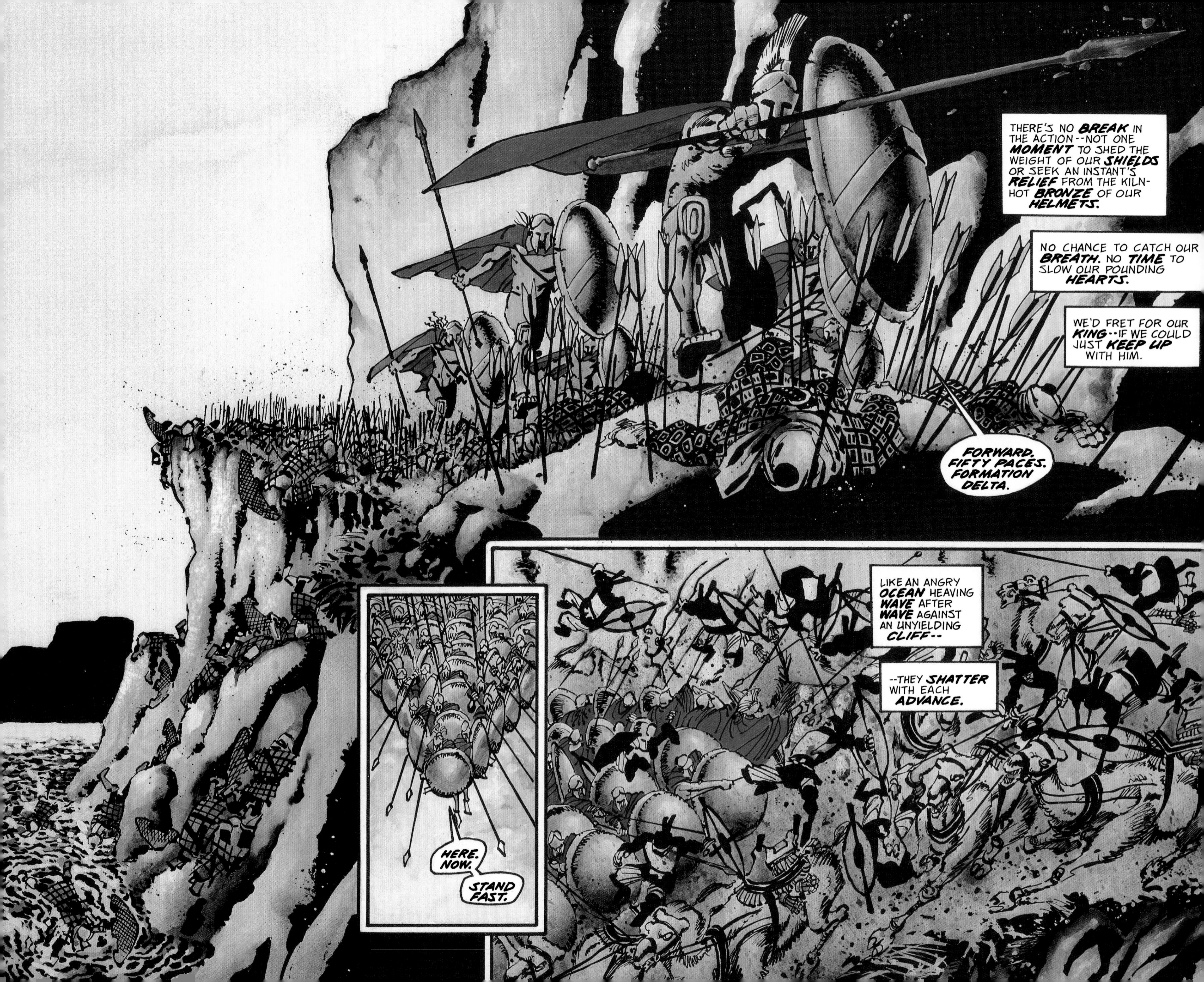
THERE'S NO BREAK IN THE ACTION--NOT ONE MOMENT TO SHED THE WEIGHT OF OUR SHIELDS OR SEEK AN INSTANT'S RELIEF FROM THE KILN-HOT BRONZE OF OUR HELMETS.
NO CHANCE TO CATCH OUR BREATH. NO TIME TO SLOW OUR POUNDING HEARTS.
WE'D FRET FOR OUR KING--IF WE COULD JUST KEEP UP WITH HIM.
FORWARD. FIFTY PACES. FORMATION DELTA.
HERE. NOW.
STAND FAST.
LIKE AN ANGRY OCEAN HEAVING WAVE AFTER WAVE AGAINST AN UNYIELDING CLIFF--
--THEY SHATTER WITH EACH ADVANCE.

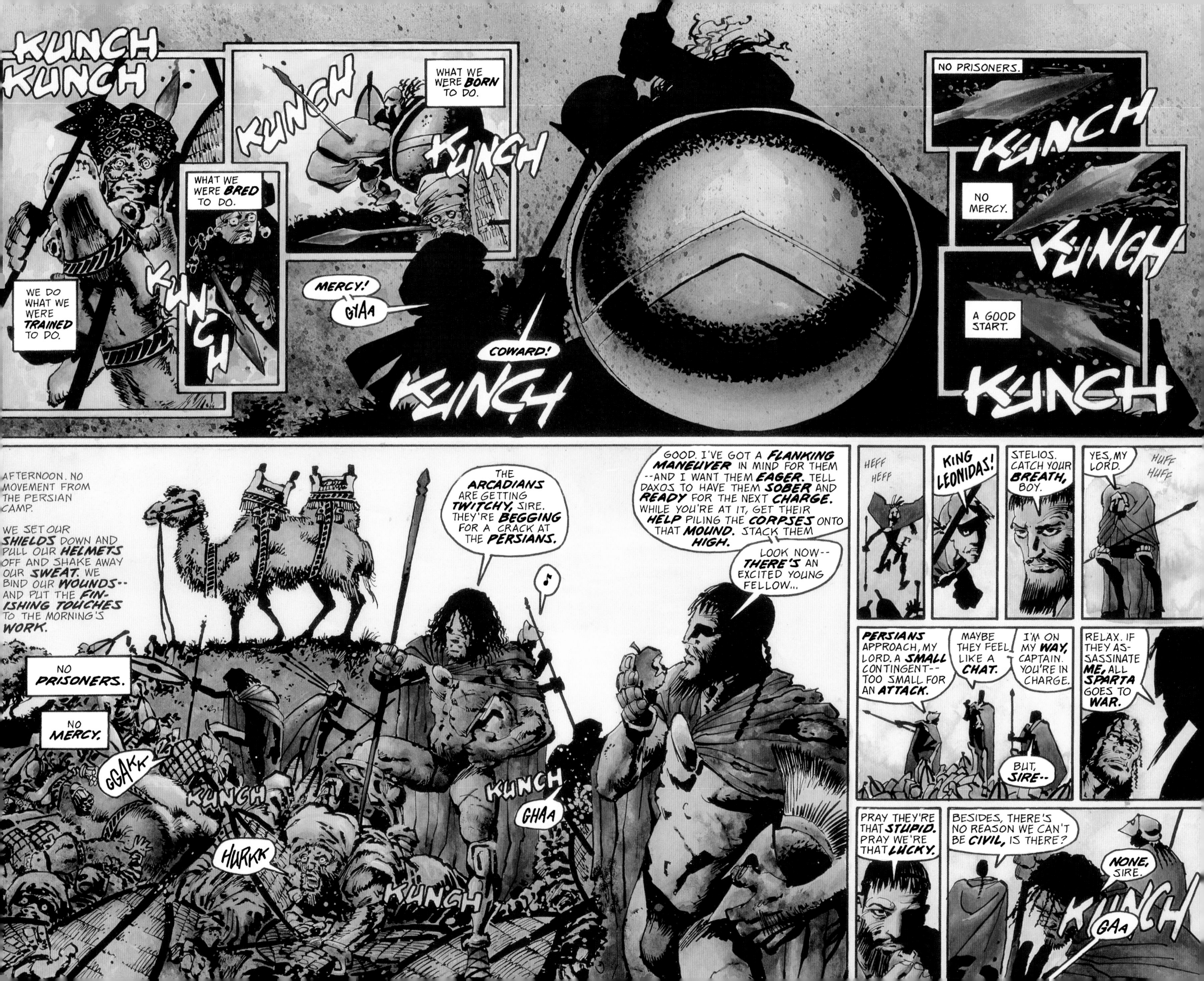
KUNCH KUNCH
WE DO WHAT WE WERE TRAINED TO DO.
KUNCH
WHAT WE WERE BRED TO DO.
KUNCH
WHAT WE WERE BORN TO DO.
KUNCH
KUNCH
MERCY!
GYAA
COWARD!
KUNCH
NO PRISONERS.
KUNCH
NO MERCY.
KUNCH
A GOOD START.
KUNCH
AFTERNOON. NO MOVEMENT FROM THE PERSIAN CAMP.
WE SET OUR SHIELDS DOWN AND PULL OUR HELMETS OFF AND SHAKE AWAY OUR SWEAT. WE BIND OUR WOUNDS-- AND PUT THE FINISHING TOUCHES TO THE MORNING'S WORK.
NO PRISONERS.
NO MERCY.
GGAKK
KUNCH
HURKK
KUNCH
KUNCH
GHAA
THE ARCADIANS ARE GETTING TWITCHY, SIRE. THEY'RE BEGGING FOR A CRACK AT THE PERSIANS.
GOOD. I'VE GOT A FLANKING MANEUVER IN MIND FOR THEM --AND I WANT THEM EAGER. TELL DAXOS TO HAVE THEM SOBER AND READY FOR THE NEXT CHARGE. WHILE YOU'RE AT IT, GET THEIR HELP PILING THE CORPSES ONTO THAT MOUND. STACK THEM HIGH.
LOOK NOW-- THERE'S AN EXCITED YOUNG FELLOW...
HEFF HEFF
KING LEONIDAS!
STELIOS. CATCH YOUR BREATH, BOY.
YES, MY LORD.
HUFF HUFF
PERSIANS APPROACH, MY LORD. A SMALL CONTINGENT-- TOO SMALL FOR AN ATTACK.
MAYBE THEY FEEL LIKE A CHAT.
I'M ON MY WAY, CAPTAIN. YOU'RE IN CHARGE.
BUT, SIRE--
RELAX. IF THEY ASSASSINATE ME, ALL SPARTA GOES TO WAR.
PRAY THEY'RE THAT STUPID. PRAY WE'RE THAT LUCKY.
BESIDES, THERE'S NO REASON WE CAN'T BE CIVIL, IS THERE?
NONE, SIRE.
KUNCH
GAA

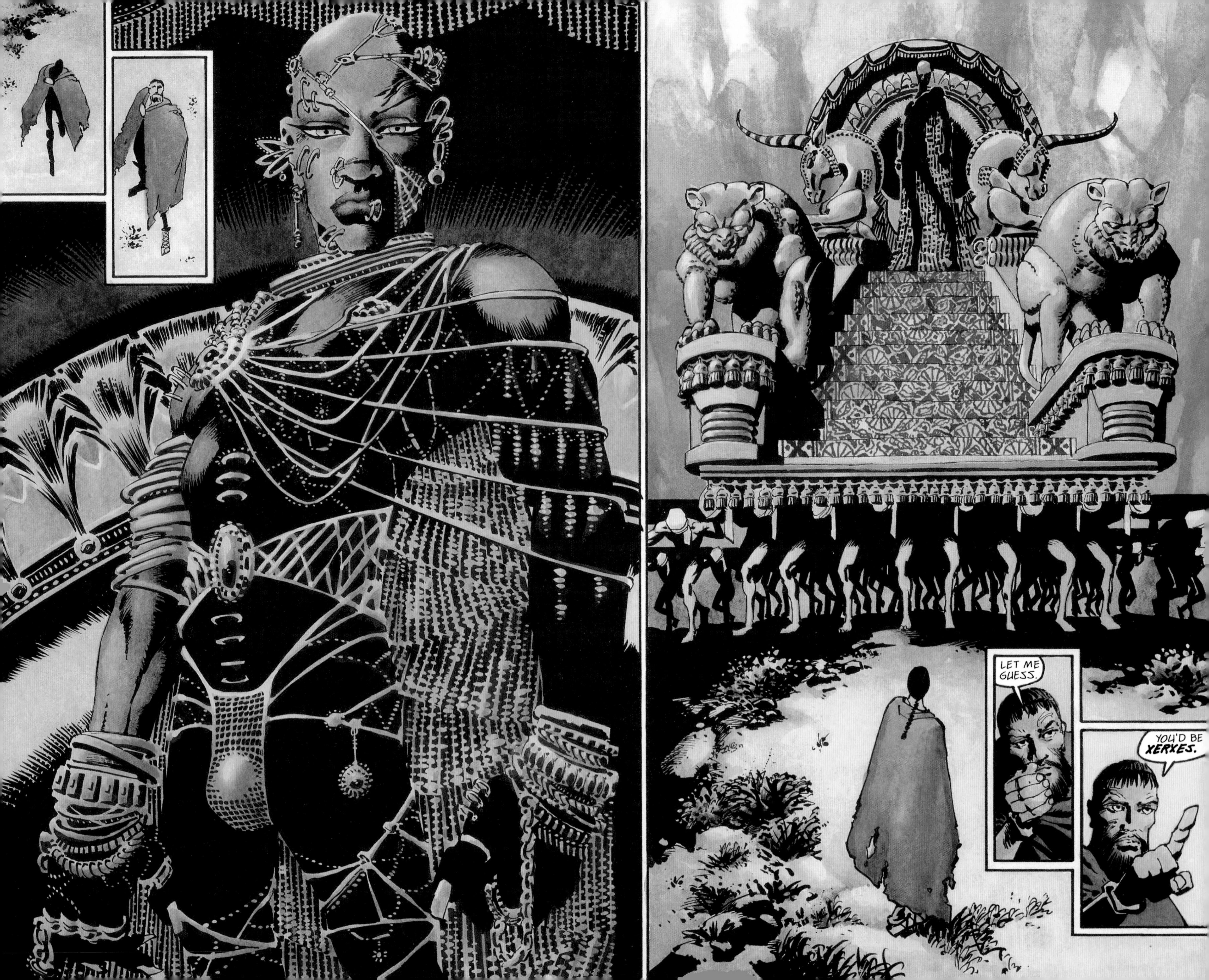
LET ME GUESS.
YOU'D BE **XERXES.**

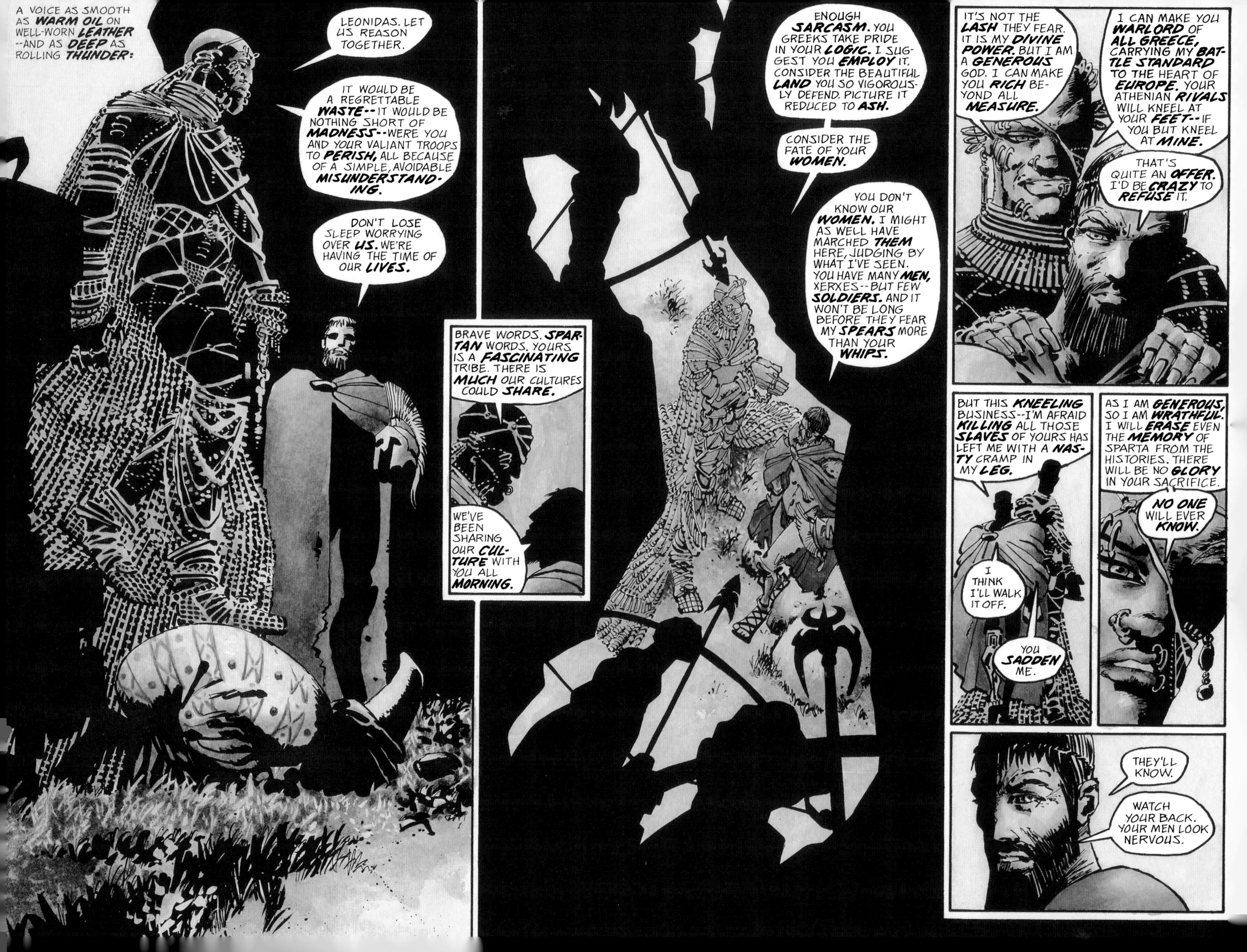
A VOICE AS SMOOTH AS WARM OIL ON WELL-WORN LEATHER --AND AS DEEP AS ROLLING THUNDER:
LEONIDAS. LET US REASON TOGETHER.
IT WOULD BE A REGRETTABLE WASTE-- IT WOULD BE NOTHING SHORT OF MADNESS--WERE YOU AND YOUR VALIANT TROOPS TO PERISH, ALL BECAUSE OF A SIMPLE, AVOIDABLE MISUNDERSTANDING.
DON'T LOSE SLEEP WORRYING OVER US. WE'RE HAVING THE TIME OF OUR LIVES.
BRAVE WORDS. SPARTAN WORDS. YOURS IS A FASCINATING TRIBE. THERE IS MUCH OUR CULTURES COULD SHARE.
WE'VE BEEN SHARING OUR CULTURE WITH YOU ALL MORNING.
ENOUGH SARCASM. YOU GREEKS TAKE PRIDE IN YOUR LOGIC. I SUGGEST YOU EMPLOY IT. CONSIDER THE BEAUTIFUL LAND YOU SO VIGOROUSLY DEFEND. PICTURE IT REDUCED TO ASH.
CONSIDER THE FATE OF YOUR WOMEN.
YOU DON'T KNOW OUR WOMEN. I MIGHT AS WELL HAVE MARCHED THEM HERE, JUDGING BY WHAT I'VE SEEN. YOU HAVE MANY MEN, XERXES--BUT FEW SOLDIERS. AND IT WON'T BE LONG BEFORE THEY FEAR MY SPEARS MORE THAN YOUR WHIPS.
IT'S NOT THE LASH THEY FEAR. IT IS MY DIVINE POWER. BUT I AM A GENEROUS GOD. I CAN MAKE YOU RICH BEYOND ALL MEASURE.
I CAN MAKE YOU WARLORD OF ALL GREECE, CARRYING MY BATTLE STANDARD TO THE HEART OF EUROPE. YOUR ATHENIAN RIVALS WILL KNEEL AT YOUR FEET-- IF YOU BUT KNEEL AT MINE.
THAT'S QUITE AN OFFER. I'D BE CRAZY TO REFUSE IT.
BUT THIS KNEELING BUSINESS--I'M AFRAID KILLING ALL THOSE SLAVES OF YOURS HAS LEFT ME WITH A NASTY CRAMP IN MY LEG.
I THINK I'LL WALK IT OFF.
YOU SADDEN ME.
AS I AM GENEROUS, SO I AM WRATHFUL. I WILL ERASE EVEN THE MEMORY OF SPARTA FROM THE HISTORIES. THERE WILL BE NO GLORY IN YOUR SACRIFICE.
NO ONE WILL EVER KNOW.
THEY'LL KNOW.
WATCH YOUR BACK. YOUR MEN LOOK NERVOUS.

THE KING CAN SCARCELY **CONTAIN** HIMSELF! WHAT FINE **FORTUNE!**

XERXES HAS BETRAYED A **FATAL** FLAW:

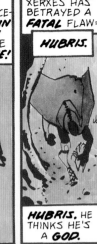

HUBRIS.

HUBRIS. HE THINKS HE'S A **GOD.**

HUBRIS. IT MAKES A FOOL OF **ANY** MAN.

EASY TO **TAUNT.**

EASY TO **TRICK.**

HE'LL **TAKE** THE BAIT. HE **WILL.**

EXCUSE ME, CAPTAIN, BUT... DID YOU HEAR WHAT HE **CALLED** ME?

WHO?

THE **KING.** HE CALLED ME **STELIOS.** THAT'S MY **NAME.** HE **DIDN'T** CALL ME "STUM-BLIOS."

I HEARD HIM CALL YOU "BOY," BOY.

MOVE IT, MEN!

PILE THOSE PERSIANS **HIGH.** UNLESS I MISS MY **GUESS--**

--WE'RE IN FOR ONE **WILD** NIGHT!

AND, **CAP-TAIN**--YOU WILL ADDRESS **STELIOS** BY HIS PROPER **NAME.**

YES, MY LORD.

HMF! ISN'T THE KING IN A GENEROUS MOOD...

THE FIRST NIGHT

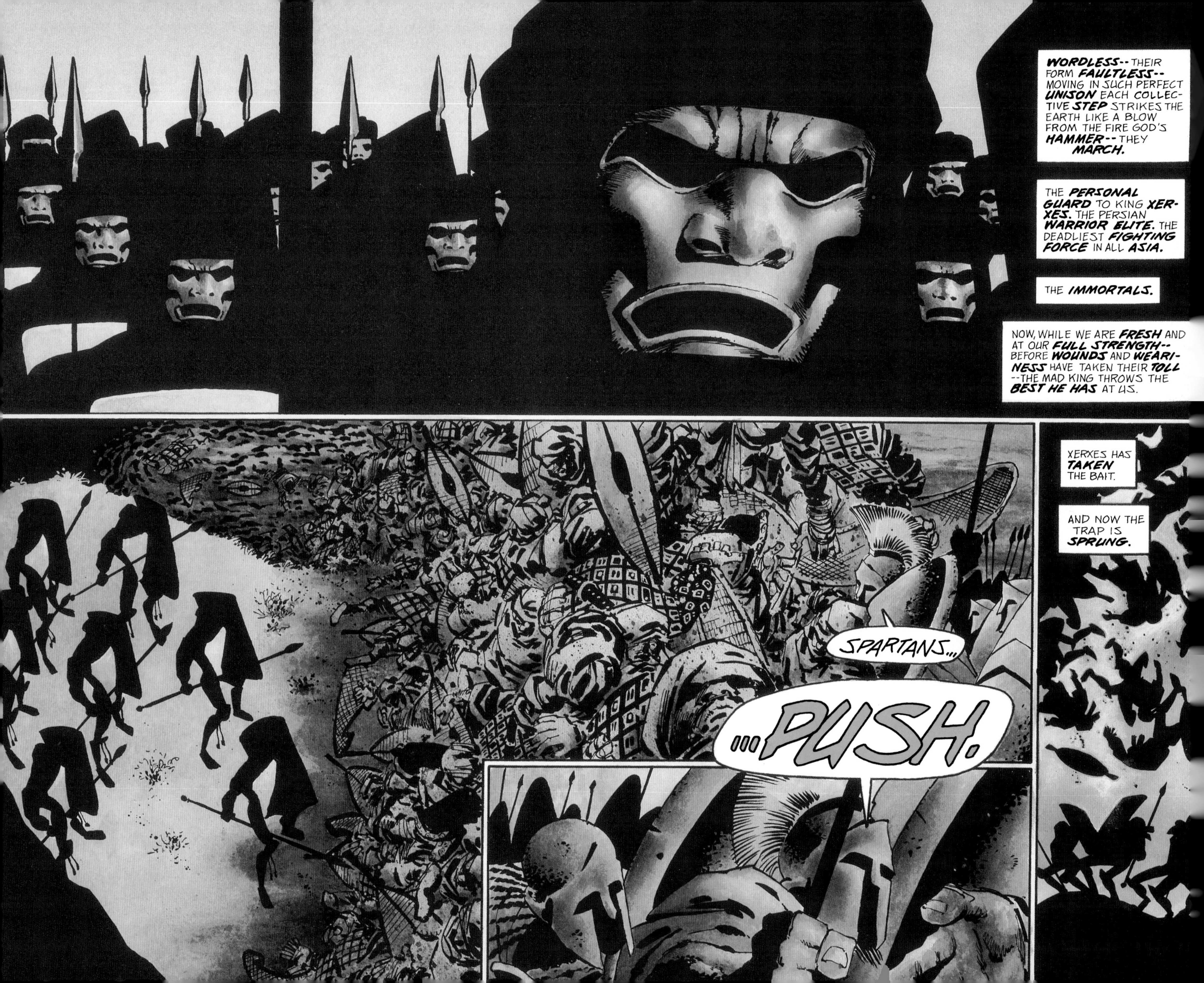
WORDLESS-- THEIR FORM FAULTLESS-- MOVING IN SUCH PERFECT UNISON EACH COLLECTIVE STEP STRIKES THE EARTH LIKE A BLOW FROM THE FIRE GOD'S HAMMER-- THEY MARCH.
THE PERSONAL GUARD TO KING XERXES. THE PERSIAN WARRIOR ELITE. THE DEADLIEST FIGHTING FORCE IN ALL ASIA.
THE IMMORTALS.
NOW, WHILE WE ARE FRESH AND AT OUR FULL STRENGTH-- BEFORE WOUNDS AND WEARINESS HAVE TAKEN THEIR TOLL --THE MAD KING THROWS THE BEST HE HAS AT US.
XERXES HAS TAKEN THE BAIT.
AND NOW THE TRAP IS SPRUNG.
SPARTANS...
...PUSH.

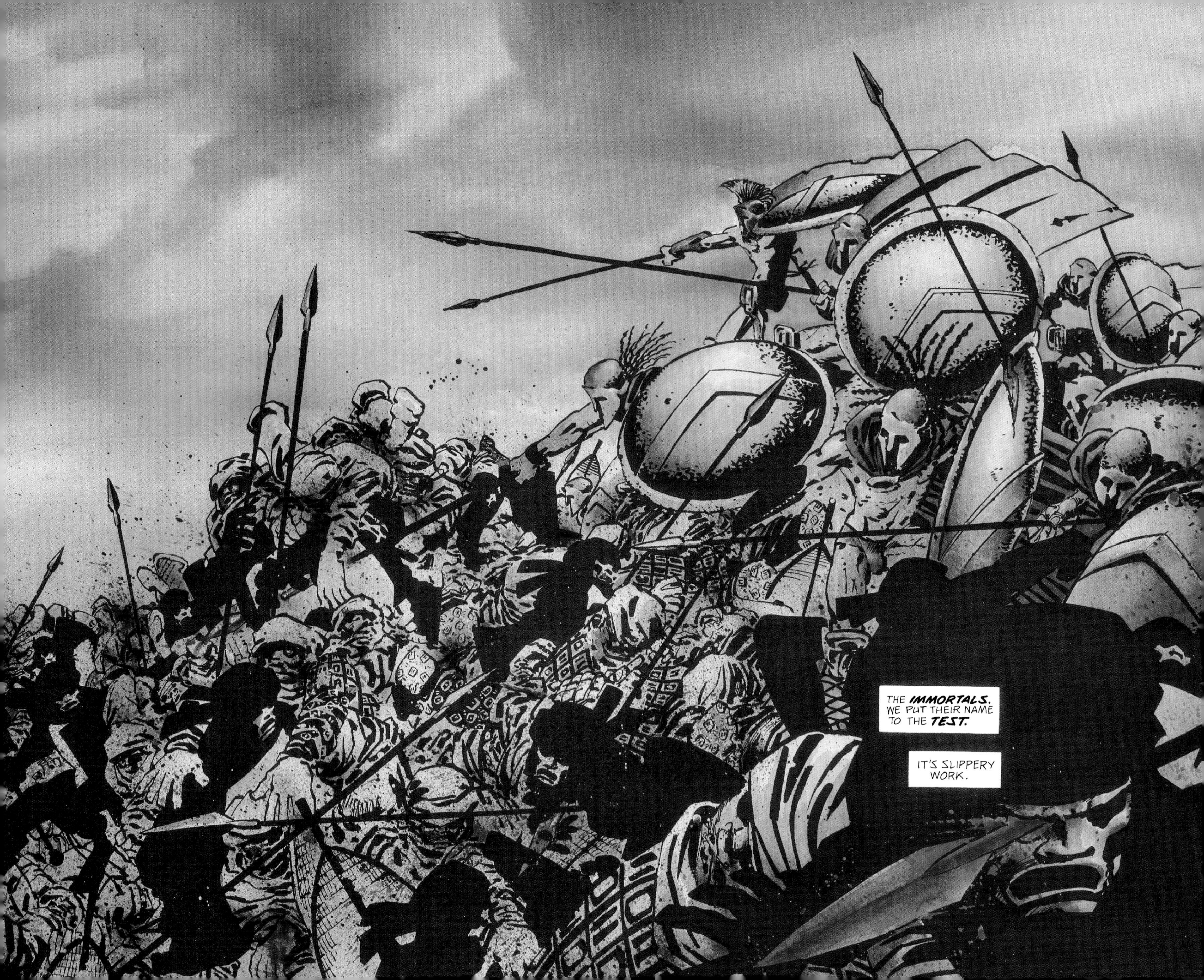
THE IMMORTALS. WE PUT THEIR NAME TO THE TEST.
IT'S SLIPPERY WORK.

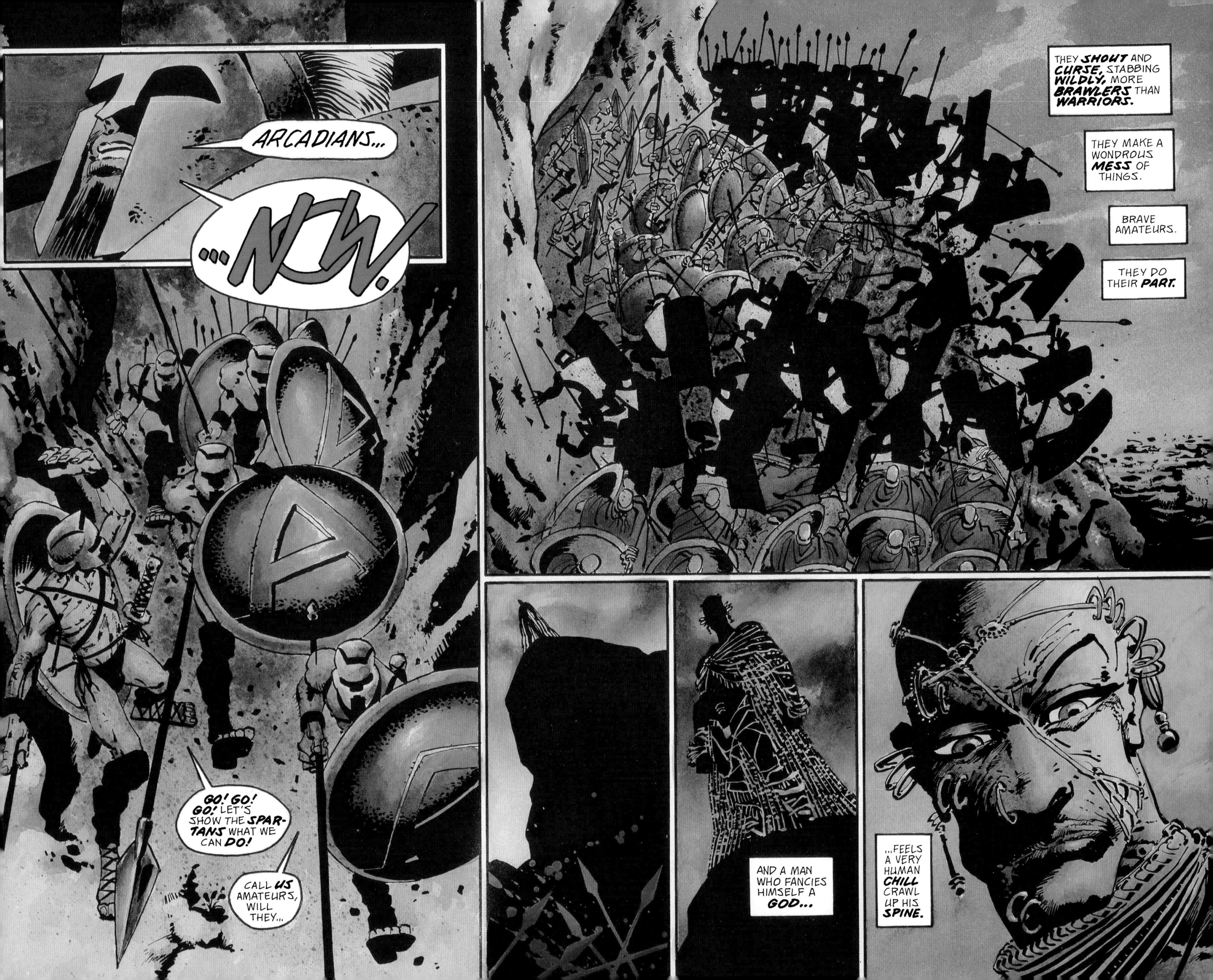

ARCADIANS...
...NOW!
GO! GO! GO! LET'S SHOW THE SPARTANS WHAT WE CAN DO!
CALL US AMATEURS, WILL THEY...
THEY SHOUT AND CURSE, STABBING WILDLY, MORE BRAWLERS THAN WARRIORS.
THEY MAKE A WONDROUS MESS OF THINGS.
BRAVE AMATEURS.
THEY DO THEIR PART.
AND A MAN WHO FANCIES HIMSELF A GOD...
...FEELS A VERY HUMAN CHILL CRAWL UP HIS SPINE.

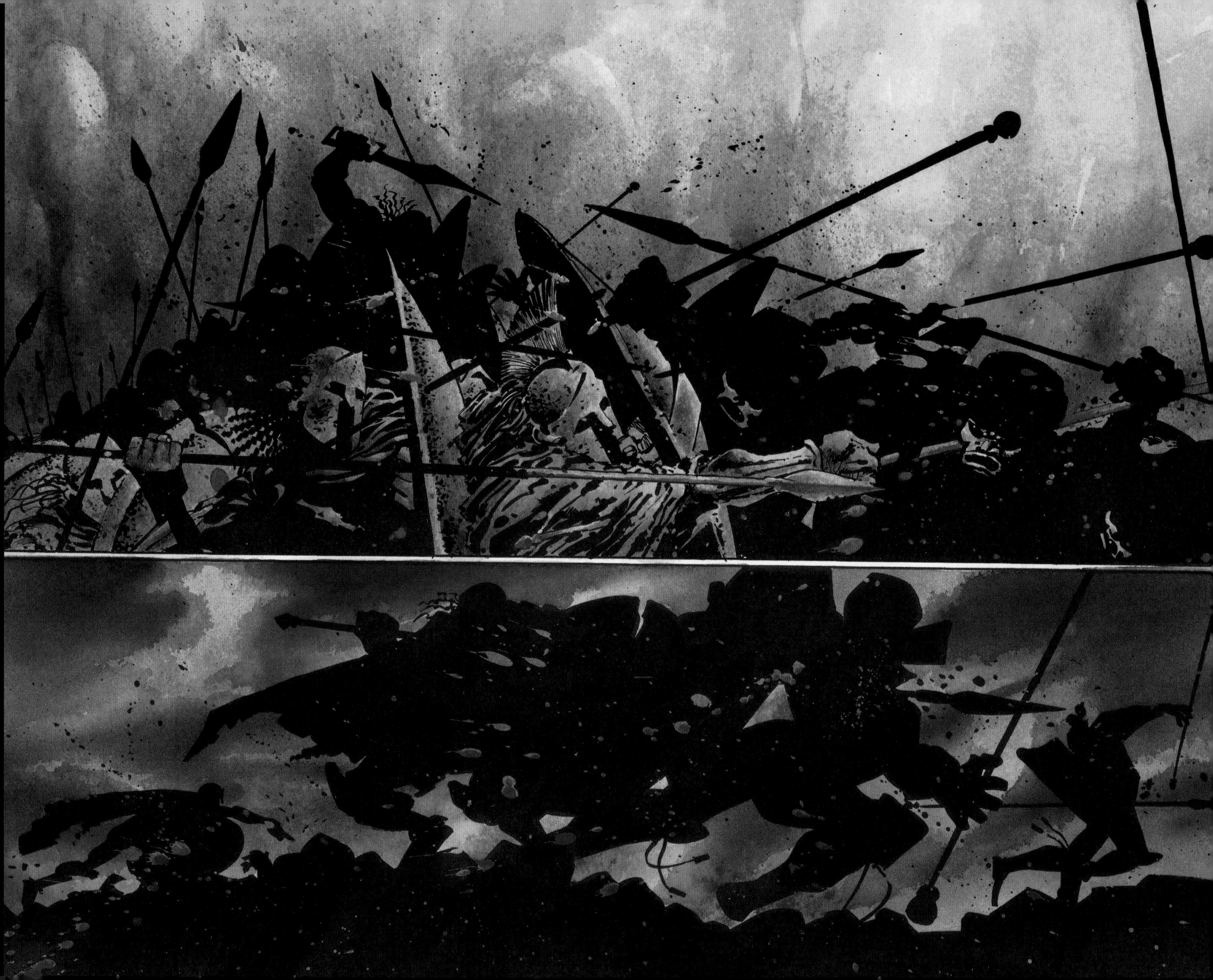

CHILDREN, CHILDREN...

TRIUMPH. THE DAY IS OURS.

THE DREAD IMMORTALS SLINK BACK TO THEIR CAMP LIKE WHIPPED DOGS--AND EVERY PERSIAN SEES IT.

WHOM WILL XERXES DARE TO DISPATCH NEXT?

AND WHO AMONG HIS LEGIONS WILL DARE TO FACE THE SPARTANS?

EVEN THE KING ALLOWS HIMSELF TO HOPE--FOR MORE THAN GLORY.

SUCH MAD HOPE--BUT THERE IT IS.

AGAINST ASIA'S ENDLESS HORDES--AGAINST ALL ODDS--WE CAN DO IT. WE CAN HOLD THE HOT GATES.

WE CAN WIN.

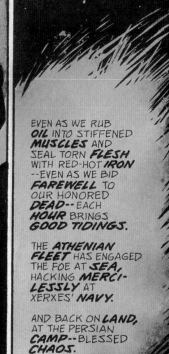

EVEN AS WE RUB OIL INTO STIFFENED MUSCLES AND SEAL TORN FLESH WITH RED-HOT IRON --EVEN AS WE BID FAREWELL TO OUR HONORED DEAD-- EACH HOUR BRINGS GOOD TIDINGS.

THE ATHENIAN FLEET HAS ENGAGED THE FOE AT SEA, HACKING MERCILESSLY AT XERXES' NAVY.

AND BACK ON LAND, AT THE PERSIAN CAMP--BLESSED CHAOS.

CHAOS! THE MEDES AND SCYTHIANS ARE IN OPEN REVOLT! XERXES IS SLAUGHTERING HIS OWN TROOPS!

HA! THERE'S NOTHING THAT CAN STOP US! NOTHING!

SETTLE DOWN, BOY. DON'T GET COCKY.

LIFE'S FULL OF SURPRISES.

KHAFF

GODS...I STILL BREATHE ...I STILL LIVE... GODS--YOU ARE CRUEL!

DAMN YOU!

DAMN YOU. DAMN YOU, GODS! DAMN YOU, FATHER! DAMN YOU, MOTHER! DAMN YOU ALL TO HELL!

HENFF

SPARTANS...

...SPARTANS! THE BOLDEST OF MEN! THE FINEST WARRIORS IN ALL THE WORLD!

DAMN YOU!

PTUI

DAMN YOU ALL!

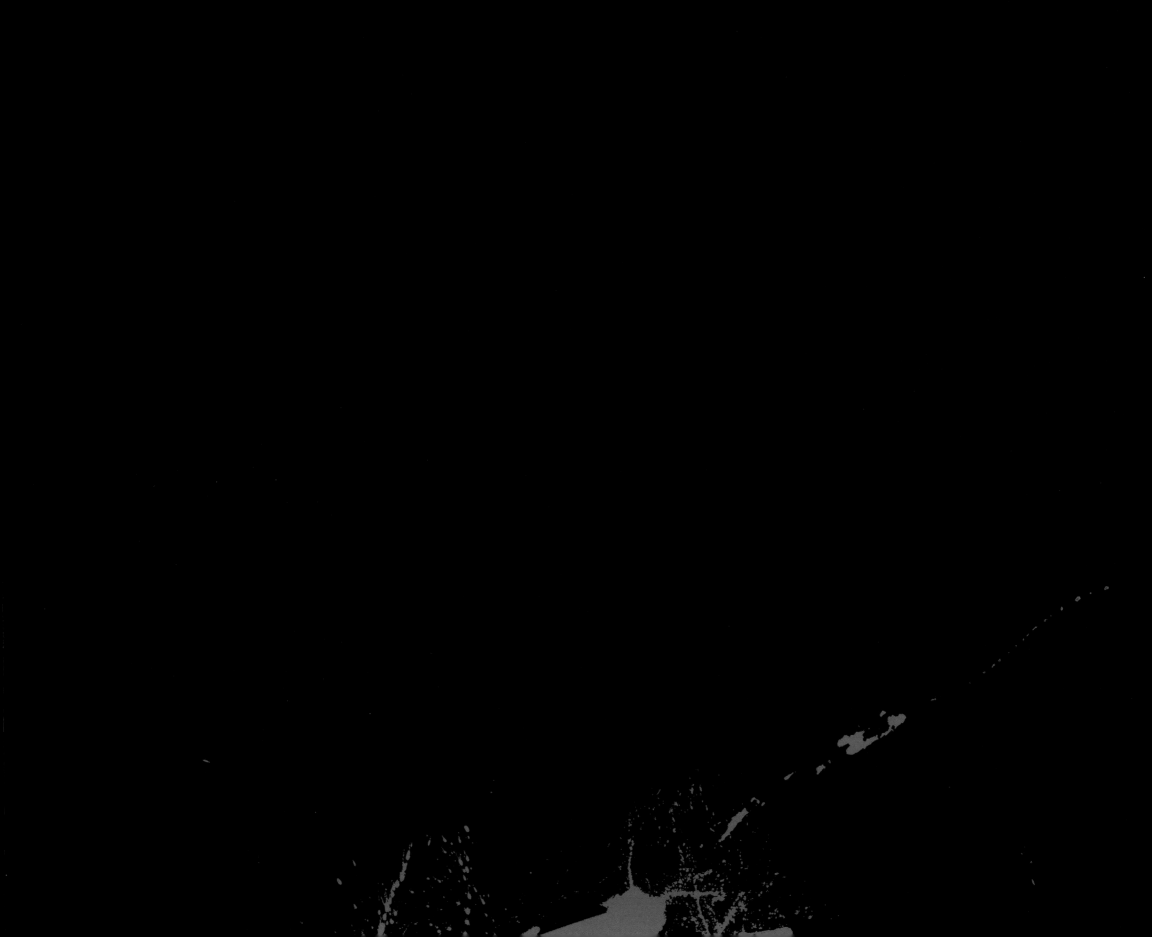

CHAPTER FIVE:
VICTORY

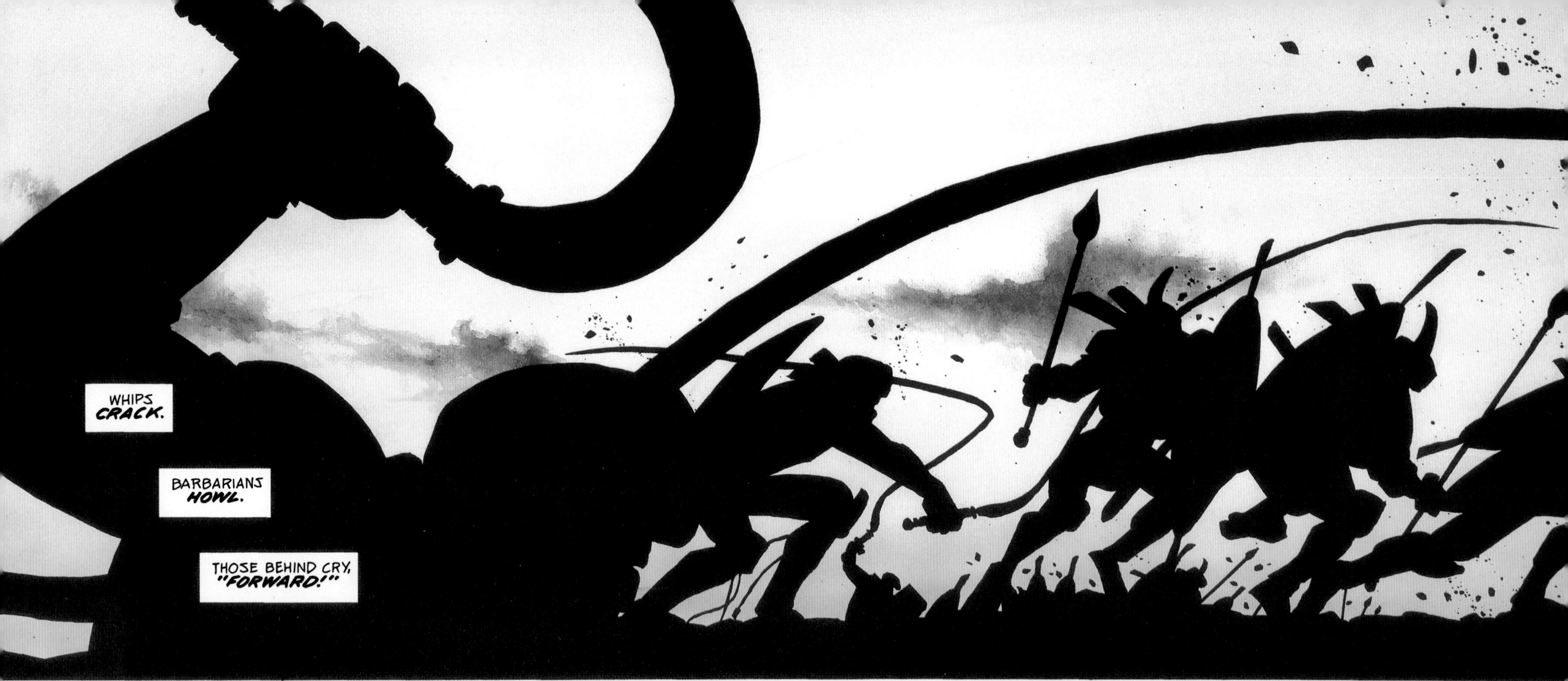
WHIPS CRACK.
BARBARIANS HOWL.
THOSE BEHIND CRY, "FORWARD!"

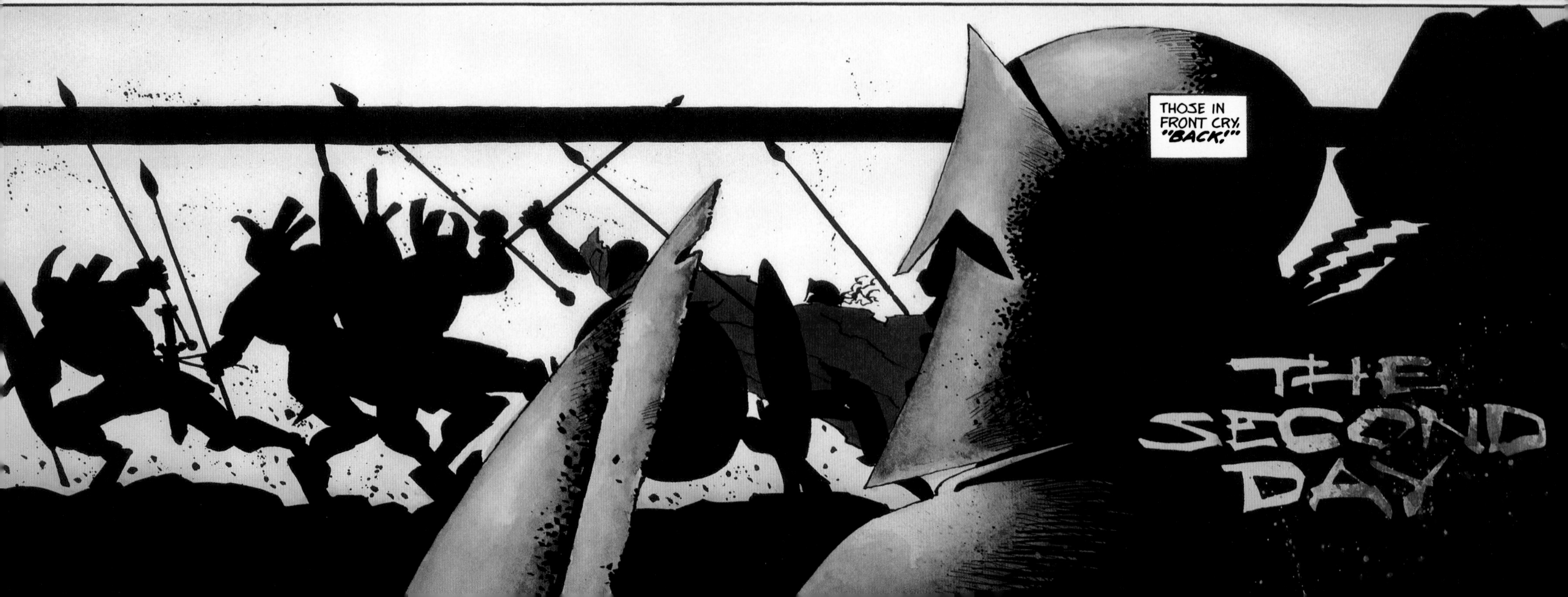
THOSE IN FRONT CRY, "BACK!"
THE SECOND DAY

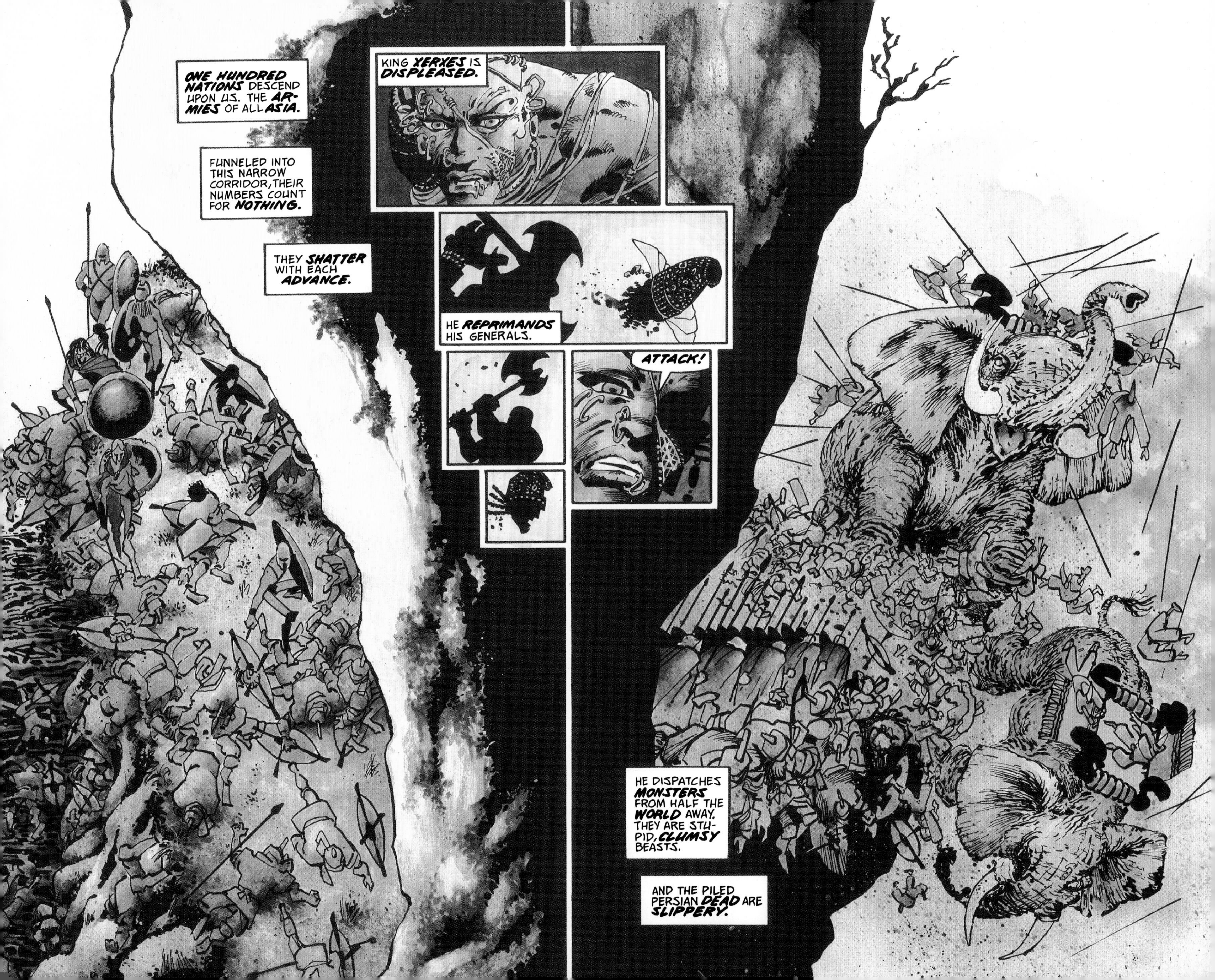
ONE HUNDRED NATIONS DESCEND UPON US. THE ARMIES OF ALL ASIA.
FUNNELED INTO THIS NARROW CORRIDOR, THEIR NUMBERS COUNT FOR NOTHING.
THEY SHATTER WITH EACH ADVANCE.
KING XERXES IS DISPLEASED.
HE REPRIMANDS HIS GENERALS.
ATTACK!
HE DISPATCHES MONSTERS FROM HALF THE WORLD AWAY. THEY ARE STUPID, CLUMSY BEASTS.
AND THE PILED PERSIAN DEAD ARE SLIPPERY.

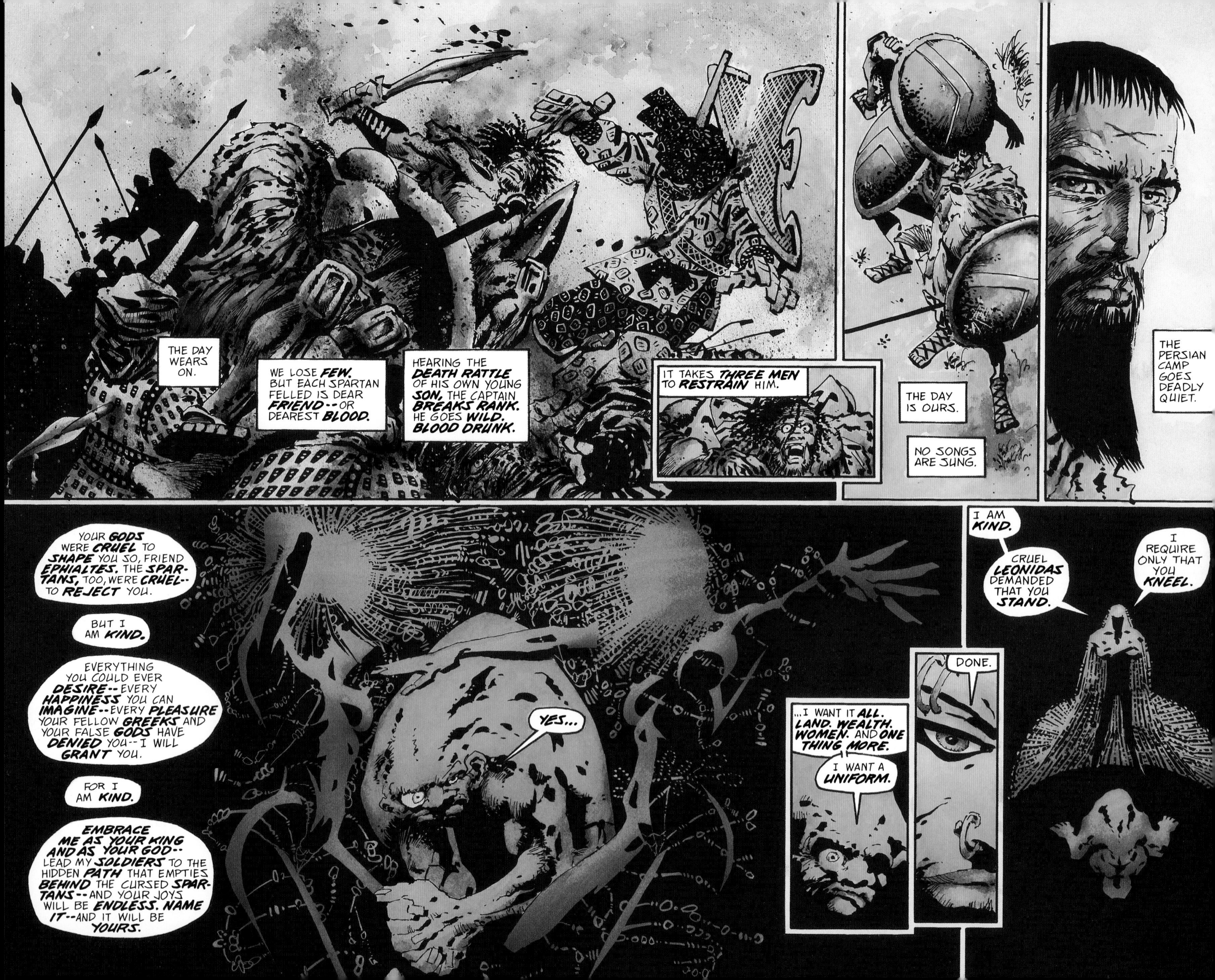
THE DAY WEARS ON.
WE LOSE FEW. BUT EACH SPARTAN FELLED IS DEAR FRIEND--OR DEAREST BLOOD.
HEARING THE DEATH RATTLE OF HIS OWN YOUNG SON, THE CAPTAIN BREAKS RANK. HE GOES WILD. BLOOD DRUNK.
IT TAKES THREE MEN TO RESTRAIN HIM.
THE DAY IS OURS.
NO SONGS ARE SUNG.
THE PERSIAN CAMP GOES DEADLY QUIET.
YOUR GODS WERE CRUEL TO SHAPE YOU SO, FRIEND EPHIALTES. THE SPARTANS, TOO, WERE CRUEL--TO REJECT YOU.
BUT I AM KIND.
EVERYTHING YOU COULD EVER DESIRE--EVERY HAPPINESS YOU CAN IMAGINE--EVERY PLEASURE YOUR FELLOW GREEKS AND YOUR FALSE GODS HAVE DENIED YOU--I WILL GRANT YOU.
FOR I AM KIND.
EMBRACE ME AS YOUR KING AND AS YOUR GOD--LEAD MY SOLDIERS TO THE HIDDEN PATH THAT EMPTIES BEHIND THE CURSED SPARTANS--AND YOUR JOYS WILL BE ENDLESS. NAME IT--AND IT WILL BE YOURS.
YES...
...I WANT IT ALL. LAND. WEALTH. WOMEN. AND ONE THING MORE.
I WANT A UNIFORM.
DONE.
I AM KIND.
CRUEL LEONIDAS DEMANDED THAT YOU STAND.
I REQUIRE ONLY THAT YOU KNEEL.

THE SECOND NIGHT

THE HOT GATES.

DILIOS. I TRUST THAT SCRATCH HASN'T MADE YOU USELESS.

HARDLY, MY LORD. IT'S JUST AN EYE. THE GODS SAW FIT TO GRACE ME WITH A SPARE.

GOOD. THE MEN NEED A BOOST. TELL THEM A STORY. ONE THAT'LL GET THEIR BLOOD UP.

XERXES REPEATS HIS FATHER'S FOLLY. TEN SUMMERS PAST, PERSIAN SLAVES SET SHORE AT THE PLAIN OF MARATHON, THERE TO FACE BRAVE GREEKS--AND OUR MIGHTIEST ALLY, THE HARSH, PROUD TERRAIN OF GREECE HERSELF.

THE PERSIANS STUMBLED FROM THEIR CROWDED SHIPS, THEIR LEGS CRAMPED, THEIR SOFT FEET RECOILING FROM THE ROCKY SOIL, THE SNAPPING, STABBING, THORNY UNDERBRUSH.

DILIOS SPINS HIS STORIES.

THE STORY OF MARATHON.

A PERFECT CHOICE.

THEY LOOKED UP-- JAWS SLACK, HEARTS LURCHING UP THEIR THROATS. ARMORED MEN CHARGED AT THEM-- AT A FULL RUN-- FROM A FULL MILE DISTANT!

ARMORED MEN. ATHENIANS. WITH THEIR LEATHER SKIRTS AND LOVINGLY SCULPTED BREASTPLATES. WHAT A PRETTY PACK THEY MUST HAVE BEEN!

ATHENIANS. AMATEURS. FOPPISH, FRILLY CITIZEN-SOLDIERS. NOT A SPARTAN AMONG THEM-- AND STILL THEY DROVE THE PERSIANS BACK TO THE SEA AND AWAY!

BROTHERS! HOW CAN WE FAIL--AGAINST FOES SO FEARFUL OF COMBAT THEY'D SHOW THEIR BACKSIDES TO ATHENIANS?

MUCH LAUGHTER.

SHORT-LIVED.

LEONIDAS! WE ARE UNDONE!

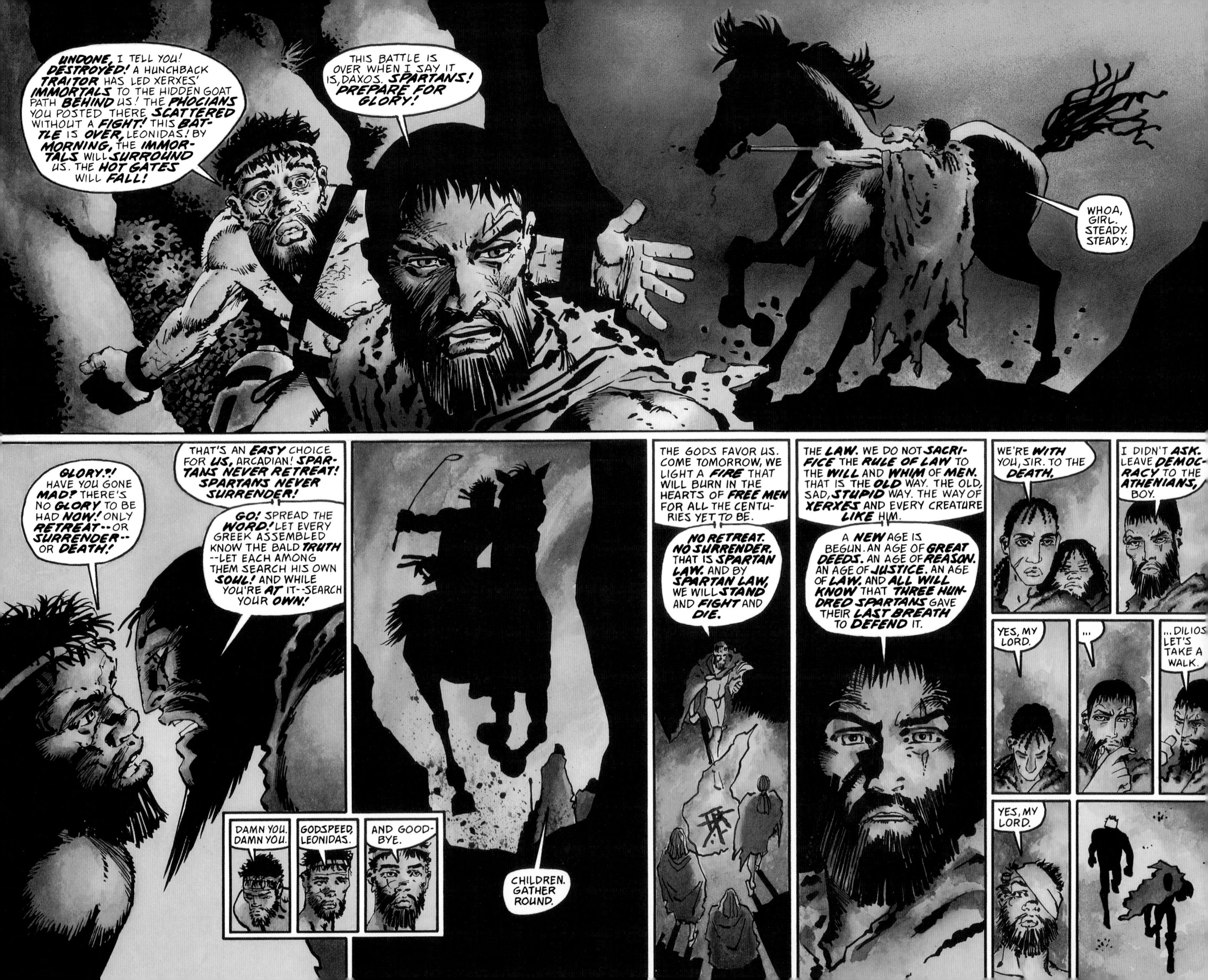
UNDONE, I TELL YOU! DESTROYED! A HUNCHBACK TRAITOR HAS LED XERXES' IMMORTALS TO THE HIDDEN GOAT PATH BEHIND US! THE PHOCIANS YOU POSTED THERE SCATTERED WITHOUT A FIGHT! THIS BATTLE IS OVER, LEONIDAS! BY MORNING, THE IMMORTALS WILL SURROUND US. THE HOT GATES WILL FALL!
THIS BATTLE IS OVER WHEN I SAY IT IS, DAXOS. SPARTANS! PREPARE FOR GLORY!
WHOA, GIRL. STEADY. STEADY.
GLORY?! HAVE YOU GONE MAD? THERE'S NO GLORY TO BE HAD NOW! ONLY RETREAT--OR SURRENDER--OR DEATH!
THAT'S AN EASY CHOICE FOR US, ARCADIAN! SPARTANS NEVER RETREAT! SPARTANS NEVER SURRENDER!
GO! SPREAD THE WORD! LET EVERY GREEK ASSEMBLED KNOW THE BALD TRUTH --LET EACH AMONG THEM SEARCH HIS OWN SOUL! AND WHILE YOU'RE AT IT--SEARCH YOUR OWN!
DAMN YOU. DAMN YOU.
GODSPEED, LEONIDAS.
AND GOOD-BYE.
CHILDREN. GATHER ROUND.
THE GODS FAVOR US. COME TOMORROW, WE LIGHT A FIRE THAT WILL BURN IN THE HEARTS OF FREE MEN FOR ALL THE CENTURIES YET TO BE.
NO RETREAT. NO SURRENDER. THAT IS SPARTAN LAW. AND BY SPARTAN LAW, WE WILL STAND AND FIGHT AND DIE.
THE LAW. WE DO NOT SACRIFICE THE RULE OF LAW TO THE WILL AND WHIM OF MEN. THAT IS THE OLD WAY. THE OLD, SAD, STUPID WAY. THE WAY OF XERXES AND EVERY CREATURE LIKE HIM.
A NEW AGE IS BEGUN. AN AGE OF GREAT DEEDS. AN AGE OF REASON. AN AGE OF JUSTICE. AN AGE OF LAW. AND ALL WILL KNOW THAT THREE HUNDRED SPARTANS GAVE THEIR LAST BREATH TO DEFEND IT.
WE'RE WITH YOU, SIR. TO THE DEATH.
I DIDN'T ASK. LEAVE DEMOCRACY TO THE ATHENIANS, BOY.
YES, MY LORD.
...
...DILIOS LET'S TAKE A WALK.
YES, MY LORD.

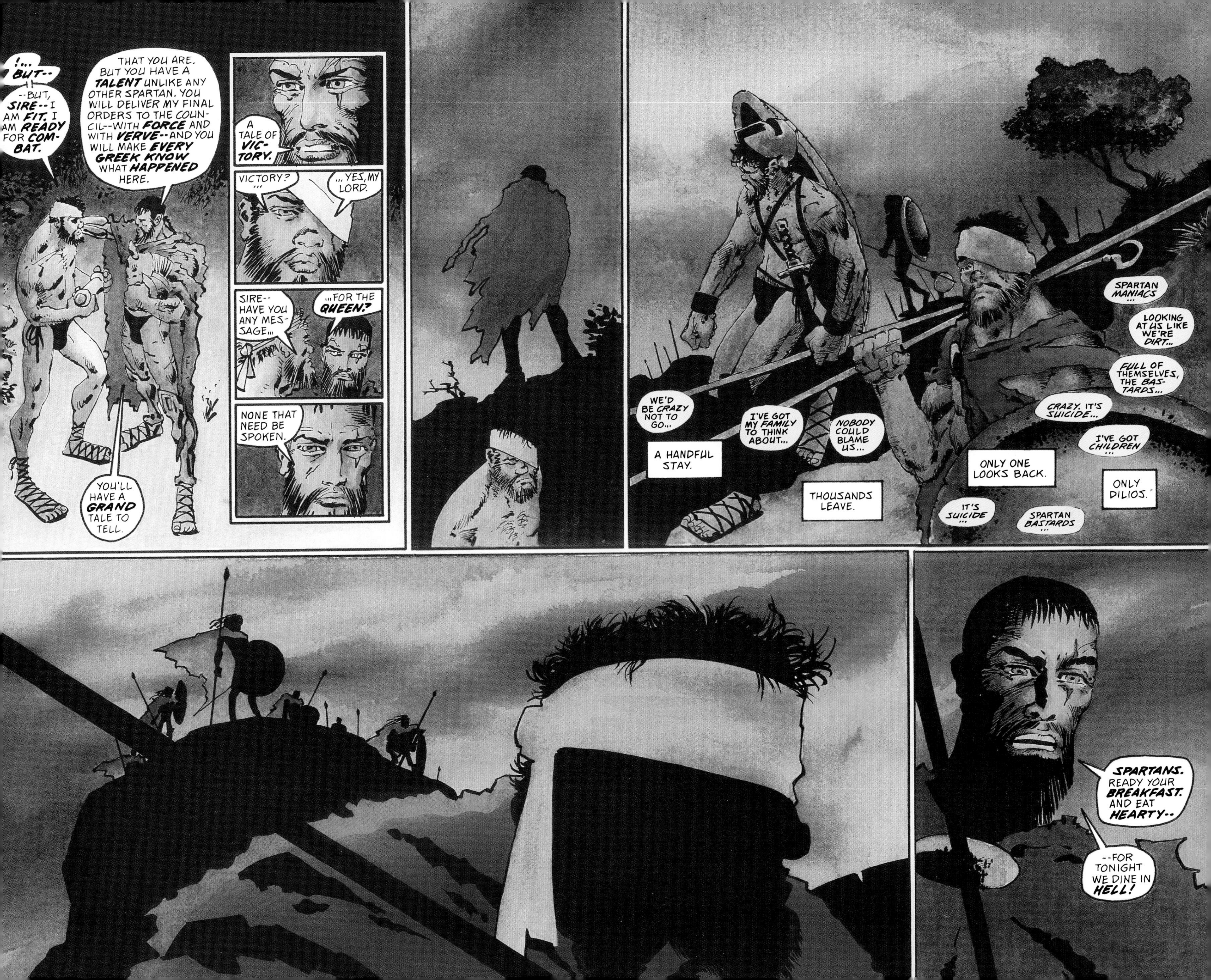
!... BUT--
--BUT, SIRE--I AM FIT, I AM READY FOR COMBAT.
THAT YOU ARE. BUT YOU HAVE A TALENT UNLIKE ANY OTHER SPARTAN. YOU WILL DELIVER MY FINAL ORDERS TO THE COUNCIL--WITH FORCE AND WITH VERVE--AND YOU WILL MAKE EVERY GREEK KNOW WHAT HAPPENED HERE.
YOU'LL HAVE A GRAND TALE TO TELL.
A TALE OF VICTORY.
VICTORY? ...
... YES, MY LORD.
SIRE-- HAVE YOU ANY MESSAGE...
...FOR THE QUEEN?
NONE THAT NEED BE SPOKEN.
WE'D BE CRAZY NOT TO GO...
I'VE GOT MY FAMILY TO THINK ABOUT...
NOBODY COULD BLAME US...
A HANDFUL STAY.
THOUSANDS LEAVE.
SPARTAN MANIACS...
LOOKING AT US LIKE WE'RE DIRT...
FULL OF THEMSELVES, THE BASTARDS...
CRAZY. IT'S SUICIDE...
I'VE GOT CHILDREN...
ONLY ONE LOOKS BACK.
ONLY DILIOS.
IT'S SUICIDE...
SPARTAN BASTARDS...
SPARTANS. READY YOUR BREAKFAST. AND EAT HEARTY--
--FOR TONIGHT WE DINE IN HELL!

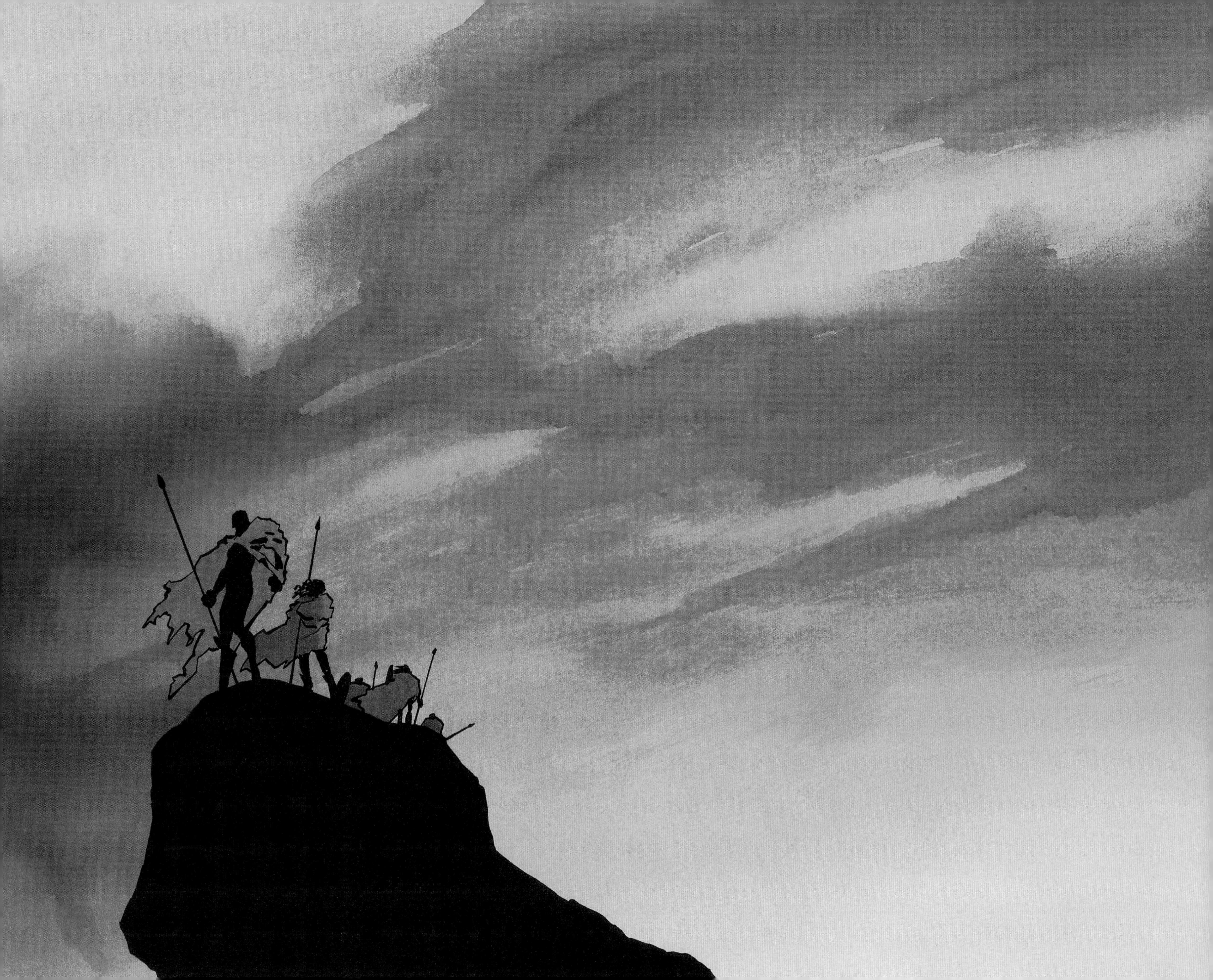

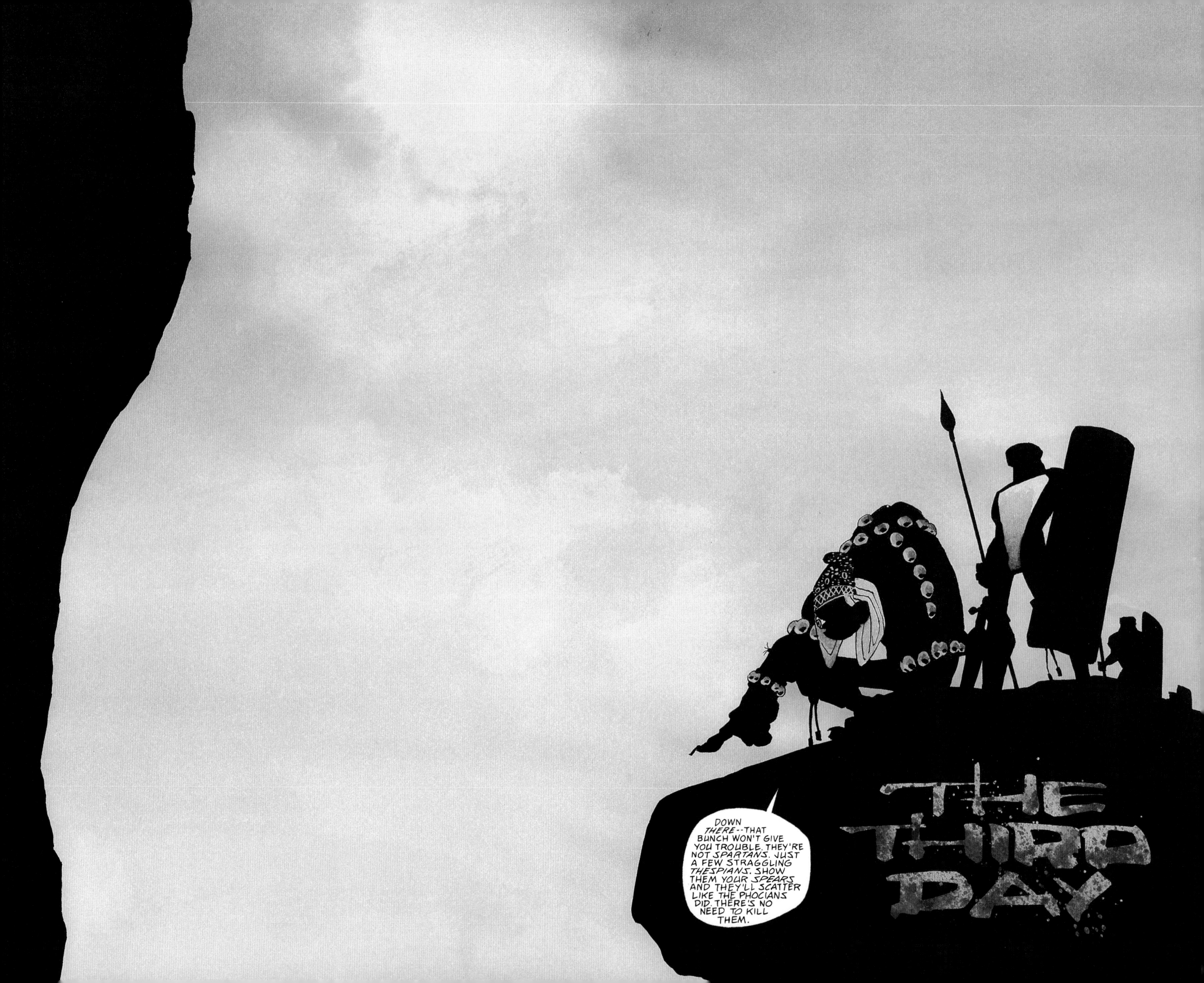
THE THIRD DAY
DOWN *THERE*--THAT BUNCH WON'T GIVE YOU TROUBLE. THEY'RE NOT *SPARTANS*. JUST A FEW STRAGGLING *THESPIANS*. SHOW THEM YOUR *SPEARS* AND THEY'LL SCATTER LIKE THE PHOCIANS DID. THERE'S NO NEED TO KILL THEM.

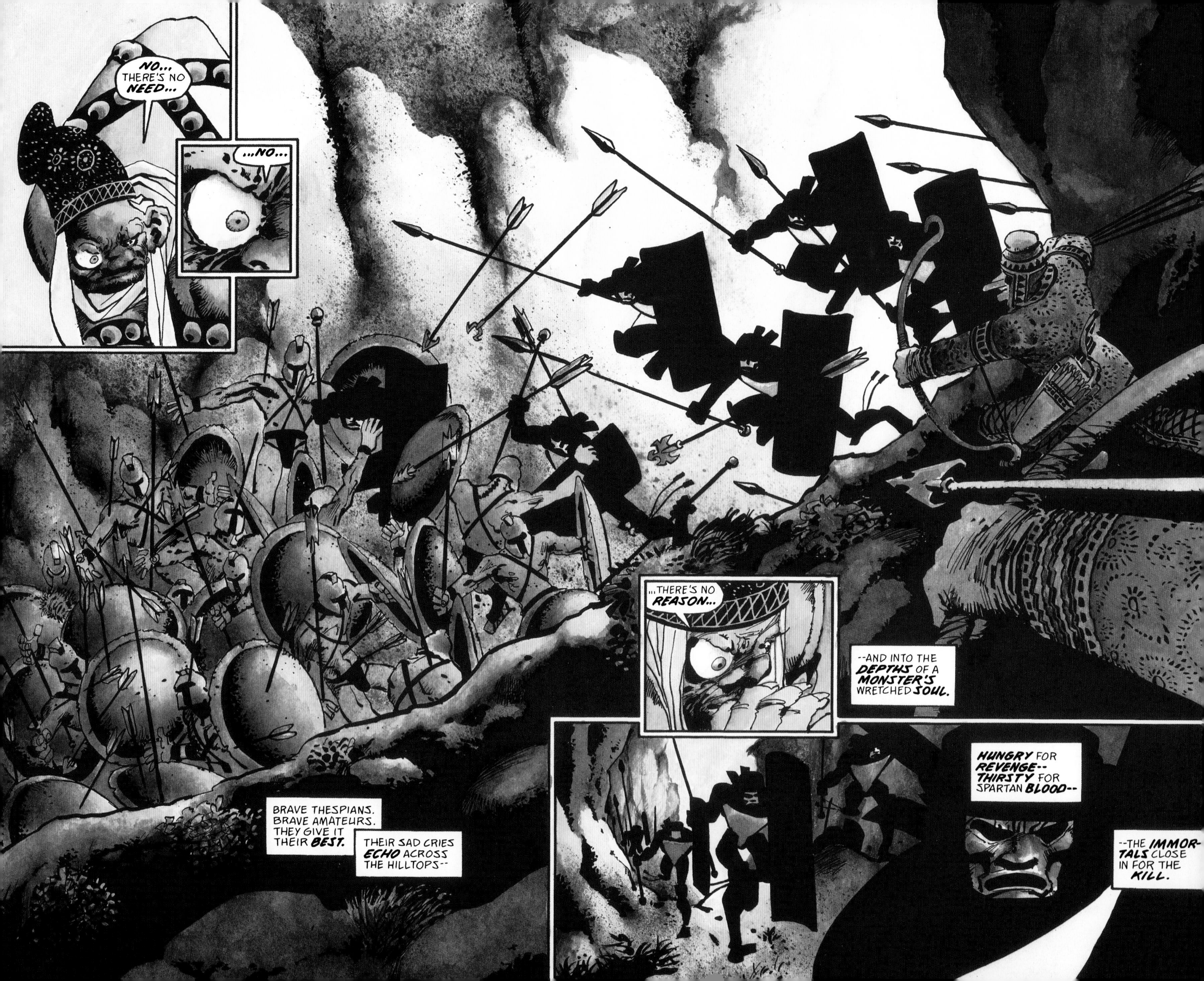
NO... THERE'S NO NEED...
...NO...
BRAVE THESPIANS. BRAVE AMATEURS. THEY GIVE IT THEIR BEST.
THEIR SAD CRIES ECHO ACROSS THE HILLTOPS--
...THERE'S NO REASON...
--AND INTO THE DEPTHS OF A MONSTER'S WRETCHED SOUL.
HUNGRY FOR REVENGE-- THIRSTY FOR SPARTAN BLOOD--
--THE IMMORTALS CLOSE IN FOR THE KILL.

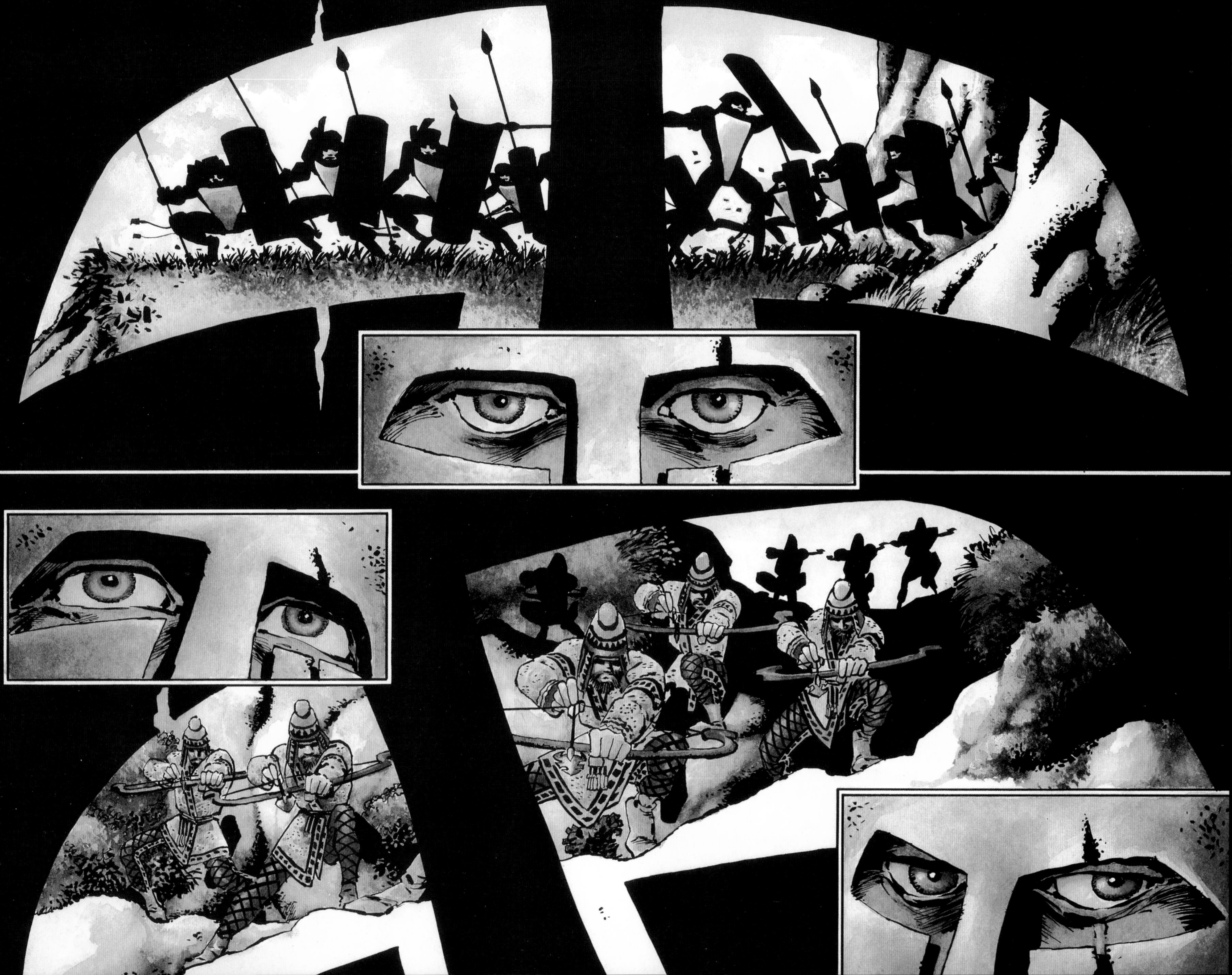

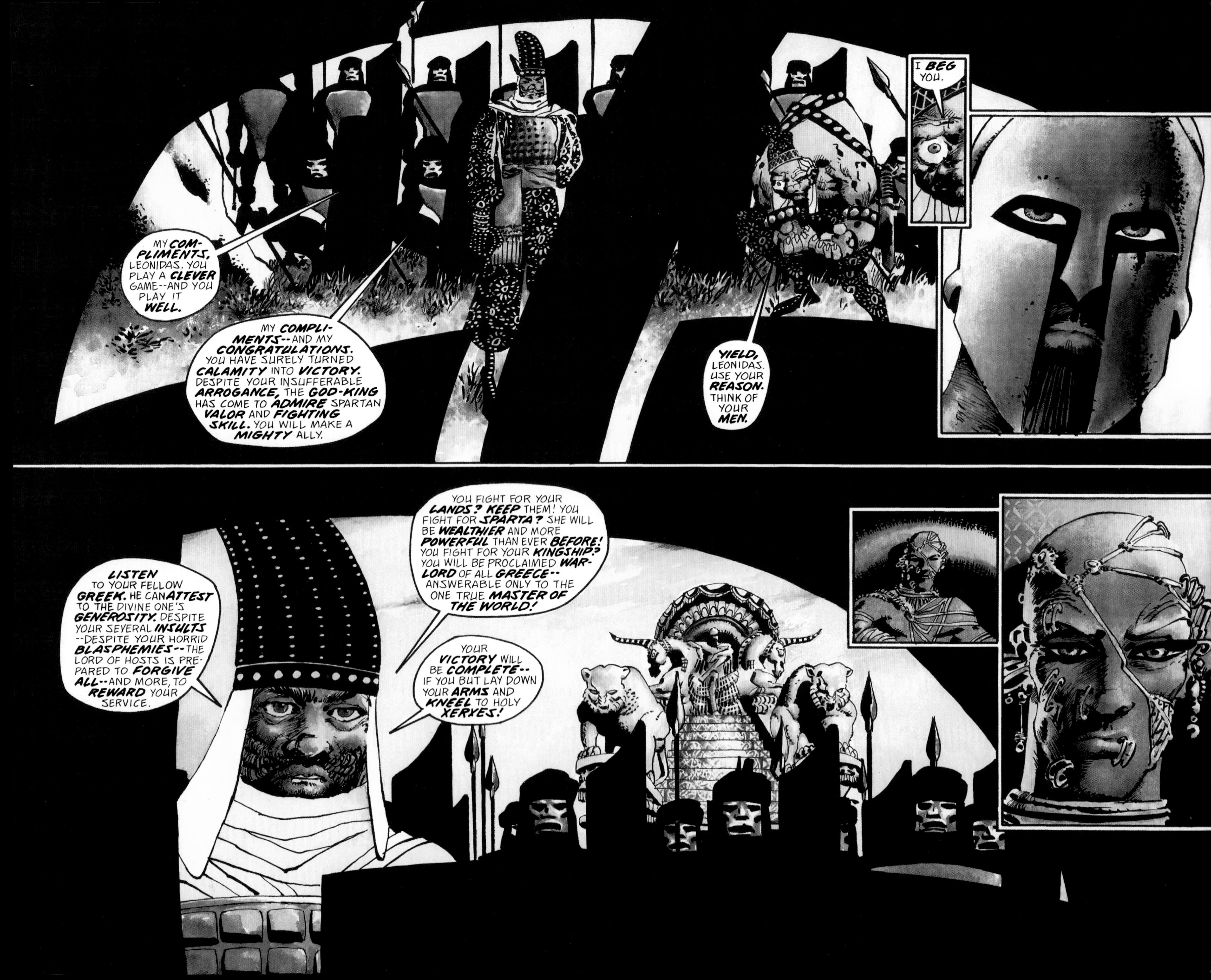
MY COMPLIMENTS, LEONIDAS. YOU PLAY A CLEVER GAME--AND YOU PLAY IT WELL.
MY COMPLIMENTS--AND MY CONGRATULATIONS. YOU HAVE SURELY TURNED CALAMITY INTO VICTORY. DESPITE YOUR INSUFFERABLE ARROGANCE, THE GOD-KING HAS COME TO ADMIRE SPARTAN VALOR AND FIGHTING SKILL. YOU WILL MAKE A MIGHTY ALLY.
YIELD, LEONIDAS. USE YOUR REASON. THINK OF YOUR MEN.
I BEG YOU.
LISTEN TO YOUR FELLOW GREEK. HE CAN ATTEST TO THE DIVINE ONE'S GENEROSITY. DESPITE YOUR SEVERAL INSULTS --DESPITE YOUR HORRID BLASPHEMIES--THE LORD OF HOSTS IS PREPARED TO FORGIVE ALL--AND MORE, TO REWARD YOUR SERVICE.
YOU FIGHT FOR YOUR LANDS? KEEP THEM! YOU FIGHT FOR SPARTA? SHE WILL BE WEALTHIER AND MORE POWERFUL THAN EVER BEFORE! YOU FIGHT FOR YOUR KINGSHIP? YOU WILL BE PROCLAIMED WARLORD OF ALL GREECE--ANSWERABLE ONLY TO THE ONE TRUE MASTER OF THE WORLD!
YOUR VICTORY WILL BE COMPLETE--IF YOU BUT LAY DOWN YOUR ARMS AND KNEEL TO HOLY XERXES!

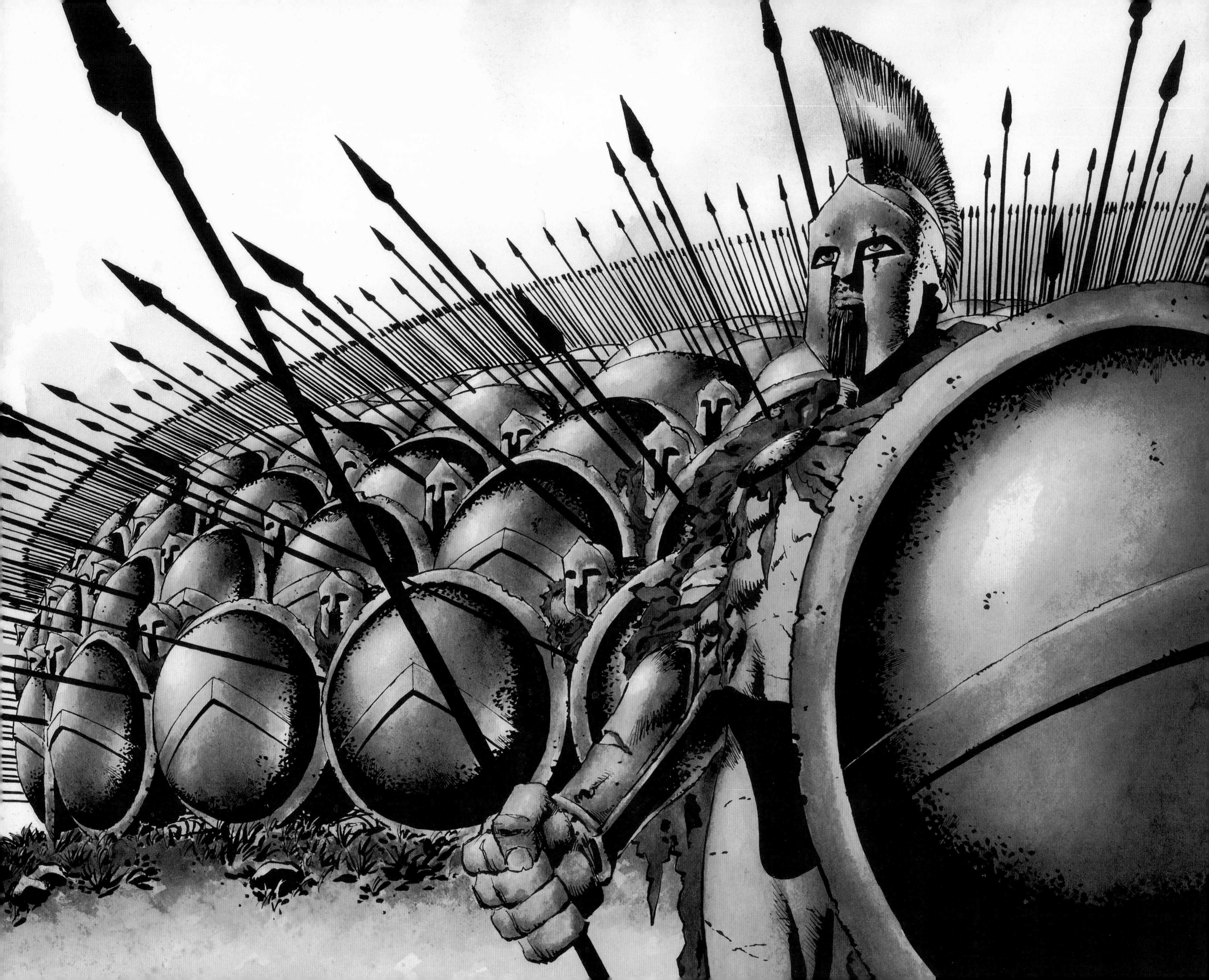

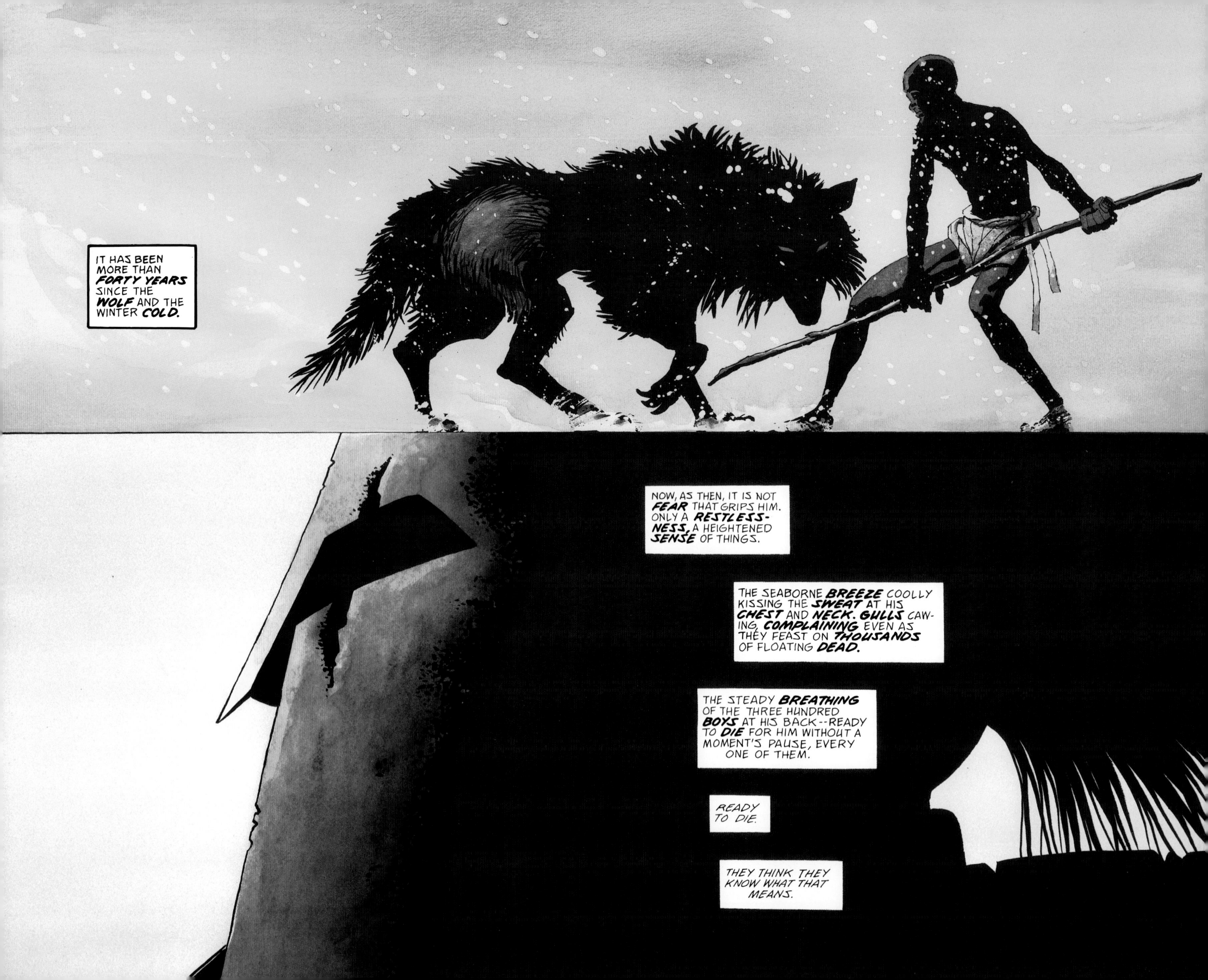
IT HAS BEEN MORE THAN FORTY YEARS SINCE THE WOLF AND THE WINTER COLD.
NOW, AS THEN, IT IS NOT FEAR THAT GRIPS HIM. ONLY A RESTLESS-NESS, A HEIGHTENED SENSE OF THINGS.
THE SEABORNE BREEZE COOLLY KISSING THE SWEAT AT HIS CHEST AND NECK. GULLS CAW-ING, COMPLAINING EVEN AS THEY FEAST ON THOUSANDS OF FLOATING DEAD.
THE STEADY BREATHING OF THE THREE HUNDRED BOYS AT HIS BACK--READY TO DIE FOR HIM WITHOUT A MOMENT'S PAUSE, EVERY ONE OF THEM.
READY TO DIE.
THEY THINK THEY KNOW WHAT THAT MEANS.

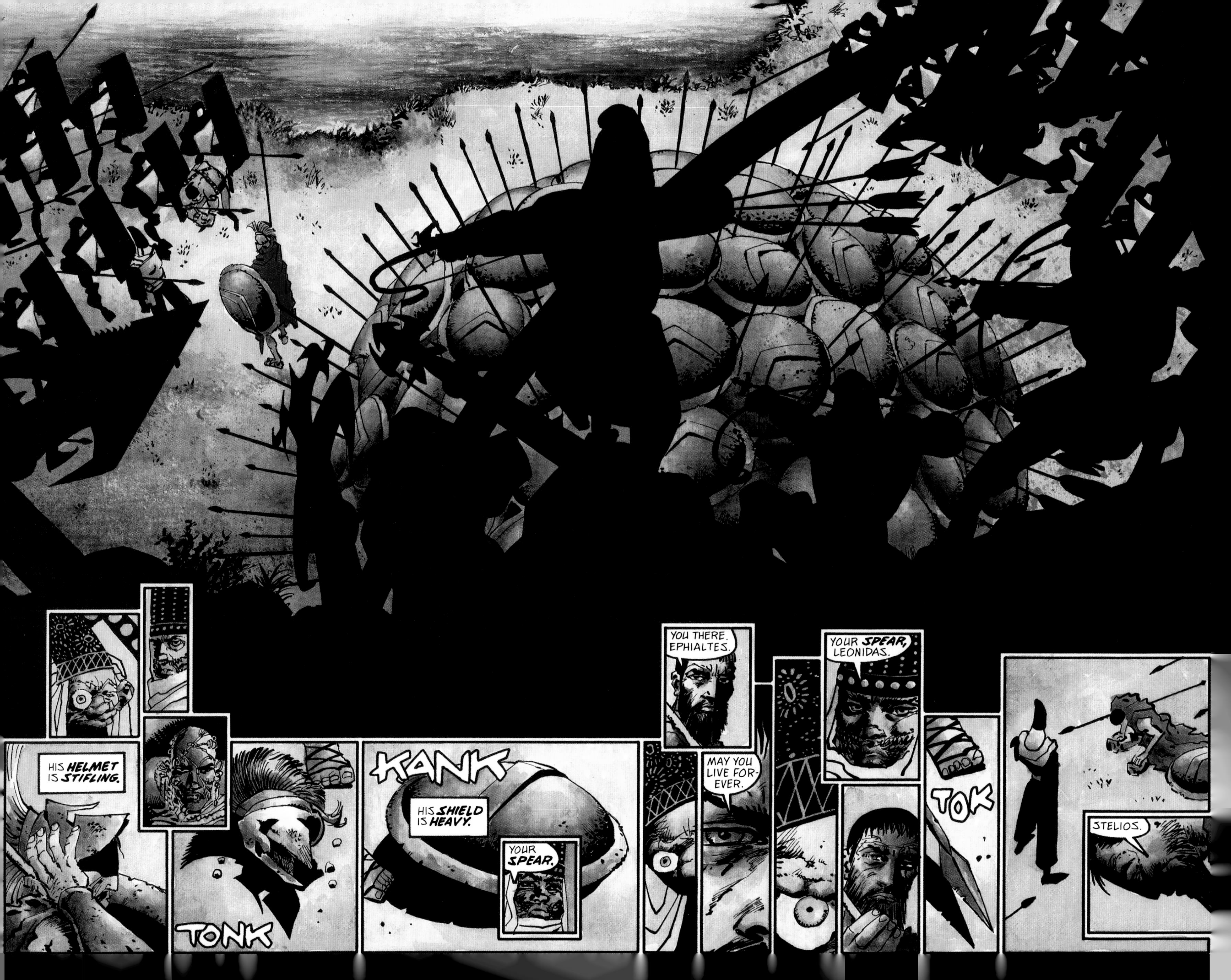
HIS HELMET IS STIFLING.
TONK
KANK
HIS SHIELD IS HEAVY.
YOUR SPEAR.
YOU THERE. EPHIALTES.
MAY YOU LIVE FOR-EVER.
YOUR SPEAR, LEONIDAS.
TOK
STELIOS.

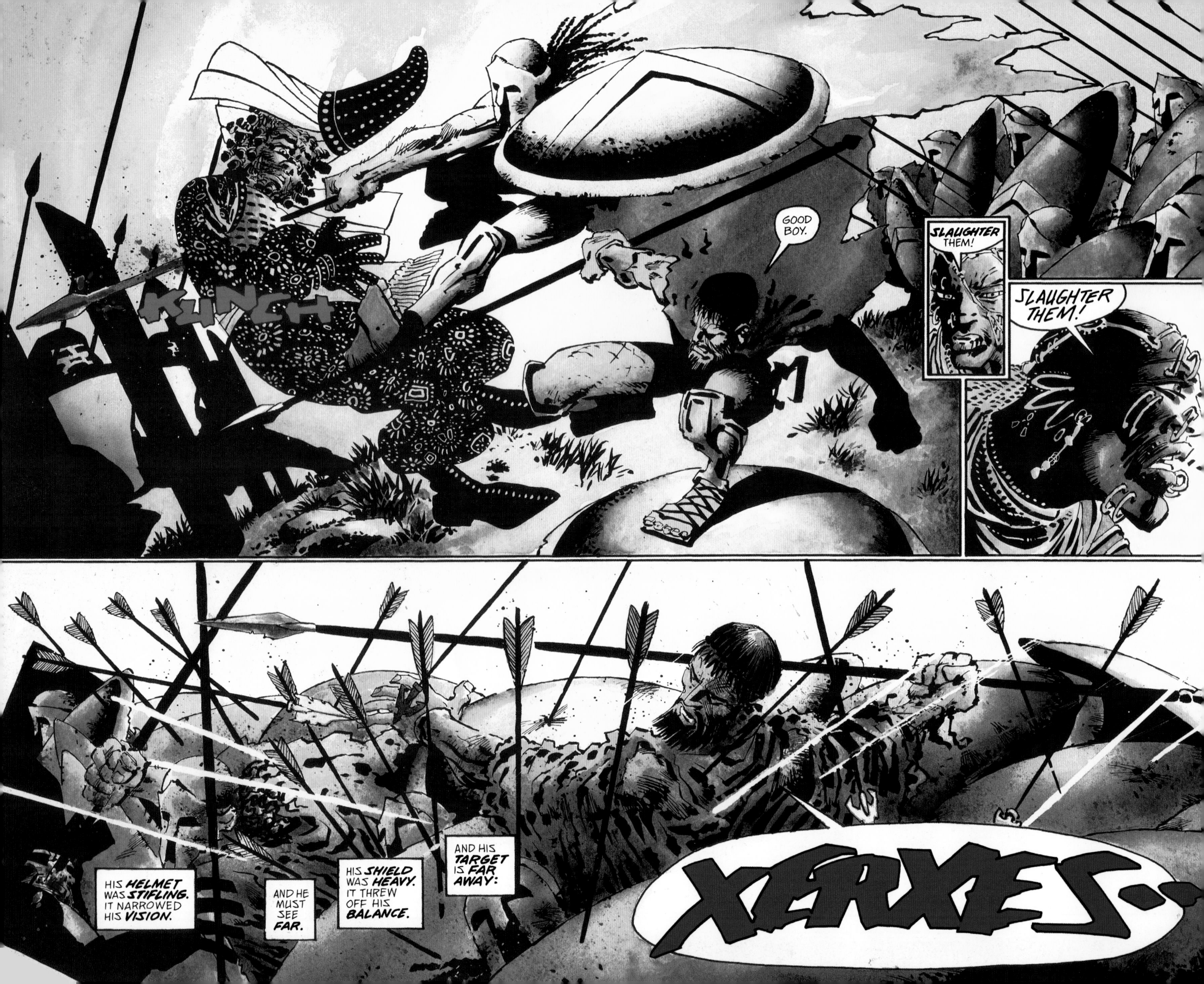
KUNCH
GOOD BOY.
SLAUGHTER THEM!
SLAUGHTER THEM!
HIS HELMET WAS STIFLING. IT NARROWED HIS VISION.
AND HE MUST SEE FAR.
HIS SHIELD WAS HEAVY. IT THREW OFF HIS BALANCE.
AND HIS TARGET IS FAR AWAY:
XERXES--

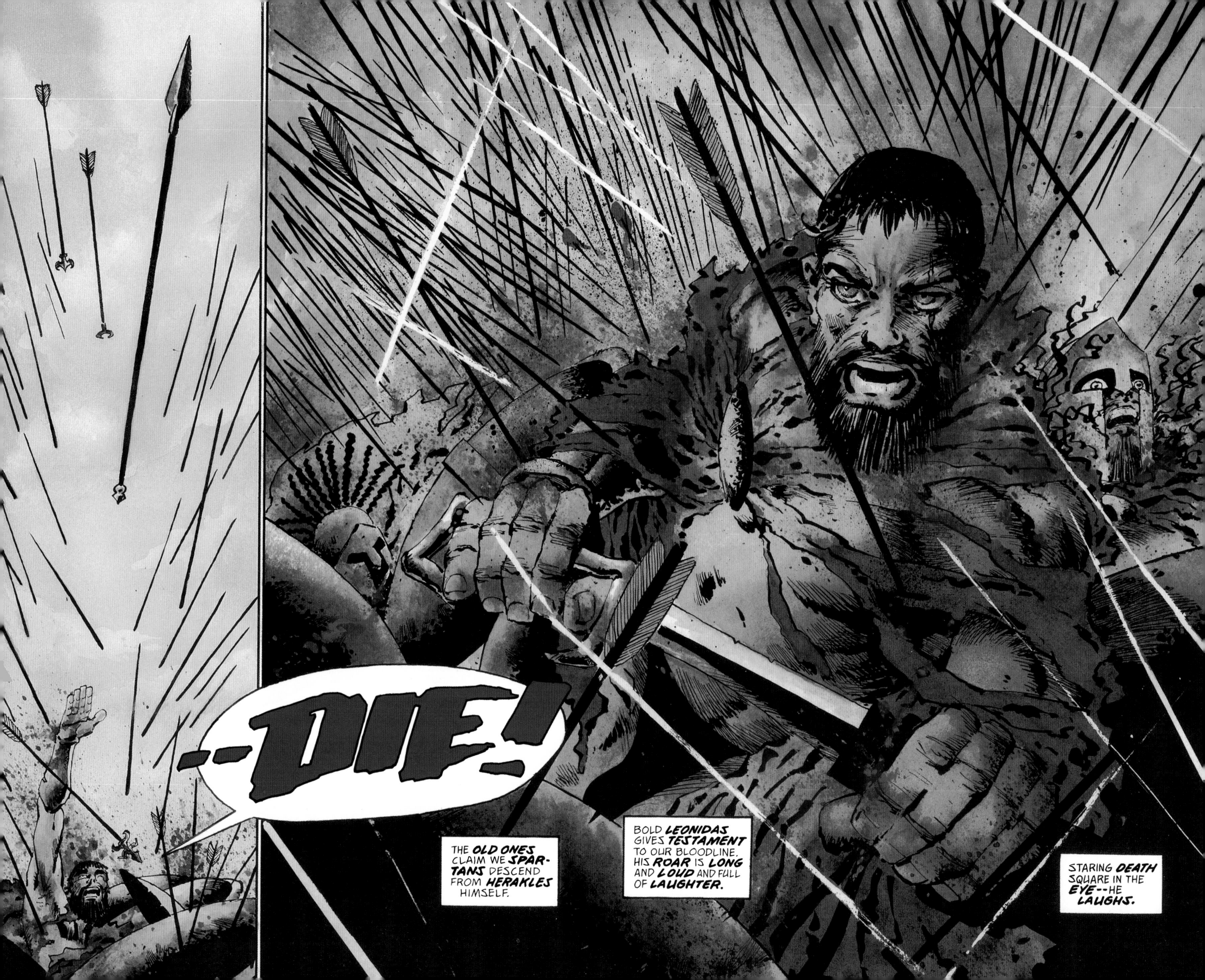
--DIE!
THE OLD ONES CLAIM WE SPAR-TANS DESCEND FROM HERAKLES HIMSELF.
BOLD LEONIDAS GIVES TESTAMENT TO OUR BLOODLINE. HIS ROAR IS LONG AND LOUD AND FULL OF LAUGHTER.
STARING DEATH SQUARE IN THE EYE--HE LAUGHS.

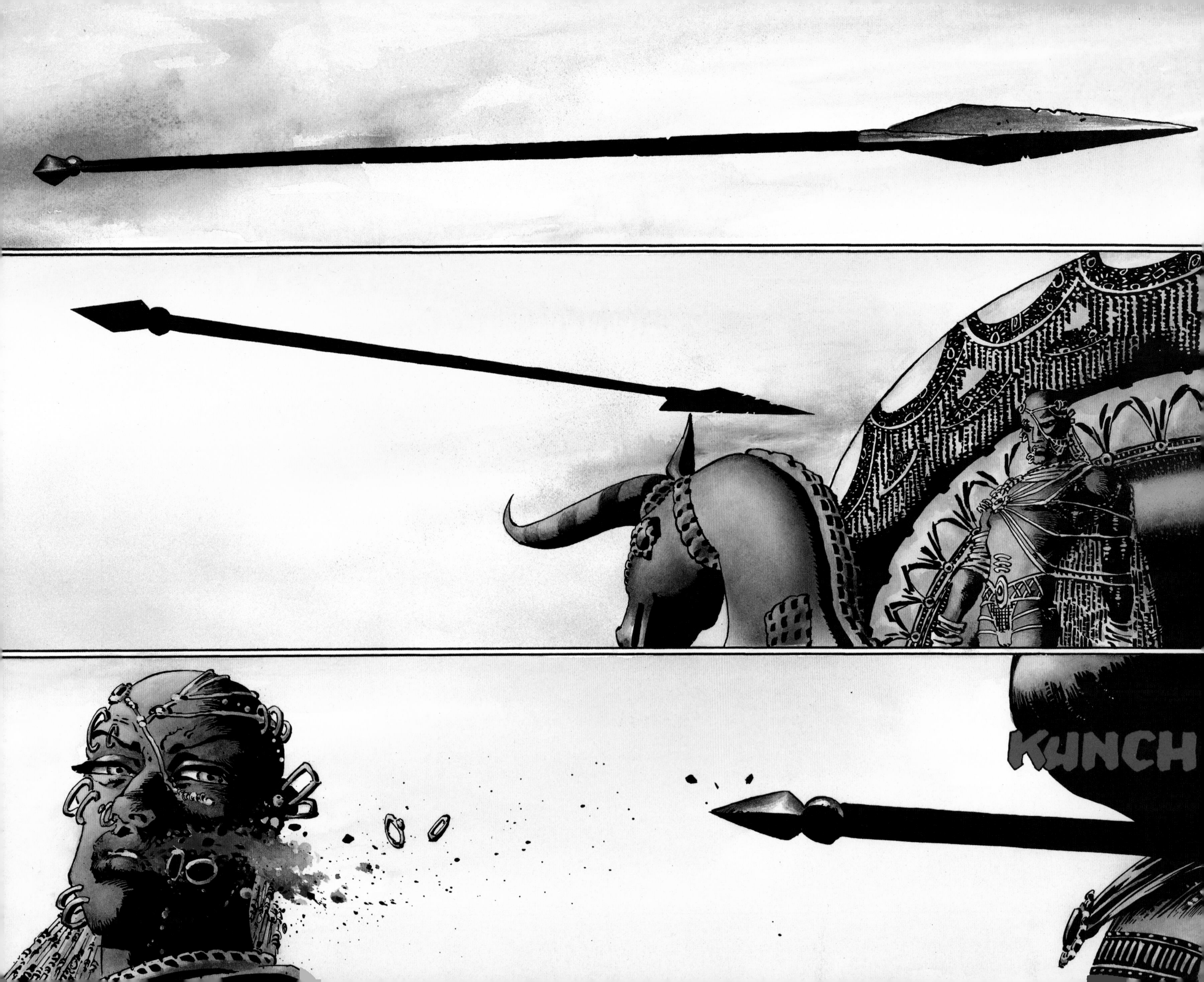
KUNCH

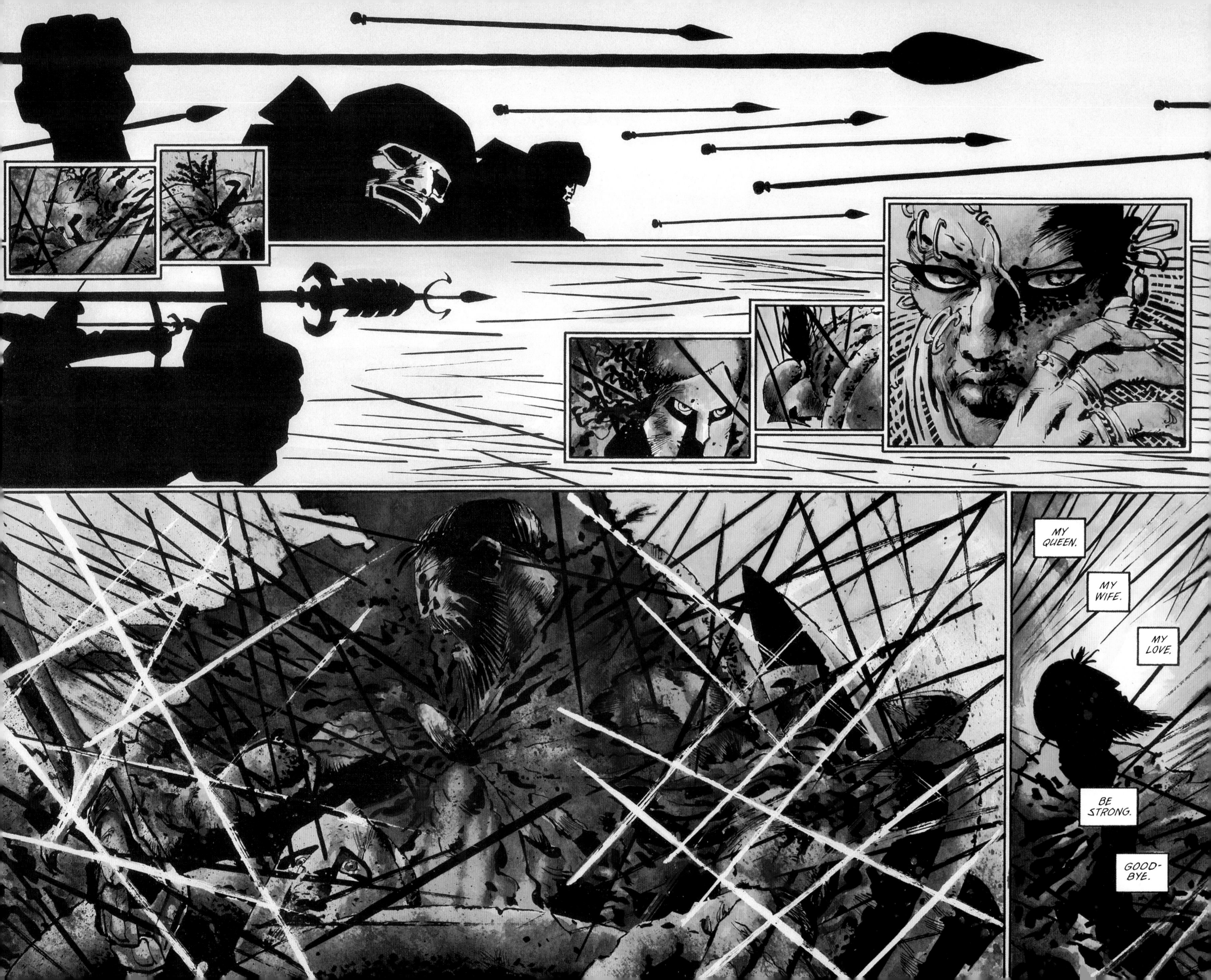
MY QUEEN.
MY WIFE.
MY LOVE.
BE STRONG.
GOOD-BYE.

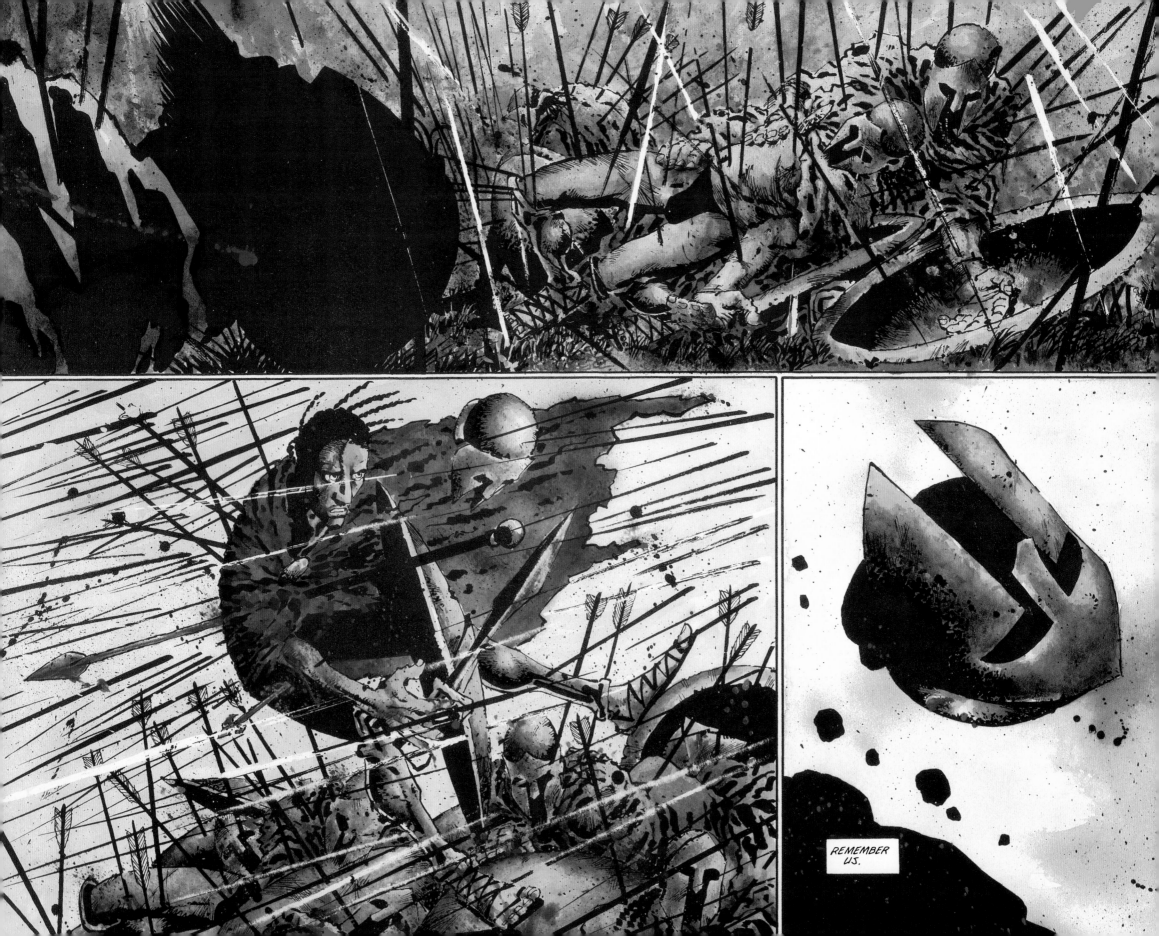

REMEMBER
US.

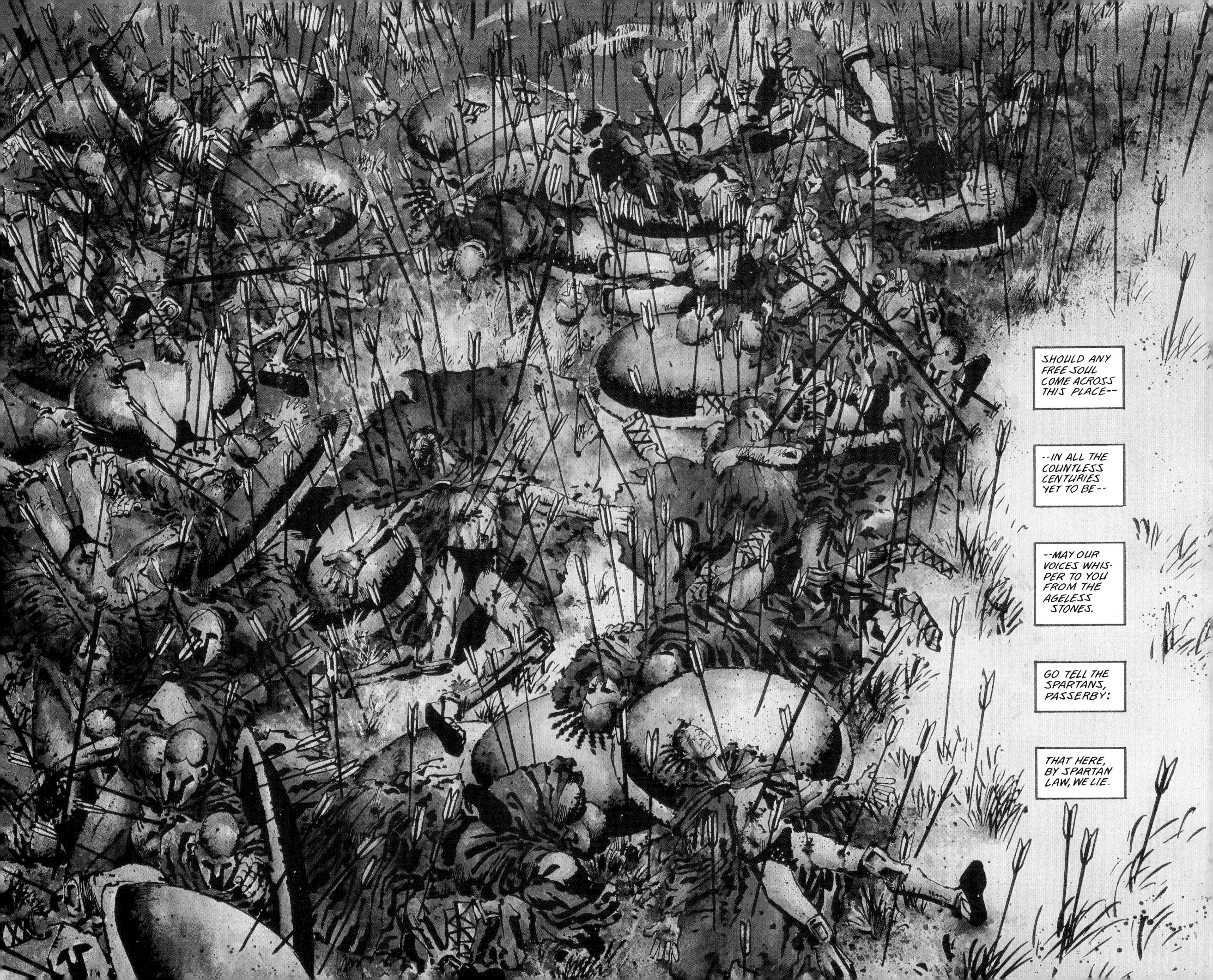
SHOULD ANY FREE SOUL COME ACROSS THIS PLACE--
--IN ALL THE COUNTLESS CENTURIES YET TO BE--
--MAY OUR VOICES WHISPER TO YOU FROM THE AGELESS STONES.
GO TELL THE SPARTANS, PASSERBY:
THAT HERE, BY SPARTAN LAW, WE LIE.

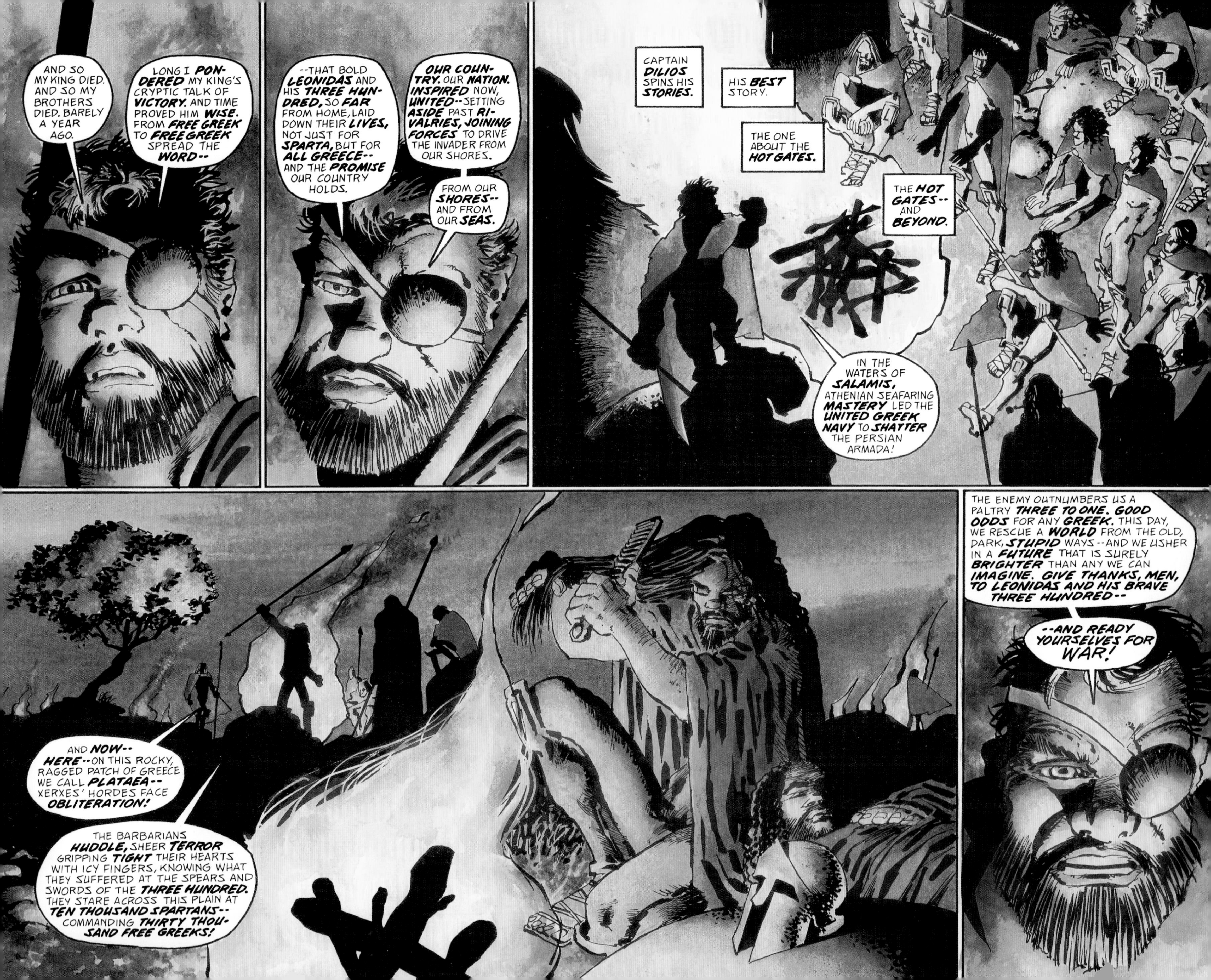
AND SO MY KING DIED. AND SO MY BROTHERS DIED. BARELY A YEAR AGO.
LONG I PONDERED MY KING'S CRYPTIC TALK OF VICTORY. AND TIME PROVED HIM WISE. FROM FREE GREEK TO FREE GREEK SPREAD THE WORD--
--THAT BOLD LEONIDAS AND HIS THREE HUNDRED, SO FAR FROM HOME, LAID DOWN THEIR LIVES, NOT JUST FOR SPARTA, BUT FOR ALL GREECE-- AND THE PROMISE OUR COUNTRY HOLDS.
OUR COUNTRY. OUR NATION. INSPIRED NOW, UNITED--SETTING ASIDE PAST RIVALRIES, JOINING FORCES TO DRIVE THE INVADER FROM OUR SHORES.
FROM OUR SHORES-- AND FROM OUR SEAS.
CAPTAIN DILIOS SPINS HIS STORIES.
HIS BEST STORY.
THE ONE ABOUT THE HOT GATES.
THE HOT GATES-- AND BEYOND.
IN THE WATERS OF SALAMIS, ATHENIAN SEAFARING MASTERY LED THE UNITED GREEK NAVY TO SHATTER THE PERSIAN ARMADA!
AND NOW-- HERE--ON THIS ROCKY, RAGGED PATCH OF GREECE WE CALL PLATAEA-- XERXES' HORDES FACE OBLITERATION!
THE BARBARIANS HUDDLE, SHEER TERROR GRIPPING TIGHT THEIR HEARTS WITH ICY FINGERS, KNOWING WHAT THEY SUFFERED AT THE SPEARS AND SWORDS OF THE THREE HUNDRED. THEY STARE ACROSS THIS PLAIN AT TEN THOUSAND SPARTANS-- COMMANDING THIRTY THOUSAND FREE GREEKS!
THE ENEMY OUTNUMBERS US A PALTRY THREE TO ONE. GOOD ODDS FOR ANY GREEK. THIS DAY, WE RESCUE A WORLD FROM THE OLD, DARK, STUPID WAYS--AND WE USHER IN A FUTURE THAT IS SURELY BRIGHTER THAN ANY WE CAN IMAGINE. GIVE THANKS, MEN, TO LEONIDAS AND HIS BRAVE THREE HUNDRED--
--AND READY YOURSELVES FOR WAR!

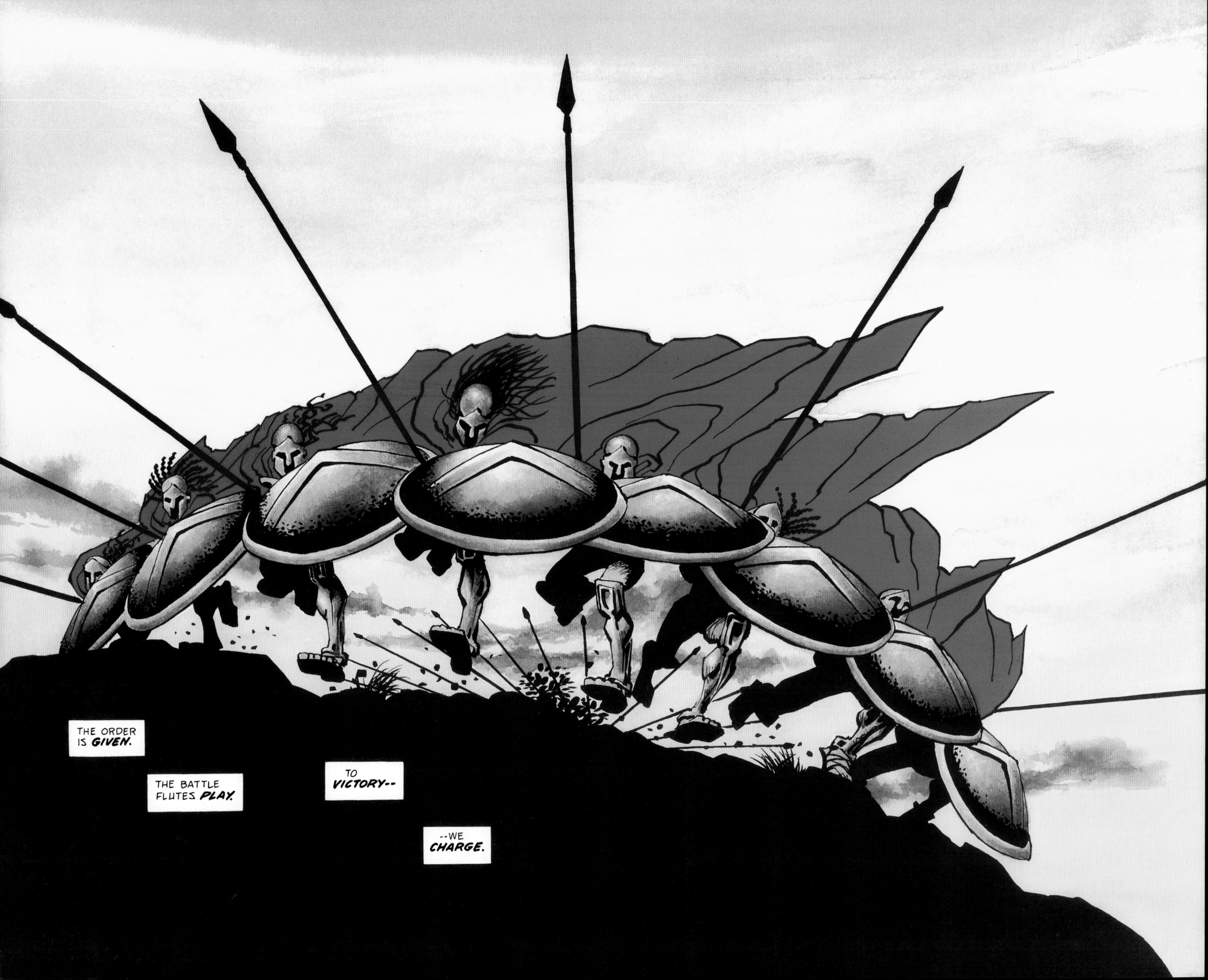

THE ORDER IS GIVEN.
THE BATTLE FLUTES PLAY.
TO VICTORY--
--WE CHARGE.

THANKS TO:

Flint Dille

Terri Dille

Harlan Ellison

Cary Grazzini

Harris Miller III

Robert P. Miller

The National Trust for Historic Preservation

Walter Simonson

Twentieth Century Fox

Don Varley Jr.

Darlene Vogel

Eleni Zachariou

Stelios Zachariou

RECOMMENDED READING

The Hot Gates by William Golding

The Histories by Herodotus

Thermopylae: The Battle for the West by Ernle Bradford

The Western Way of War by Victor Davis Hanson

OTHER COMIC BOOKS BY
FRANK MILLER AND **LYNN VARLEY**

RONIN

BATMAN: THE DARK KNIGHT RETURNS

ELEKTRA LIVES AGAIN

BATMAN: THE DARK KNIGHT STRIKES AGAIN

FRANK MILLER's SIN CITY

THE HARD GOODBYE

A DAME TO KILL FOR

THE BIG FAT KILL

THAT YELLOW BASTARD

FAMILY VALUES

BOOZE, BROADS, & BULLETS

HELL AND BACK

THE ART OF SIN CITY